WHISTLING
IN THE
DARK

TIME CAN BE AN ALLY OR AN ENEMY.

ALSO BY

GORDON BONNET

Kill Switch

Lock & Key

Sephirot

Gears

Signal to Noise

The Fifth Day

The Shambles

Sights, Signs, and Shadows

SNOWE AGENCY MYSTERIES

Poison the Well

Dead Letter Office

Face Value

Past Imperfect

Room for Wrath

THE BOUNDARY SOLUTION

Lines of Sight

THE BOUNDARY SOLUTION BOOK TWO

WHISTLING IN THE DARK

TIME CAN BE AN ALLY OR AN ENEMY.

GORDON BONNET

FLEET PRESS

an imprint of

THE OGHMA PRESS

OGHMA

CREATIVE MEDIA

Bentonville, Arkansas • Los Angeles, California
www.oghmacreative.com

Copyright © 2020 by Gordon Bonnet

We are a strong supporter of copyright. Copyright represents creativity, diversity, and free speech, and provides the very foundation from which culture is built. We appreciate you buying the authorized edition of this book and for complying with applicable copyright laws by not reproducing, scanning, or distributing any part of it in any form without permission. Thank you for supporting our writers and allowing us to continue publishing their books.

Library of Congress Cataloging-in-Publication Data

Names: Bonnet, Gordon, author.
Title: Whistling in the Dark/Gordon Bonnet. | Boundary Solution #2
Description: First Edition. | Bentonville: Fleet, 2020.
Identifiers: LCCN: 2019952076 | ISBN: 978-1-63373-547-7 (hardcover) |
ISBN: 978-1-63373-548-4 (trade paperback) | ISBN: 978-1-63373-549-1 (eBook)
Subjects: | BISAC: FICTION/Science Fiction/Alien Contact |
FICTION/Science Fiction/Action & Adventure | FICTION/Horror
LC record available at: https://lccn.loc.gov/2019952076

Fleet Press hardcover edition January, 2020

Cover & Interior Design by Casey W. Cowan
Editing by Gil Miller & Trinity Greco

Published by Fleet Press, an imprint of The Oghma Press, a subsidiary of The Oghma Book Group.

To my twin brother from another mother, Andrew Butters.
Read on, write on, rock on.

ACKNOWLEDGEMENTS

AS ALWAYS, I AM DEEPLY grateful to Casey Cowan of Oghma Creative Media for his unwavering support and encouragement, and for overseeing the publication of *Whistling in the Dark*. A sincere thank you as well to my eagle-eyed editors, Gil Miller and Trinity Greco, for their amazing talent at tightening up my writing. I couldn't have done this without their support, skill, and expertise. I also owe Casey and Gil a debt of gratitude for another reason. Without them, I wouldn't have written The Boundary Solution trilogy in the first place. The idea came out of a discussion between the three of us spurred by my short story "Hitching a Ride," in which I first considered the urban legend of the Black-eyed Children. Casey and Gil thought the idea was fantastic, and Casey said, "Why don't you turn this into a novel?"

Then one novel became three, and "Hitching a Ride" became a prequel to Kerri's adventure fighting the Children. (If you're curious, the incident with Matt Giles, mentioned a couple of times in Lines of Sight, references the events in "Hitching a Ride.")

I also want to give a big thank you to Cyndy Prasse Miller and Vivian Cummings for their invaluable assistance with marketing and promotion, as well as to Venessa Cerasale, Amy Cowan, and Dennis Doty, who keep all the wheels at Oghma oiled and turning.

My deepest thanks go to my inimitable cheerleading squad, who keep me putting words on the page: Cly Boehs, Carla Dugas, K. D. McCrite, Jennifer Gracen, Abby Ives, Andrew Butters, and Allison Stitt. And last, to my lovely wife, Carol Bloomgarden... you're always there with love, support, encouragement, and glasses of wine. What else could I ask for?

*"Hitching a Ride" is available as part of my short story collection Sights, Signs, and Shadows, also available through Oghma Creative Media.

WHISTLING
IN
THE
DARK

TIME CAN BE AN ALLY OR AN ENEMY.

CHAPTER
1

"FREEZE! AND NO SUDDEN MOVES unless you want me to blow your fucking head off."

Kerri Elias held her gun leveled at the slight, balding man who cowered by a flowering hedge along the edge of the squat brick building. He was standing near a neatly-engraved sign saying, *Chauvin Pediatrics. Paul C. Chauvin, MD.* The early evening air was heavy, humid, filled with the sound of crickets chirping and the whine of mosquitoes.

The man raised his hands and froze as commanded. A shudder passed through his narrow frame.

"If you want my wallet, take it." His voice was thin, tremulous.

"We don't want your goddamn wallet." Kerri's partner, Aaron Vincent, strode forward and grabbed the man by the shoulder, whirled him around. Aaron was a good eight inches taller and probably outweighed him by forty pounds of lean muscle, and the balding man stumbled and almost fell into the bushes. The man was sweating, his gold-rimmed glasses askew. He had a thin mustache and a weak mouth, and his watery blue eyes darted back and forth as if he were trying to find a means of escape.

Pediatrician?

Like anyone with any sense would leave their kids alone with this guy.

Aaron patted the man down, then turned toward Kerri. "No weapons."

"I still don't trust him as far as I could kick him." Kerri kept her gun aimed at the man's head. "We've been through this before."

"Please," he said. "Please don't hurt me. I swear, I'll do whatever you want, just don't hurt me."

"You're Paul Chauvin."

He frowned. "Yes."

"What do you know about the Black-eyed Children?"

The frown deepened. "I… I'm a pediatrician. I see a lot of children. I don't know who…."

"He's lying." Kerri's voice was filled with disgust. "We knew he would."

"We should get going." Aaron's gaze flickered toward the road. "There have already been a couple of cars by. Someone sees us and thinks we're robbing him, calls the cops, it could be awkward."

Kerri nodded. "Okay, *Doctor*, listen carefully. You're going to walk, nice and easy, to the white Honda in the parking lot. You're going to get in the back seat. My partner's going to tie your hands, just in case you were thinking of trying anything cute. Then we're going to your house. You live on Rosie Street, correct?"

Chauvin's brows drew together. "How do you know that?"

Kerri gave a harsh sigh. "Cut the crap. The innocent routine is *not* going to work here. We know what you are."

Aaron flashed a glance at Kerri. His face showed some worry as well. Uncertainty clouded his handsome features. "Are you sure…?"

"I'm sure." She turned back toward Chauvin. "I will have my gun on you the whole time. If you run, or fight back, or do anything other than what we tell you, I will not hesitate to use it. Do you understand?"

The doctor's Adam's apple bobbed in his throat, and he nodded.

"Good. Now turn, nice and slowly, and head toward the car."

Chauvin nodded again, turned, and tottered across the neatly-clipped lawn along the side of the building to the parking lot, currently occupied by two cars—Kerri's rental car and a dark blue Renault that was probably the doctor's. He opened the back door of the car and sat down, his face looking resigned.

Aaron pulled zipties out of his pocket and quickly cinched his wrists and ankles, then maneuvered the man into the back seat and slammed the door. He looked around, climbed into the driver's seat. Kerri holstered her gun and jogged around to the passenger side.

"I'm not sure about this." Aaron started up the engine as Kerri dropped into the seat and closed the door behind her.

"You were sure this afternoon."

"Yeah, I know, but… look at the guy."

Kerri gave a glance over her shoulder. A more pathetic figure she couldn't imagine. He looked as if he were near tears.

"If we're wrong…." Aaron said.

"We're not wrong."

Chauvin's wheedling voice came from the back seat. "I just don't… I don't want you to hurt me. I swear, if you let me go, I won't call the police."

"Not too bloody likely." Kerri's voice was grim. "And remember, they've all looked harmless. Remember Martinez? She was a special ed teacher, looked like she wouldn't have swatted a fly. I don't trust him."

"But what do you want with me?" There was the quiver in the voice again. Either authentic, or damn convincing.

A jolt of uncertainty pulsed through Kerri, but she pushed it away. They had to be right. Chauvin had been both on the database himself and seen with others on the database. His office had been a regular Grand Central Station of individuals whose names showed up on the file for this part of Louisiana. If he wasn't some kind of central player, they were completely off-base.

And that didn't bear thinking about.

"What we want with you is for you to answer some questions." She turned to face front again. "But we're not going to get into that until we get back to your house."

The drive from Dr. Chauvin's office to 100 Rosie Street only took fifteen minutes. The rush hour traffic was thinning, and when they turned off the main thoroughfare of Kaliste Saloom Road onto Silverbell Parkway, they left behind most of the noise and congestion for an upscale subdivision filled with expensive homes, immaculate landscaping, and well-manicured lawns.

"Who the hell comes up with these names?" Aaron said. "Silverbell Parkway and Rosie Street? I keep expecting to see Bambi Drive or something."

The GPS beeped. *"Your destination is on the right."*

"This it?" Kerri gestured toward a curving driveway ending in a closed garage door.

"Yes." Dr. Chauvin's voice sounded reluctant.

Aaron turned into the driveway and braked to a stop.

Kerri turned back to the doctor cowering in the back seat. "Okay. Same drill as before. My partner is going to open the door. He'll cut the ties on your feet. You'll then walk, calmly and nonchalantly, toward your front door, unlock it, and let us in. You need to make it look like we're your best friends come for a visit. Do you understand me?"

He nodded again, a jerky, frightened movement. "Yes."

Man, if he was lying, he was damn good. What would happen if a neighbor spotted them and called the police? It was almost dark by now, so it was unlikely. But the last thing they needed was the complication of explaining to a cop that no, they weren't kidnappers, and as unlikely as it looked, the weasel-ly-looking man with the wire-rim glasses was actually the ringleader of a group of collaborators trying their hardest to sell out their fellow humans to an alien race bent on sweeping the Earth clear of sentient life.

Dr. Chauvin, however, did what he was told. Aaron used a pocket knife to cut the ziptie binding his ankles, and he walked a little unsteadily toward his front door.

"I can't get to my keys unless you cut my hands free."

Kerri's voice was stern. "Which pocket are your keys in?"

"Front right."

Kerri slid her hand into Chauvin's pocket, suppressing a shudder of revulsion at having to touch the man. She retrieved his keys, unlocked the door, and ushered the doctor inside. There was a moment as they passed through a narrow foyer that Kerri wondered if Chauvin might try to get away or fight back, but he docilely continued into a well-furnished living room with an elegant roll-top desk, a massive teak coffee table with a polished slate top, a sofa set that probably cost several thousand dollars, a fancy recliner, and a huge flat-screen television.

"Sit," Kerri said.

Chauvin plunked down onto the sofa. Kerri sat in a rolling chair in front of the desk, and Aaron dropped into a rocker near a set of built-in bookcases.

"Can you untie my hands?"

"Not yet. Not until we get some information." Kerri leaned back and gave the quivering man a close look. "How long have you been working for the Black-eyed Children?"

"I don't know what you're talking about."

She scowled. "Let's start over. I'll repeat it slowly. How long have you been working for the Black-eyed Children?"

Chauvin's eyes widened, and the furtive look was back. "I swear, I have no idea what you mean. What children?"

"What if they don't know they're being controlled?" The uncertainty was back in Aaron's face. "Okay, he's a collaborator, but it's yet to be proven that they know what they're doing."

"If he doesn't know, then why was he in touch with the others? I don't buy that they're just passively waiting for orders, all innocent until suddenly they're given a task. I think at least some of them know perfectly well what they're doing, even if they're powerless to stop it." She nodded toward Chauvin. "I'd bet my next month's salary this guy is one of them. And I want some answers."

"Who are you people?" The little man's mouth quivered, but there was a cagey glitter in his blue eyes. "At least tell me that much."

Clever. See what information he could obtain before divulging any of his own. She caught his gaze and held it. "Two people who will fight you every step of the way."

There was a sudden white glow through the fabric of her jeans. With a pulse-pounding rush of panic, Kerri reached into the pocket and pulled out a little glass half-dome, glowing like a miniature sun.

She whirled toward Aaron. "We've got company. Secure him. We cannot lose him."

Dr. Chauvin was edging his way down the couch, mouth set in a knowing smirk, but before he could get up, Aaron tackled him. He let out a squawk and began to struggle, but Aaron subdued him and within moments had his ankle secured by a zip tie to a leg of the heavy wood-and-slate coffee table. Chauvin snarled at him, expression nearly inhuman, pulling on the restraint but unable to break it.

The wall near the built-in bookcase shimmered and rippled.

"Behind you!" Kerri aimed her gun at the distortion. "Get ready!"

Through a wall swirling like a gauze curtain in the breeze stepped what appeared to be a child of about twelve. He had blond hair, raggedly cut, wore a torn t-shirt and dirty canvas pants, and was barefoot. He glanced around the room with eyes like polished globes of onyx—no irises, no whites, all pupil.

The Child's lips pulled back in a sneer, and he stepped toward them, skinny arms reaching out, grasping fingers extended.

Kerri pulled the trigger. The Child rocked back, looked down with astonishment at a bloodless hole in the middle of its chest. Its knees buckled and it sank to the floor, finally pitching forward in a faceplant.

Another Child came through, then another, then another. Aaron fired, then Kerri, taking them down one after the other. In moments, six corpses lay on the spotless linoleum of Dr. Chauvin's living room floor. There was still no blood. There would not be. These things didn't bleed, because they had no circulatory systems.

No organs at all, in fact.

A breathless minute passed as they waited for more Children to come through the portal. Then the shimmer on the wall and the light from Kerri's beacon winked out at the same time. There was a low crunching noise as a piece of the bookshelves collapsed, the wood crumbling as if it had been hit by a sudden case of dry rot. A set of encyclopedias spilled to the floor, thudding down next to the fallen Children.

"I think we may have discouraged them." Aaron holstered his gun. "Wish we'd brought our tranq rifles."

"Ordinary guns are enough for now. Whether they return to collect the shot ones so they'll regenerate or return just to take another crack at us, they'll be back. By then I want to be long gone." Kerri turned back toward the doctor, who stared at them with an expression of mingled hatred, fear, and anger. "So, Doctor Chauvin. Are you still going to try to claim you're a helpless victim who has no idea what we're talking about?"

He yanked futilely at the ziptie lashing his ankle to the coffee table. The table slid a little, but the tie held. "I have no reason to tell you anything."

"No? Don't you think your masters are going to be a little upset that you let yourself get caught and were sitting there helpless as six of their soldiers were killed?"

"They won't stay dead." He laughed, ending in a harsh snarl. "You can't kill them, you know. You're fighting a losing battle."

"You're wrong about that. But I'm not here to discuss it." She gestured at him with her gun. "What I want to know is where your headquarters is. You are the hub of activity around here, but the Children don't appear to be organizing their activities out of your office or your home. Don't play dumb. I want to know where it is. We had two leads on locations, and both turned up nothing. I want to know where the base of operations is."

"What's in it for me?"

"We don't shoot your ugly head off." Aaron's voice was grim.

He laughed again. "You wouldn't. Humans have too many scruples. I don't believe you'd harm me. We know all about you two. We know your history. We've taken great interest in you." He gave her a smile. "So don't pretend you would shoot me while I'm tied and helpless. I simply don't believe you."

Kerri hesitated, gave Aaron a sideways glance.

Chauvin smirked. "Not bothering to deny it? At least you're that honest."

Her mouth tightened. "Maybe you'll respond better to a possible reward than a threat."

His brows drew together, and one corner of his mouth quirked upward. "What do you think you could possibly tempt me with?"

"How about amnesty? You tell us what we want to know, we protect you from the Children. We get you away from here."

He threw back his head and laughed. "You? Protect me? Soon you'll be fleeing for your lives. You've only seen the first, tentative fingers of this invasion. Plans are being laid. When they come to fruition, there will not be one human left alive on the Earth."

Aaron gestured at him angrily. "What did they do to you? You were human once. We've seen what happens when your kind dies. It's not like them." He jerked his head toward the fallen Children. "You have blood, guts, nerves, a heart. You feel pain. How did they turn you into a slave?"

A sudden understanding washed through Kerri. She looked at Chauvin, and sympathy overtook her anger and revulsion. Who had this man been before? He had family, friends, loved ones, all of whom had been harmed beyond repair by what the Children had done to him. Who had all of the people in the database been, prior to their conversion into mindless automata?

When she spoke, her voice was quiet. "We can try to reverse whatever it was they did to you. Give you back what you once were."

There was silence in the room except for the ticking of a clock and the low purr of the air conditioner.

Chauvin stared at her, mouth hanging open, all of his superior self-possession gone. That bolt, apparently, had hit home. She got a glimpse—a faint one—of the man he'd once been. His expression was one of suspicion mixed with the faintest trace of longing.

"You can't do that." His voice slurred, as if he had to force the words to come out of his mouth. "It's... it's in too deep to ever be removed."

"You don't know that. We have medical professionals on staff. We can get you access to the best doctors. They can restore you."

"I…." He looked from one of them to the other, licked his lips, and gave a little tug on his leg, still tied to the coffee table. "What if you're lying?"

"We're not lying. But we can't promise success. All I'm telling you is that we can give you a chance. If there is any of the original Paul Chauvin inside you, you know I'm speaking the truth. If you come with us, tell us what you know, we'll do everything in our power to stop the Children from controlling you."

The little man's face twitched, as if he were undergoing a horrible internal struggle. "You can offer me nothing. If I let the Children use me, they'll make sure I'm spared when the rest of you are taken."

"That's bullshit, and you know it. Once they're done using you, they'll let you die. They break their tools."

"They told me… told me if I cooperated…." He stopped, breathing hard. Whenever he said anything revealing what he knew about the Children, or suggesting that he would fight them, his words came out only with a struggle. However they were controlling him, it took a supreme act of will to counter it.

"What? What did they tell you?"

Now it seemed that even opening his mouth took effort. His face reddened, and sweat broke out on his forehead. "That… if I cooperated, they'd reward me."

"Like the one of you who tried to kill us in New Mexico?" Aaron's eyes glittered with anger. "The one they commanded to strap on a suicide vest and blow himself to bloody shreds? That's the kind of reward the Children have in store for you. We're giving you a chance. It might be the only one you'll get."

The sweat beaded, ran down the side of his face. His shirt, an expensive-looking, tailored, pale green, dress shirt, was dark with sweat stains. The words came out in a tumbling rush, as if some kind of internal barrier had been broken.

"All right. Please. But you have to do it fast. Get out of here. You were right that they'll be back. They're always watching. If you'll let me go… I'll help you… I'll….." Chauvin's watery blue eyes flew open wide, and he gave a gasping intake of breath. "No." His voice thinned to a strangled squawk. "No. Don't."

He toppled sideways with a crash, tied hands flailing in front of him and sweeping a stack of magazines and a coffee cup onto the floor. His restrained ankle twisted awkwardly, the zip tie biting into the flesh. His body thrashed for a moment, and his head tipped backwards, mouth open. Then, just as suddenly, he went completely limp.

Kerri ran toward him, put two fingers against his jawline, but she knew what she would find already from his staring, unfocused eyes.

"Fuck." She closed her eyes, then gave a harsh sigh and looked up at Aaron. "He's dead. They killed him."

"How?" Aaron's eyes were wide with horror.

"I don't know. But I'm not leaving him here to be taken by the Children when they come back to collect their own dead. Paul Chauvin was a human once. He deserves better." She stood and holstered her gun. "Cut him free. We're taking his body with us. Maybe if our doctors have him to study, they'll be able to figure out how he was being controlled, so we can help others like him. Let's move."

CHAPTER 2

W HAT THE HELL IS THIS?" The young man who met them in the empty parking lot behind the medical examiner's office looked somewhere between irritated and downright angry. His dark hair stood on end, his clothes were rumpled, and he needed a shave. Clearly he'd rolled out of bed, thrown some clothes on, and gotten in the car. "I get a call at eleven p.m., something about an emergency autopsy? The fuck is an 'emergency autopsy,' anyway? The patient isn't gonna be any deader tomorrow morning."

"You're William Daigle, the assistant ME?" Aaron asked.

"Yeah. Who are you, by the way? Or is this gonna be one of those sketchy, the-less-you-know-the-better deals you see in the movies?"

Kerri pulled out her badge. "Kerri Elias. DHS. My partner, Aaron Vincent."

Aaron held up his ID as well, and the young doctor squinted at it. "IDs can be faked, you know."

Aaron scowled. "I gave you the number to call to confirm that we're here under the auspices of the DHS. Did you call?"

He pulled his fingers backward through his hair and gave a harsh sigh. "Yeah. I called. I wouldn't be here otherwise. I just want to know what's going on before I put my foot into something I can't pull it out of."

"We'll explain once we're inside," Kerri said. "At least as much as we're able."

"Where's the body?"

Kerri met her partner's eyes for a split second, and then looked back at the young doctor. "In the trunk of our car."

"In the trunk...." His eyes went from one of them to the other, registering incredulity. "You know what this looks like, right?"

"Yeah. We also know we may not have a lot of time. So let's stop fucking around here, okay? Like my partner just said, we can discuss the details once we're inside."

He sighed again, and rubbed his eyes. "Fine. I'll get a gurney."

Five minutes later, they were wheeling a gurney with Paul Chauvin's body down a long hallway, floored with tile, in which only every third light was on. Dr. Daigle turned and pushed the gurney through some double doors marked *Autopsy Room #3* and stopped the gurney by stepping on a metal lever to clamp a brake onto the wheels.

"So you say this guy just pitched over and died?" Dr. Daigle pulled the sheet back and looked at Paul Chauvin's face. Daigle's brows drew together. "Jesus," he said in a hushed voice. "I know this man." He looked up at Kerri. "I mean, he's not a friend or anything, but I know who he is. He's a pediatrician who works down on the southside. My sister brings her kids to him. I've seen him on commercials advertising his practice."

"We're trying to find out what killed him." Kerri gazed at the young doctor steadily. "I know this sounds suspicious, but you need to believe us that it's critical. This is much bigger than just one death."

Daigle nodded. "Yeah. That's what the guy said at the number you gave me to call. It was like, 'Cooperate if you know what's good for you.'" He swallowed. "Tell me how he died."

"We were questioning him," Aaron said. "His eyes opened wide like he'd received some kind of jolt, and he fell over to his side. He was dead five seconds after he hit the floor."

"There's not much that kills that quickly. Aortic aneurysm is one of the only things I can think of. Even a massive cerebral hemorrhage takes more than a second or two."

"It wasn't an aortic aneurysm," Kerri said. "This was more like something in his brain switched off. Like all of a sudden, he went offline."

He looked from one of them to the other. "That's not how the brain works. You can't just… turn it off."

"Even so. That's where we want you to start. Whatever happened to Doctor Chauvin, it was his brain, not his heart. I just hope we can tell something once you've got him opened up."

Daigle took a deep breath. "Okay. Look, autopsies aren't pretty. You want to wait out in the hall? I'll update you when I know something."

Kerri shook her head. "No. We need to see this. We can handle not pretty." Aaron nodded his assent.

"Okay. Then suit up. If you're staying, you need to take precautions."

The three of them donned gowns, gloves, masks, and face shields. Daigle switched on a light over Chauvin's body. "Help me to get his shirt off. Usually I don't have to do that part. They're generally naked by the time they get here."

Aaron lifted Dr. Chauvin's body, and they unbuttoned and maneuvered him out of his shirt, still damp with sweat from his final moments. They laid him back down on the gurney. He looked pathetic and vulnerable, skin pale and freckled, face slack in death.

Anger rose in Kerri's chest, not at Chauvin, but at the Black-eyed Children who had done this to him. No one deserved this, to have his life shut off at a whim, to end up on an autopsy table because he'd been about to do something counter to his programming. She hoped that whatever they learned from the autopsy, it would help her stop this from happening to anyone else.

As in the case of the autopsy of the Child she'd witnessed in Tacoma, Washington, the doctor incised the skin around the forehead and pulled it backwards, exposing the skull. Unlike the Child, however, this man was human. Instead of an undifferentiated mass of muscle-like tissue, he had bone and blood and a heart and a brain. She steeled herself against what the next step was as Dr. Daigle switched on the electric bone saw and began to cut through the man's skull.

Even Aaron looked a little pale underneath his surgical mask, but he kept his eyes on the man on the gurney. In only a couple of minutes, Daigle gave gentle pressure and lifted the top of the cranium off. He made a quick incision of the layers of membrane covering the brain, and retracted those as well.

Then he said, in a hushed voice, "What in the actual fuck is that?"

Paul Chauvin had a human brain, the typical pink and gray, folded into convolutions, split down the middle into two hemispheres. But covering it was a web of green fibers, shining under the intense light from the lamp. The web covered the entire brain, but the fibers were denser in some places than others, forming a nearly opaque emerald-colored spider web over the glistening nerve tissue.

Daigle looked up at Kerri and Aaron. "Well?" He stopped, swallowed. "What am I looking at?"

Aaron's voice was somber. "That is why Paul Chauvin died."

There was a silent moment in which the young assistant ME looked from one of them to the other. "Okay. But that doesn't tell me what it is. I'm not going one step further until you give me more information, and convince me that cutting into this won't release some kind of pathogen and cause a plague."

"We don't think that's how it works." Kerri's voice was tentative.

Daigle dropped his scalpel onto a metal tray with a clatter. "You don't think? Well, you know what? That's not good enough. I want some answers. Or so help me, I'll call the cops and have you two taken in for questioning. I don't give a damn what the higher-ups at the DHS say."

"Have you ever heard of the Black-eyed Children?" Aaron's voice was level, unemotional.

Kerri frowned. "Aaron, do you think...?"

He held up one hand. "Look, I'm sick of this secrecy, this what-they-don't-know-won't-hurt-them bullshit. Doctor Daigle's right. We can't expect cooperation without understanding." He paused. "Rendell can go fuck himself if he disagrees."

"Rendell can go fuck himself for a variety of other reasons," Kerri muttered. "Okay, go for it."

He turned toward the doctor. "Look, I'm going to give you the abbreviated version. Assuming you believe us and don't call the police, we can tell you more after we're done here. The quick version is that there is a threat, not just to the United States but the whole Earth. There is a race of creatures who take on the shape of children to infiltrate people's homes and induce people to stop their cars to help. They abduct the people they come into contact with. Our current understanding is that they feed on neural energy, mostly on the energy associated with the memory centers in the brain."

"That's not possible." Daigle's voice was flat.

Kerri shook her head. "It is possible. I've witnessed it." She didn't add that she was the one who'd had a memory stolen, removed from her brain as easily as someone would pull a splinter out of a finger. The young doctor was already having a hard enough time with this. No need to make it worse.

Aaron nodded. "But not all of the people they contact are abducted. Some are… changed. Altered so that they follow commands. We've met three of them, but there are hundreds, probably thousands, more. One of the three escaped us. Her whereabouts are currently unknown. The second tried to kill us in a suicide bombing."

"Jesus," Daigle said under his breath.

"We were damn lucky to survive. This guy is the third. We want to know how he's being controlled, and if there's any way to reverse it."

Kerri spoke, voice taut with anger. "When the Children knew we'd contacted Doctor Chauvin and offered to help him, to try to get him away from their control, they terminated him. He was making noises about wanting to take us up on our offer of amnesty, and bam. Like Aaron said, whatever killed him did it quickly. It really did look like they simply flipped a switch and turned his brain off. He got a couple of words out—apparently he had a second or two of realization of what was happening—then he fell over. Dead by the time he landed."

Daigle didn't respond for a moment. He looked back down at the eerie green spider webbing covering the man's brain, then pulled a magnifier attached to a flexible cable between his face and Chauvin's body.

"I…." He stopped, gave a little shudder. "It sounds like science fiction."

Aaron gestured with one gloved hand. "Look at what's in Doctor Chauvin's skull. That's not fiction. You can see it for yourself."

"We need your help," Kerri said. "Aaron said there were thousands of people who are being controlled the way Paul Chauvin was. I think the number is more like tens of thousands. We need to find a way to stop this. To stop the Black-eyed Children."

Daigle looked through the magnifier at the fibers, and Kerri peered over his shoulder. Even though they were linked to a dead man's brain, they looked strangely alive. The young doctor swallowed audibly. "They're concentrated in a few regions. The parts of the brain associated with speech" —he pointed with one gloved finger— "here in the frontal lobe. They're called the Broca's area and the Wernicke's area. Also around the prefrontal cortex. That's basically the decision-making part of the brain. The part that evaluates circumstances and context and tells you what to do."

"Makes sense," Kerri said.

He pointed again. "Up here on the very top, too. That's the motor cortex. It's one of the parts of the brain that coordinates movement. There seem to be less in the visual and auditory centers. It's like they plug into the part that controls what you do but don't affect so much what you experience."

"Which squares with what we've observed." Kerri looked down at the body, pathetic and helpless on the autopsy table. "They're completely normal until they're not."

Daigle nodded. "To find out more, I'll have to cut into the brain. What assurance do you have that cutting into these fibers is safe?"

Aaron shrugged. "None."

"You're free to stop here," Kerri said. "We're not going to coerce you. That's what the Children do."

Daigle nodded again, then spoke in a quiet voice. "Jesus. I swear, if this is a dream, I'm never eating an entire fucking pepperoni pizza before bedtime again."

He picked up his scalpel, and with a forceps lifted one of the fibers from where it turned and dove deep into Dr. Chauvin's gray matter. He slipped the scalpel underneath it, and in one quick motion severed it.

Immediately all of the other threads writhed, pulsing like the tentacles of a jellyfish.

Kerri's throat constricted with fear.

They watched as the cut fiber, wriggling like a severed earthworm, slid forward, extending, probing as if looking for something. It reared up like a striking snake, darted at Daigle's gloved finger. He pulled it away just in time, and it missed his index fingertip by a fraction of an inch. He took one terrified inhalation and stepped back, staring. The fiber wove back and forth, moving with what looked like deliberation and volition, and finding no other target finally punched into the brain tissue at precisely the location where the original thread had entered.

"Holy flying fuck," Daigle said in a hushed voice.

"Believe us now?" Aaron sounded shaken as well.

"Yeah." The doctor's tone was breathless. Once more, the glowing green network had settled into immobility, covering Paul Chauvin's brain like frost on a windowpane. "That'd complicate surgically removing it, though." He shuddered. "Not that it'd be surgically removable in any case. I'm not a neurosurgeon, but I know enough to see that this... whatever it is has infiltrated the brain so completely there's no way to remove it. Not with any surgical technique I've ever heard of. And that's not even taking into account that it seems to be... to be alive."

"So there's no way to reverse it." Kerri scowled. "Shit."

"Well, not surgically. There might be, I dunno. Drugs, medications, something that could get rid of it, the way chemo does with cancerous tissue."

"We know of only one chemical that affects the Children. And it's toxic to humans, too."

He looked up at them. "What more do you need to know? I've got to tell you that right now, I'm scared shitless to touch this guy again. That... that thing, that thread, it looked like it was trying to jab itself into me."

"That's what it looked like to me, too." Aaron pointed at Chauvin's exposed brain, making sure to keep his distance. "If it had stuck itself into you, it could well have…." He left the sentence unfinished.

"Turned me into one of them." Daigle gave another convulsive shiver. "It might… I don't know, this is speculation. But that might be how it works. Once introduced into the body, those fibers might find nerve tissue to infiltrate, then make their way to the brain. So you could insert a piece of it anywhere, and it would eventually end up where it wanted to go, then grow to cover the brain. And any point on the body would work as a starting point. The nervous system runs through the entire body." He took a deep breath. "It'd be a remarkably good strategy for a parasite. That sort of thing is not unknown in the animal world. There are wasps that parasitize cockroaches. The female lays an egg in the cockroach's brain and poisons the part of it that controls volition. The larva then has a docile, controllable food source."

The analogy was all too apt. Kerri shivered. "In any case, we can't risk your getting parasitized yourself. We were damn lucky. I say close him up and get a hold of headquarters. There's nothing more we can do here without exposing Doctor Daigle and ourselves to unacceptable dangers."

"Agreed," Aaron said.

"What do I… um, what do I do with the body? This is seriously not following protocol. If there's a body here tomorrow morning, the ME will wonder how the fuck he got there and why his head is cut open."

"If we can manage it, the body will be long gone by then." Aaron stepped back, shucked his gloves, gown, face shield, and goggles, and pulled out his phone. "We need to get him somewhere that will keep his death out of the public eye, get you off the hook for helping us, and have the ability to conduct an examination using remote tools to avoid anyone getting infected. If all goes well, we'll be out of your hair in an hour or two."

———

IT TURNED OUT TO BE closer to three hours. It was approaching four in the morning by the time two grim-looking men came in equipped with a body bag, and with barely a word other than a quick flip of the ID and query as to where the body was located, secured Dr. Chauvin's corpse and carried it into the back of an anonymous white van. Dr. Daigle looked shell-shocked through all of this. Understandable, considering the extent to which this must have overturned his conception of the world.

Kerri watched the young man with a measure of empathy. Her own introduction to the Black-eyed Children had been traumatic, too, beginning with the abduction of her boyfriend right out of their apartment. Since then, her life had accelerated into a continuous barrage of terrifying encounters.

At some point, would she become inured? Did that ever happen, even to people who were confronted with death every day? Would there come a time when the next shock, the next assault, would produce no emotional response, nothing but a reaction of doing what needed doing?

If so, that time was still far in the future. Seeing that questing, probing, green thread tonight, looking for living tissue to penetrate, had sent the adrenaline coursing through her veins. She still felt the effects of it—the shuddery, wobbly-kneed come down. She needed sleep, but if she went to bed now it would still be hours before she could relax.

"Doctor Daigle," she said. The young doctor turned toward her, eyes wide. "You want to get a cup of coffee? You look like you need one."

He nodded. "Sure. And call me Will."

"Okay, Will. I think Aaron and I could use some caffeine, too."

Aaron came over to where they stood, near the back entrance to the Medical Examiner's building. The van with Doctor Chauvin's body had taken off ten minutes earlier, but they hadn't left. Each of them seemed to be trying to process what they'd seen, make sense of a universe that contained such things.

"If I don't get some coffee, I'm going to fall asleep standing up," Aaron said. "What's nearby?"

"There's a café over on University. It's open all night."

"Meet you there?" Kerri held the door for him.

Daigle nodded, then turned to lock the door behind them. "Yeah. If I don't faceplant into the steering wheel on the way."

The café they entered fifteen minutes later was empty except for a bored-looking counter clerk who glanced up at them with a raised eyebrow and a heavy sigh. They ordered three large coffees, and after a brief stop for cream and sugar, retreated into the back corner of the café. The only sound was the low murmur of a television set on Fox News and the whoosh of an occasional car passing by.

"So the two of you are…." Daigle began, and took a sip of his coffee. "I dunno. Like Mulder and Scully, or something?"

Kerri laughed. It felt like the first time she'd smiled in days. "Hardly. Well, Aaron might be Mulder, but I'm sure not Scully. I'm still trying to figure out how I ended up here on the front lines."

"But I'm guessing this isn't a regular branch of the DHS, that you could, like, look up on Wikipedia."

She shook her head. "Nope. In fact, if you asked any of the government higher-ups, they'd deny we even exist."

"Special ops."

"Basically."

"And these things… the Black-eyed Children. You called them "a race of creatures." That's some kind of euphemism for aliens, right?"

"That's our understanding, yes," Aaron said. "We don't know much about them except that they parasitize sentient life. Most of their victims don't end up like Chauvin did. Most of them just have their neural energy sucked away for food, and they're killed when they're emptied."

"Jesus. I've never heard of this. How can this be happening, and no one's heard of it? How can it not be headline news every night?"

"They're careful and stealthy. At least they have been up to now. We have reason to believe that's changing. But so far, they take a person here, a person there, and people are usually abducted when they're alone. It looks like a kidnapping, eventually goes into the 'Unsolved Crimes' folder, and that's that."

"How did they catch Chauvin, though? Man, I'd rather be killed than end up like that."

"Me, too. We suspect that Chauvin and the others like him were caught and then released. But before the Children let them go, they introduced into them a means for controlling their actions so that they could have some human slaves to use." Aaron sipped his coffee. "Now we know how."

"So this is going to be some kind of invasion?"

Kerri nodded. "That's what we think, yes."

"Where do I sign up to fight?"

She leaned back in her chair. The doctor looked younger than she was—maybe twenty-three or twenty-four—but his youthful appearance must be to some extent misleading, because no doctor that young would end up as assistant to the Medical Examiner. More like twenty-eight, possibly even pushing thirty.

What would Rendell do if he found out they'd recruited someone without going through proper channels? Oh, well, they'd broken enough rules in the past twenty-four hours that this one surely couldn't count for much.

"You sure you know what you're asking?" She looked into the doctor's dark eyes. "It's dangerous. In the past month I've seen one person killed and another one abducted. There's no guarantee of safety."

"Sounds like there's no guarantee of safety even if you don't volunteer."

Aaron chuckled. "Can't argue with that."

"So what the hell do I do? Is there some kind of *X-Files* recruitment office, or something?"

"Not exactly. I...." At that moment, Kerri's attention was caught by the television in the corner, and a screen captioned *Mysterious Deaths Last Night Number in the Hundreds, Possibly Thousands.*

Aaron followed her eyes, and after one glance at the television screen, said, "Holy shit." He stood, strode over to it, and pushed the volume button.

A shaken young woman was reporting, holding a microphone in trembling hands. Behind her was a police car and an ambulance, lights flashing. "*...unknown if this is a terror attack. In Baltimore alone, over fifty unexplained,* *and nearly simultaneous, deaths occurred last night. The victims were of all ages and walks of life, and all witnesses report the same thing. There was a moment's reaction, as if the victim was struck by a sudden pain, followed by collapse. In many cases CPR was attempted, with no success. Reports are coming in now from other major cities, and the fear is that the deaths in Baltimore are only the tip of the iceberg."*

The anchor, too, showed horror in his expression, however much his training to remain impassive attempted to cover it up. *"And Lisa, there's no unifying factor linking the victims?"*

"No, Steve, nothing known yet. From the victims so far identified, it appears unlikely that they even knew each other."

"And speculation about the cause of death?"

"Doctors have yet to weigh in. It's too early for any autopsies, of course, so we'll look for that information in the coming hours and days. For now, we can only hope and pray that whatever this is isn't as bad as it seems, and that it doesn't spread to claim more victims."

"We're with you there. That was Lisa Maldonado, reporting live from Baltimore. This story is still unfolding, and we'll keep you apprised of further developments when we have them. Now, on to our other big story, which is the bombing of the British embassy in...."

"My God," Kerri said quietly. "They killed them. They killed them all."

"Somehow they must have figured out that we had a database of names. We confronted Martinez, and then Gil, then Christina Vine, and now Chauvin. They put two and two together and decided to cut their losses."

"Gil hardly counts. They sent him after us, not the other way around."

"Do you realize...?" Will Daigle looked at them over the top of his coffee cup with a stricken expression. "These people, they all died suddenly and mysteriously. So there'll be autopsies. When the brain is opened, and the doctor doing the autopsy cuts into the fibers...."

Kerri's heart thudded against her ribcage. She didn't think she had any adrenaline left, but there it was. The back of her arms prickled into gooseflesh.

"Aaron, I think it might be time for a call to Rendell. Also to your supervisors in Atlanta and Washington. This could be bad. This could be beyond bad." She looked from one of them to the other. "I think the invasion is beginning."

CHAPTER

3

THE NOTE WAS UNEQUIVOCAL.

ATTENTION all doctors, medical examiners, and assistants who are handling the bodies of anyone who died between 1 p.m. and 10 p.m. Eastern Standard Time on Tuesday, August 20—Do NOT conduct an autopsy or in any way cut into the tissue of the deceased. The CDC will be taking charge of the remains and will conduct the appropriate examinations under controlled conditions. THIS IS URGENT AND IMPERATIVE and is to prevent the accidental exposure of civilians to the causative agent. Please forward this information to any relevant agencies. HOWEVER, the contents of this document should not be made available to the general public, to forestall panic and unnecessary fear and distress. More information will be made available when possible.

It was a forlorn hope that such a document would not be leaked to the press, and immediately afterward generate the panic that the secrecy was intended to prevent. The headlines on the morning of August 21, even from reputable mainstream media, were nothing short of terrifying.

The Washington Post: **10,473 Confirmed Dead in Unexplained Sudden Mortality Event Worldwide, CDC Urges Calm.**

The New York Times: **Autopsies Forbidden by CDC Directive, Authorities Fear Spread of 'Causative Agent.'**

The Chicago Tribune: **Even Medical Personnel Forbidden From Touching Victims of August 20 Mass Death, No Explanation Forthcoming.**

The more alarmist segments of the media were even less measured.

InfoWars: **CDC Hiding Evidence of Man-Made Plague, US Govt. Claims No Responsibility.**

Before It's News: **Contact With a 8/20 Victim Means You Could Be Next!**

World leaders were strangely silent on the topic except to offer condolences to families of the victims. Press conferences were immediately terminated as soon as statements were completed, any questions asked met with stony silence or a terse "No comment."

Kerri stood next to Aaron in Rendell's office, staring at their boss across his expanse of mahogany desk. Rendell looked furious, but for once, not only at her.

"Jesus Maxwell Christ," he snarled, flipping through the pages of her report. "Under whose authorization did you conduct the action against Doctor" —he looked down at the paper— "Chauvin. What made you think he was connected to the Children?"

Kerri gave a brief glance at Aaron, and Rendell's eyebrow rose. Okay, so he was already aware she wasn't going to give him the whole truth.

He probably knew that anyway.

She met his eye steadily. "Danielle was convinced Chauvin was a collaborator. I got his name before she died, and while we were in Louisiana, we decided to conduct surveillance on him. He exhibited suspicious behavior, and when confronted, acted in such a way that we both felt deserved further questioning. We were not prepared for an attack from the Black-eyed Children in his home, nor did we have the slightest clue that he would be… be terminated."

Rendell snorted. It was obvious he recognized her deception about where she'd gotten Paul Chauvin's name, not that she intended to tell him more. Even if everyone in the database had died on August 20—a possibility yet to be verified—there was no way she was going to mention the database and the circumstances under which it had been found, not unless they had no other option.

He was her boss, but she still didn't trust him. And at least attributing their targeting Chauvin to Danielle meant he couldn't prove they were lying.

Rendell glared at both of them in turn. "Let me make it clear to you. I do not want agents running off and conducting their own investigations without prior authorization. In your case, Elias, that means authorization from me. I don't care who further up or down the ladder has told you to do something, you clear it with me or it doesn't happen. Is that understood?"

"Yes, sir."

"Now, what about the guy you brought back here?"

"His name is Will Daigle," Aaron said. "He's a doctor."

"I know that. That much is in your report."

Kerri tried to keep the annoyance out of her voice, and mostly succeeded. "After seeing the results of the autopsy on Chauvin, Daigle volunteered to join the Boundary."

"Did he?" Rendell leaned back in his chair. "So now you two are not just agents, you're recruiters?"

"Excuse me, sir," Kerri said, "but I think we need all the help we can get. If we don't have a full-blown panic on our hands, we will soon. And Aaron and I are of the opinion that this mass killing of collaborators—assuming that's what they were—is the prelude to an equally large-scale action by the Children. Daigle has medical experience, is willing and able to help. Plus, he already quit his job with the Lafayette Medical Examiner's Office."

"I don't give a flying rat's ass if he gave up his position as center forward for the Boston Celtics. How do you know he can be trusted?"

Aaron shrugged. "At this point, sir, I think we have to. He saw the filaments in Chauvin's brain and damn near got stung by one of them. It's anyone's guess what would have happened had his glove been pierced, but he's of the opinion that it would have led to his being parasitized, and I agree. He knows enough it would be foolish simply to turn him away."

Rendell's eyes narrowed. "You two presume far too much. Your disrespect for authority—no, your complete disregard for authority—is trying my patience."

Having known Rendell for three years, Kerri was surprised he had any patience left to try, but she kept her mouth shut.

His mouth twisted as if he had just tasted something sour. "I will approve Daigle's appointment as a Boundary agent on a provisional basis, but do not take this as approval of your actions. He'll be expected to go through the usual training and probationary period. As far as the two of you, I will be having a conversation with my own superiors regarding your behavior and what punitive steps, if any, need to be taken. Dismissed."

They exited the office past Rendell's secretary, and once more Delia gave them a pitying smile. How many times exactly had Kerri gotten that look in the last month?

She'd lost count.

"Well, that went better than expected," she said in a flat voice, as they emerged into the hall.

Aaron burst into guffaws. "He's blowing smoke. Don't forget that Rendell's superiors are the same as my superiors, even if he doesn't know that. And I've already talked to my superiors, and they've given us their blessing, both for what we've done and to welcome Will into the fold."

"Have you told them about the database? Someone else has to know, if for no other reason, so the knowledge won't die with us if we're killed."

"Cheerful thought."

"Necessary thought."

Aaron nodded. "Yes. I'm in daily contact. Don't worry about that. We've got the go-ahead from the people who are really in charge to proceed investigating the leads we have."

She gave him a sidewise look and a smile. "You ever going to tell me who your actual boss is?"

"When they tell me I can. You're not going to pull some kind of Mata Hari thing and seduce me to get me to spill the beans, are you?"

"I already seduced you. You didn't tell me any secrets, although I do recall some pretty good moans of pleasure."

"As I recall, I wasn't the only one making noise."

They passed a bench where Will Daigle sat, dressed in slacks, a dress shirt, and a tie. He looked up at them, wide-eyed. "Well?"

Aaron reached out a hand. "Congratulations and welcome to the Boundary."

Will grinned and shook Aaron's hand. "Cool. I was wondering just what the fuck I was gonna do if your boss said no."

"Wasn't an issue. I have some pull with people who have our backs. I'd already confirmed with them that if Rendell pitched a fit and said no, he was gonna be overridden before an hour had passed. But it's good that he agreed. With Rendell, it's always better if he thinks things are his idea."

"Well, I'm glad y'all found me. My boss back home was such a dick, if you gave him Viagra, he'd get taller."

Kerri laughed. "I'm not sure Duke Rendell is an improvement in that regard."

Will shrugged and followed them down the hall. "Can't be worse. In any case, I'll have to go back soon and pack up my apartment, if I'm gonna be moving to New Mexico. Shouldn't take long. I don't have that much, at least not much that I want to move across the country. Most of my furniture is Early American Garage Sale."

"Sounds good. They'll tell you who to report to for training. It's not quite boot camp, but prepare yourself to be challenged mentally and physically."

Kerri held the door into the stairwell for the other two, and they headed down toward the first floor. "With any luck, Asha Choudhary will take charge of your training. She's our direct supervisor, now that Danielle's...." She stopped, unwilling to complete the sentence.

"Still fucking hurts, doesn't it?" Aaron's voice was barely audible over their footsteps on the tile of the wide, sunlit foyer. "You think you're done grieving, then it hits you again."

"I still feel like we should have been able to prevent her death." Kerri's mouth twisted. She could almost taste the bitterness of the words. "Maybe

Rendell was right. Maybe it was stupid to go launching out on our own." She looked over at him. "You sure your bosses know what they're doing, trusting us with investigating the database?"

"It's not like Rendell's made the best decisions, either. He's the one who slowed us down and allowed the Child we'd captured to get rescued and lost us a seasoned agent in the process. My intuition is still that we're right not to tell him everything, nor to let him run what we're doing against our better judgment. I'd take your good old-fashioned common sense, and mine too, for that matter, over his bureaucratic bullshit." This time he held the door for Kerri and Will, and they exited into the heat and sunshine and dry wind of a New Mexico late morning. "And don't forget—my orders from higher up are still the same, not only about us but about Rendell. Keep an eye on him, and if we notice anything suspicious, let the upper echelon know immediately."

"Do you have any idea what we're supposed to be suspicious about?"

Aaron shrugged. "If they know, they haven't told me. Honest to God, when I realized the Children pulled the plug on a bunch of the people on the database, I was half expecting to find out Rendell had a mysterious heart attack, too."

"You think he's a collaborator?" Will gave Aaron an incredulous look. "Your boss?"

"I won't say it hasn't crossed my mind. But it's just a thought. He could well be nothing more than a past-his-prime paper-pusher who is determined to accomplish as little as possible, whose sole reason for existence is making the lives of his subordinates a living hell." Aaron pushed a button on his key fob, and the lights flashed on his Renault as the doors unlocked.

Will laughed. "Jesus. He sounds like Doctor Rob Trahan. My boss. Ex-boss, now. I gotta say, every day I went to work I thought, 'I went to medical school for this?'" He climbed into the back seat as Aaron and Kerri got in the front. "By the way, there's one thing I still want to know. How the hell did y'all know to call me? I wondered at the time why you didn't get a hold of Doctor Trahan, who's the Medical Examiner, after all. I was just an assistant. Flunky, more like. But I'm the one you called in the middle of the night to do the autopsy."

Aaron started the engine and looked over his shoulder as he pulled out of his parking place. "I called my own boss when Chauvin died. Not Rendell—one of the people who is really in charge. She gave me your name and phone number." He grinned. "I guess somehow you must have attracted some attention from the good guys, because she said you were the man to call."

Will shook his head. "Damned if I know why. I mean, it's a good thing. Doctor Trahan would probably have told y'all to fuck off, and your boss, too. Either that or he'd have decided you were organized crime trying to get away with a hit, or some such shit. He was always going on about conspiracies and how there was some kind of evil plot to take over the world."

"He's not wrong about that," Kerri said.

Will absorbed this in silence.

"Anyhow, let's get some lunch. I know a good Mexican place. Boys, if you're going to live in New Mexico, you might as well learn about the Official State Question right now."

"Which is?" Will said.

Aaron shrugged. "Beats the hell outta me. I've only lived here for a few weeks myself."

Kerri grinned. "Red or green?"

Will looked from one to the other in puzzlement. "Red or green what?"

"Chili sauce."

Will snorted with laughter. "Oh, hell, I don't care. I'm a Cajun, man. As far as I'm concerned, pepper is one of the four food groups. As long as it's hot, I'm good."

THEY DUG INTO THREE PLATES of enchiladas and tamales—all with green sauce—then cooled down with a bottle each of Lagunitas.

Kerri watched Will eating with an amused expression. "I thought Aaron shoveled food down fast, but it's a tight race."

"I'm the fifth of six kids," Will said around a mouthful of tamale. "You had to eat fast or you didn't get any."

"Okay, then, what's your excuse, Aaron?"

He shrugged and grinned. "No excuse. I'm an only child. I just like food."

"Nothing wrong with that." Will chased his mouthful with a swallow of beer. "So when do you think they'll start my training?"

"Next few days is my guess. They usually don't mess around once they've decided to take someone on."

"Cool." Will gave them a dazed grin and shook his head. "Man, a week ago I wouldn't have believed you if you told me where I'd be today. I still want to know how they knew about me, though. It's flattering but a little creepy."

"I'll ask my boss," Aaron said. "No guarantees she'll tell me, of course. They have classified access to information beyond anything I'll ever be trusted with."

Kerri leaned back in her chair. "While you're at it, you might want to ask your boss what our next move should be. Because I'm beginning to wonder if the database might not have been a false flag."

Aaron frowned. "How do you mean?"

"We're assuming that the people who died on August twenty were terminated by the Children, right?"

"I can't see any other reasonable explanation."

Kerri nodded. "Agreed. Then don't you think they cut them loose without much provocation? We talk to one, she disappears. A second one blows himself to smithereens in an unsuccessful attempt to kill us. A third one we tail to a mall, and she comes up and basically says, 'Hey, we know who you are, and we know what you're doing.' We catch a fourth one, and *bam.* They pull the plug on ten-thousand-odd collaborators. Why? We're obviously vastly outnumbered. The Children can jump through portals anywhere they want, not to mention healing from gunshot wounds. Right now, we've got a database and two fucking tranq rifles as the only assets on our side of the ledger."

"Tranq rifles?"

"It's the only thing we've found that kills the Children," Aaron said. "It's a plant extract that attacks the fibers that hold them together. Shot with a syringe full of it, they kind of melt."

"That I'd like to see," Will said.

"It's not pretty."

"I do autopsies for a living. You think I'm bothered by not pretty?"

"But guys, to get back to my point," Kerri said. "They've got strength, numbers, are damn near invincible, and have thousands of humans to act as go-betweens. Why would they kill the ones they'd parasitized? It makes no sense."

"Maybe they were done with them," Will said.

"Done how?"

"Remember my telling you about the wasp that parasitizes cockroaches?"

Kerri shivered. "All too well. The image has shown up in several nightmares since then."

"Well, once the larva has fed, it can let the cockroach die. It's served its purpose. The larva pupates, and an adult wasp breaks out of the dying roach's body to repeat the cycle."

"Great. That adds another nauseating twist to the story."

Will shook his head. "I don't mean that the Children were using people like Chauvin for food. You told me they could extract what they need without going through something crude like a neural implant. What if the collaborators were used only as sentries and gateways? They keep watch, let the Children know if anyone's getting too close, finding out too much. You told me that the chick in Las Cruces whose house you went to had a portal in her garage, right?"

Aaron nodded. "The drywall was about to collapse it was so brittle."

"So she, and others like her, not only funnel information to the Children but provide a safe spot they can appear and disappear. But if they're moving into a more open phase of the war, they don't need them anymore. Let's assume that the web in the brain is not only some kind of implant that allows the Children to control them but also links them brain-to-brain. So you talk to one of the people who is already parasitized, the whole network knows."

"That'd explain why they terminated Chauvin. They heard the offer we made him and knew he was considering accepting it."

"Right. So they figured out you were on to them while you were talking to Chauvin. Chauvin looks like he's going to talk, maybe appeal to you for asylum, so they pull the plug. They don't want that kind of thing spreading through the entire network. Plus, they realize that you somehow know the identity of four of the people with implants, they figure you probably know more of 'em. And maybe they say, 'I guess it's time to end the covert approach. Ditch the human collaborators. All-out war.'"

"God, that makes sense," Kerri said. "Which is scarier than hell."

"We've been warned that the Children were going to launch the real offensive soon." Aaron leaned back in his chair. "Maybe this is the first sign of it. But what do we do? I'm still not sure how we approach this other than reactively, and that's not working. We did one proactive thing, and it backfired rather spectacularly."

"We couldn't have anticipated the Children would respond this way."

"No, but it does make me want to think hard about what we're doing before we do it."

Kerri frowned. "Maybe we should see if we can contact Saul again."

"I thought about that."

Will looked from one of them to the other. "Saul? Who's Saul?"

"Damned if I know," Aaron said. "He's this guy that one of the teams picked up in Arizona near the site of an attempted abduction. He claimed he'd returned to the place because he knew they were coming for him. Called himself a Pleiadian and said he was on our side and would give us help. So far all he's given us is a warning device that tells us when the Children create a portal nearby and some weird advice that sounded like Yoda on acid."

Will snorted laughter. "Advice about what?"

"Oh, about Kerri being the Chosen One and the future influencing the past, or something like that."

"Okay." Will looked at Kerri with a questioning expression.

"He's making Saul sound crazier than he was," Kerri said. "It was pretty clear he knew what he was talking about, with the possible exception of my having some pivotal role to play, which I'm still not seeing. But he said his people had been fighting the Children for generations. And he said he'd help us when we needed it."

"When's that going to be, though?" Will said. "I mean, what constitutes 'need?' Does he mean rescuing you when you're in a fight, or telling you how to defeat the Children, or something else? Sounds pretty vague."

"It's not the first." Kerri looked down at her empty plate. "Our friend Danielle got killed in a fight with the Children, and Saul was nowhere to be found."

"Maybe things have to get bad enough that he decides it's time to intervene."

Kerri's cellphone pinged, and she pulled it out. "Asha," she said with a smile. "Hey, Will, I bet she's letting me know when your training starts." She touched the screen with her finger, and immediately her smile vanished. She stared at the words in front of her, but her brain refused to take them in. She reread them over and over, certain they had to mean something else than what they said.

The temperature in the room felt like it fell fifteen degrees, and her cellphone pinged again as another text, and then another, appeared.

"What?" Aaron said. "What's wrong?"

"There's been…." She stopped, shook her head, swallowed. "There's been a massive attack on headquarters. It's a text from Asha telling us to stay away, get out of Las Cruces, make sure we don't get caught." She looked up and met first Aaron's eyes, and then Will's. Her heart was thudding in her chest. "She said she was trapped in a storeroom with Evan Reed and a couple of the others, but she was sure they wouldn't make it out alive."

Aaron looked stricken, Will terrified. Neither one responded.

She knew she had to tell them what Asha had said, the last text that came through, but it was an effort to keep her voice from trembling. She took a deep breath, held it, let it out slowly.

"The last thing she wrote is, 'Don't try to rescue us. That is a direct order. Your survival is paramount. Keep one step ahead of them, and keep fighting.'"

CHAPTER
4

WE CAN'T GO BACK TO our apartments," Kerri said. "It's too risky. They know where we live."

Aaron nodded as he pressed a button on his remote and unlocked the doors of his Renault. "Agreed. That's what they'll be expecting."

"What about headquarters? We can't just ignore them."

"What can we do? We're three people. How many Children would it take to mount a coordinated attack on headquarters? Hundreds, if not more. It'd be suicide. Besides, Asha gave us a direct order to get out of Las Cruces."

Kerri felt hot tears rise to her eyes, but she forced back the reaction. "They're our friends and coworkers. We can't just…."

Aaron climbed into the driver's seat. Will got into the back, Kerri took shotgun. "I know. It sucks. But I think we have to follow her orders." He paused. "Anything more from Asha or anyone else?"

Kerri glanced at her phone and gave a short, sharp shake of her head.

"Hey, guys?" Will said. "Can I just interject here that I'm scared shitless?"

"You and me both, pal." Aaron backed out his parking space. "You'd be crazy if you weren't."

Kerri pointed back toward the restaurant they'd just exited. "Look."

Heading toward the entrance were three slender figures with narrow, child-like features, all dressed in ragged clothes. All were wearing sunglasses. As Kerri watched, one of them turned toward her and lifted a skinny arm, index finger extended. The other two swiveled their heads around and all three began to walk, then run, toward them.

"Get us the fuck out of here!" Kerri shouted.

Aaron gunned the motor and screeched out into traffic, narrowly missing an old gunmetal gray pickup truck, whose driver honked the horn and flipped him off.

The pursuing Children were left behind as Aaron turned onto University Avenue, heading toward the intersection with I-10. The last thing Kerri saw was the three of them slowing to a walk, watching their prey escape with faces devoid of any expression, eyes hidden behind reflective lenses.

"Guess this means we can't assume they won't be active in the day anymore." Aaron's voice was light, but Kerri caught a tremor in it.

"I'd say we can't assume anything. Where are you headed?"

"Asha said to get out of Las Cruces, right?"

"Yes."

"I'm taking her advice. And also what you said earlier, about getting back in touch with Saul."

"Any ideas of how to do that?"

Aaron shrugged. "Maybe the same way Asha did. Drive up to the spot where we dropped him off, and see if he's there waiting for us."

"That feels like flailing around and hoping for the best."

"Do you have a better strategy?" He put his turn signal on, then pulled onto the on-ramp for I-10 West.

"No, not really. At the moment, Saul seems like our only hope."

Will gave a tight little laugh. "God, how can you talk about this all so calmly? If you're right, we're looking at the first battle of a fight that could destroy the human race. How are you not huddled in a corner, pissing your pants?"

Kerri turned and looked into the young doctor's earnest face. His dark eyes were wide with fear. "Will, don't make any mistake about it. We're as scared as you are. If we're able to talk about it calmly, it's just whistling in the dark."

"You regretting joining up?" Aaron gave Will a raised eyebrow.

"At the moment, I'd rather be here than in Baltimore, that's for fucking sure." Will's mouth curled upwards in a little smile that vanished almost instantly. "I'm good so far. But seriously. A week ago, the worst I had to deal with was an obnoxious boss. Now we're being chased by aliens who want to suck out our souls. I'm having a hard time processing this."

"Understandable." Kerri gave him what she hoped was a reassuring smile. "Look, we're not going to pretend this isn't dire. We don't know the extent of it yet. But I can also tell you that Aaron and I aren't going to give up without a hell of a fight. Maybe you're not safe here with us—the Children are gunning for us pretty hard right now, seems like—but ask yourself if you'd be any safer back in Lafayette, not knowing about any of this."

He swallowed and nodded. "I'd feel better if we knew more. More about what we're running from, and what we might be running into. And I was thinking maybe… maybe we could find out more on the radio. Maybe if there have been other attacks, we could find out that way."

"Not a bad idea." Aaron punched a dial with his index finger.

But the first three preset stations had nothing but static. The fourth, KRWG 90.7, caught a terrified-sounding female voice in mid-report.

"… are getting reports in from all over the country of attacks. The primary targets seem to be government offices, military installations, and television and radio stations."

Kerri's heart gave a little stutter-step. She met Aaron's eyes for a moment, then turned back toward the double ribbon of I-10 unspooling in front of her, westward into the desert.

"The identities of the attackers are unknown, but more than one witness has described that they're groups of young people who appear to be unarmed. Other information is unavailable at the moment."

A male voice cut in. "Can you describe for our listeners what you're seeing?"

"I'm standing in the alcove of a bank building entrance on the seventeen hundred block of Connecticut Avenue."

"They hit Washington?" Will's voice was hushed, disbelieving.

"We're still seeing small groups of people running by but nothing like an hour ago. The streets are mostly empty except for abandoned cars. When the… the events began, it was chaos, and the streets were clogged with people. There were accidents, and people panicked and left their cars to flee on foot. We saw groups of… of what appeared to be children, attacking those who were fleeing."

"When did you realize the attacks were occurring?" the male reporter asked.

"We… we were on the third floor of the Washington Square Building, and there was a sudden noise. Screaming, footsteps running. Three people came down the hall saying that there was a terrorist attack, to get out of the building. One of them had blood on her face. We ran along with them, down the stairs and outside."

"Did any of them describe the nature of the attacks?" The announcer seemed to be controlling his own horror only with some effort.

"Just that there was a sudden rush of attackers, seemingly from out of nowhere. Some of the victims were dragged off. Others that fought back were injured or killed. A few were able to escape. We saw some of the attackers—they looked so young, but were somehow able to subdue people twice their size. There were so many of them, they were swarming the streets, looking for people who'd gotten away."

"How did you manage to escape?"

"I…." The woman's voice hitched, and she couldn't answer for a moment. She took an audible breath. *"I'm sorry. We hid, first in a bookstore, then made a run for it, trying to get back to our car. Jerry—one of the sound technicians—he had a sprained ankle and couldn't move fast enough. We tried to help him, but he fell…."* She broke off into wracking sobs.

"Can you tell us any more about how these massive attacks were coordinated?"

There was no response at first, and when she finally spoke, it was with the hard edge of anger. *"No. No. I have no idea. I don't know what's happened or why. I just need to get back to our…."* She stopped, and her voice suddenly changed from near hysteria to an abject, despairing plea. *"No. Please. Jesus, please don't—"*

There was a crash, and the feed was cut off.

"Valerie?" The male reporter's voice was thin, strained to the breaking point.

"We're trying to reestablish contact with Valerie Hoekstra, reporting live on the terrorist attacks in Washington, D. C. We...." He seemed to run out of ideas of what he could possibly say. *"I'm... I'm trying to—"*

Then his voice, too, was cut off, and the radio station was replaced by a soft purr of static.

"God help us," Will said quietly from the back seat.

Kerri looked over at Aaron. "Do you think all of this was precipitated by what we did with Doctor Chauvin?"

"No way to know for sure. But if I had to guess, I'd say no. From the sound of it, there were hundreds of attacks today, maybe thousands. There's no way they could have set all this up in only a few days. It might be that Chauvin is what triggered them to act, but it was already planned."

"What the hell can we do to stop them?" Will sounded near the edge of hysteria himself. "If there really are thousands of attacks, today, all over the world, there must be a hundred thousand, maybe a million Children invading the Earth right now. Far as I can see, we're fucked."

Neither Kerri nor Aaron answered.

"And we're heading out into the desert to meet with some guy who's supposedly on our side, who you think will just be there waiting for us?"

Kerri shook her head. "I don't know what else we can do."

Will's voice rose to a shout. "What the hell is the military doing? What are the police doing? They're supposed to protect us. Isn't that what they're for? To keep us safe? For fuck's sake, why is this happening?"

"The reporter said that the military installations were the first targets. Those, and radio and television stations. It makes sense. Stop the people who are best equipped to fight back, and stop us from communicating with each other."

"Jesus Christ." The young doctor sounded near tears. "I've been trying to text my parents and my brothers and sisters. No answer from any of them."

"Don't assume the worst," Kerri said. "Stations are down. Just because you can't get through doesn't mean they're in harm's way. Under normal circumstances, if someone didn't reply right away to a text, you wouldn't panic."

"I think I've got a good fucking reason to panic." He looked down at his phone screen. "I'm on Twitter. The hashtag *#ChildAttacks* is at the top of the trending list. Apparently, it's not just in the US. I saw people mention Tokyo, Beijing, New Delhi, Cairo… it's everywhere. All at once. One person I saw wrote, 'I'm the last one left in my office. They're looking for me. I'd ask for help but it's too late.'"

"Holy shit."

Will took a deep breath, let it out slowly. "Okay. All right. We're still alive, and we made it out of Las Cruces. But Jesus, guys. We've got no food or water. We can't count on anywhere we stop not to be swarming with Children. Eventually, we're going to need gasoline for the car. I'm trying not to freak out completely, but I gotta say, it's hard not to estimate our chances at very nearly zero."

"I'm not going to give up." Kerri swiveled to look Will full in the face. "I know it doesn't seem like much, but Saul told us that we're going to win. That something we will do would defeat the Children."

"Something you will do," Aaron corrected.

"Okay. But right now, that's all we have to cling to. It'll have to be enough, unless you want to find the nearest bunch of Children and surrender."

"We may get our chance," Aaron said in a low voice. "Guys? Look ahead. I think we're driving right into a road block."

Will gave an inarticulate moan of terror.

Aaron slowed the car, and Kerri peered forward, shading her eyes against the sun. "It's not Children. They're adults, at least the ones I can see."

"Collaborators? Or allies?"

She gave a helpless shrug. "How could we tell until it was too late?"

"Then fuck it. Hang on to your hats, folks." Aaron's hands tensed on the steering wheel, and he shoved the accelerator to the floor.

The force of their speed slammed Kerri backward into her seat. Aaron, face set in a grim scowl, leaned forward toward the windshield, gaze fixed on a wooden barrier that was the only weak point in the road block. The rest was made up of parked cars.

And humans. The ones Kerri could see were male. None were dressed in official uniforms. The nearest ran toward them flailing their arms and shouting, but when it became obvious Aaron wasn't going to stop, they jumped aside.

The front bumper of the Renault struck the crosspiece of the wooden barrier with a crash. It snapped in half, and a piece of it flew toward the windshield, striking it near the top and leaving a long crack snaking its way down the glass. The other piece was flung outwards and narrowly missed a balding man with metal-rimmed glasses, who ducked and shouted an angry curse as they roared past.

"Goddammit." Aaron's voice was a tense whisper as they zoomed away from what was left of the road block. "I have had this car for three years and not a single fucking scratch."

Kerri laughed, half from the hysteria of relief. "If that's all the damage that's done over the next few days, you can count yourself lucky." She turned back toward Will. The young doctor's eyes were huge, his face a sickly pale. "You okay?"

He cleared his throat. "I think we'll get to check how good your upholstery's stain-proofing is. Because I may have just shit myself."

Aaron glanced in the rear-view mirror. "At least it doesn't look like they're gonna try to chase us."

In the side mirror, the men and cars were already receding into the distance. Kerri watched the tiny figures until the Renault took a curve in the highway and the remains of the road block were lost to sight.

"Do you think that was meant for us personally? Because if it was, now it's obvious what direction we're going. If there are others out there, all it would take is a text or call to let the next ones know we're heading their way."

"It could have been trying to stop people from getting in or out of Las Cruces. Maybe it was a bunch of weekend warriors who decided to seal the borders around Cruces for some reason."

Kerri shook her head. "I don't buy that. Stop people from getting in, okay. You can see why people would do that. Why would they place a road block to stop people from getting out?"

"Who knows? Maybe they think they'll be the ones to catch the bad guys. Stop 'em from escaping."

"Still not buying it. Whatever reason they had for the blockade, I'd lay odds it wasn't that."

"Okay." Aaron shrugged. "I'll admit I'm only speculating. But whatever reason they had, we got through. We'll have to hope our luck stays good. After what's happened in the last week, people are going to panic. Panicked people make stupid decisions. That alone makes travel dangerous."

"We don't have much of a choice."

"No. I still want to see if we can contact Saul. I'm counting on his knowing what to do. It's obvious this isn't his first rodeo. Maybe he'll decide he needs to do more than to give us some vague advice. Now that the invasion has begun, it's time for him to act." Aaron's mouth tightened. "Fish or cut bait."

"Where are we supposed to be meeting this dude?" Will's voice was stronger, having lost some of its tremor.

Kerri swiveled around in her seat. "I looked at the report. Fortunately. Asha told us that her team had run across Saul at the same spot where he'd been picked up hitchhiking a few months ago. I was curious and dug the story out of the archives. Guy named Matt Giles, works for a copper mining concern down in Bisbee. He was on his way from visiting the work site, heading north on Highway 80. If I remember right he was maybe thirty, thirty-five miles north of Bisbee, and Saul was just standing there by the side of the road with his thumb out. If we're lucky, Saul will be there waiting for us, the same way he was with Asha."

"This guy is telepathic or something?"

"Beats the hell out of me."

"He claimed to be able to jump back and forth through time." Aaron chuckled. "He scared the piss out of Rendell by jumping back and stealing his pen, and then handing it to him as if he'd plucked it out of thin air. When Rendell did his usual bluster and bullshit, Saul did it again, this time having Rendell's appointment calendar delivered to him by parcel post. That convinced him, even though he didn't want to admit as much. Anyhow, Saul said he knew where to meet Asha's team because he was able to figure out when they'd be there, and then jump to that point. Don't ask me to explain it, but it makes as much sense as anything else we've seen."

Will snorted. "That's not saying much."

Kerri looked out of the window at the desert swishing past, the rocks and cactus and mesquite scrub blurred by their speed. "I hope like hell he's there. If he's not, I'm out of ideas of where to go or what to do next."

Aaron nodded, but a muscle twitched in his jaw, revealing tension kept carefully hidden from his voice and words. "Then let's concentrate on getting into Arizona. The next step can worry about itself for now."

KERRI SQUINTED INTO THE WESTERING sun until her head throbbed, looking for signs of another blockade. Deming slipped past, then Lordsburg, and they encountered no further resistance. Hardly anyone was on the interstate. Even in this thinly-populated stretch of I-10, there was usually more traffic than this. In an hour, Kerri had seen a grand total of just two cars in the eastbound lanes, and no one at all sharing the westbound lanes with them.

This was simultaneously a relief and a little surreal. She finally stopped glancing into the side view mirror every two minutes, checking for pursuit, but the emptiness of the parallel ribbons of highway was unnatural.

It was dusk before they reached the intersection of I-10 with Highway 80. Aaron put on his turn signal to inform no one that they were taking the exit, pulled into the off ramp, and crossed over to head south toward Bisbee and the hoped-for rendezvous point with Saul.

"It's gonna be dark by the time we get there." Kerri spoke in an offhand manner, as much to assuage her own doubts as Aaron's.

"I know. I don't see that we have another option."

"Have you given any thoughts to where we can spend the night? We're going to have to sleep at some point."

"One thing at a time. I've been thinking about that, though. Even if the Boundary headquarters was attacked, and, what did the news report say? Military bases, police, government buildings, TV and radio, that sort of thing. There's gonna be some people left in towns and cities, just trying to keep things on an even keel. We can't be the only ones left already. Even the Children can't move that fast."

"So what do you suggest?" Will's voice, from the back seat, sounded edgy with fear and fatigue. "Stop at the next Motel Six and hope for the best?"

"Worst comes to worst, we can sleep in the car. Find a place where it's not visible from the road, pull off, take a nap, then keep going. I'd like to find better accommodations at some point, though. Catnaps in the car only get you so far. We're going to need a good night's sleep eventually."

Kerri had to suppress a shudder. "I doubt the Children have to stop to sleep. Or eat. Or pee. Our animal needs are going to make us vulnerable."

"I don't see any way around that." Aaron gestured at the darkening desert ahead. "I'm still holding out some hope that Saul will know what to do. Hell, I'm hoping that he'll step in and take over the whole fucking shooting match." He paused, and when he continued, his voice was grim. "I doubt our luck will carry us quite that far, though. In my gut, I have this feeling that whatever's going to happen, it's going to be up to the three of us."

CHAPTER
5

I T WAS KERRI WHO NOTICED the shimmer by the side of the road, about twenty miles south of I-10. At first she thought it was heat haze, but by this time it was nearly dark, and the air was cooling. It had the same rippling, ghostly appearance, a little silvery, almost like a gauze curtain swaying in the wind.

She pointed it out with a frown.

Will cupped his hands around his eyes to shield against the reflection in the window. "What the fuck is that? Captain Picard beaming down?"

Aaron eased back on the accelerator, and the car slowed as they approached the spot. The apparition hadn't moved. It hovered about ten feet off the road, in a clear patch between two clumps of mesquite.

"A portal for the Children?" Aaron's voice was low, cautious, as if he were afraid of being overheard.

Kerri glanced down at her lap and extracted the little glass half-dome from her pocket. It was dark. "Don't think so. At this range, the beacon would have activated."

"I don't have the faith in that thing you do."

"It's saved my life more than once. I'm going to trust it until proven otherwise. Whatever that is, it's not a portal."

By this time, they were nearly alongside the thing, whatever it was, and

Aaron braked to a stop. He didn't turn the motor off, and no one made a move to exit the car.

"Is this where your friend met Saul the first time?" Will sounded like he was keeping his voice level with an effort.

"Near enough. I don't remember the exact place where we dropped him off. But I'm guessing this is it."

"And he's supposed to somehow just know we're here and show up?"

"That's what he did with Asha."

"I dunno. Sounds kind of bizarre to me. How the hell would he know we're coming? What's your opinion on all of this, Aaron?"

"We all saw him do his magic trick with Rendell's pen and appointment calendar, as if it was the easiest thing in the world. And Kerri's right, that's exactly how it went down. Asha and her team were driving along, just doing a check of places where there'd been suspicious activity, and he was standing there waiting for them."

"But the Children know about him, too."

Aaron nodded. "I expect so."

Will gestured toward the ghostly apparition, which hadn't moved since they first saw it. "So is this Saul? Or a trap? Or something else entirely?"

Kerri took a deep breath. "Only one way to find out. Aaron, cover me." She cautiously opened the door, drew her gun, and stood facing the shimmering column of light. It was no more than a dozen feet away. She heard Aaron put the car in park, and his door opened, but she didn't turn toward him to see where he was. She would just have to trust that he was in place.

She took a tentative step forward. "Saul?"

No response.

"Saul. If that's you, it's Kerri Elias, from the Boundary. We need help. If you can hear us, let us know."

The rippling curtain of light shuddered, and its indistinct outline coalesced. Kerri had the sensation she was watching energy transmute itself into matter. But somewhere before reaching solidity, the change stopped. Saul was there, but wavering, translucent. He looked out at her from the swirling column, and she saw immediately the change in his expression from the first time she'd seen him. His youthful face was creased with worry, and the lightness and ease he'd had in their previous encounter was replaced by tension, perhaps even fear.

"We don't have long." The voice coming from inside the column sounded tinny, like a poor-quality recording. *"The Children know of this place. If they're not watching now, they won't be far behind you. I hoped you'd come here."*

"Thank God it's you." She re-holstered her gun, and let out a long, slow breath. "The headquarters was attacked. A lot of the agents... well, we honestly don't know. Chances are there were a lot of casualties. But Asha told us to get out of Las Cruces."

Saul nodded. *"You're safer out. If you'd stayed in the city, every Child in the area would be trying to find you. You have more chance if you're out in the open and keep moving."*

"What do we do now?"

"I can only tell you what I know, which isn't much. First, it's not as dire as you probably think, at least not yet. The Children always start the same way. They target defense and communications, and whatever acts as a command center. This means that a lot of places in the periphery are probably substantially untouched. The usual plan is to kill the nerve centers of the civilization, then they have their leisure to move from there and take out community after community. Your best chance will be to stay out of big cities. And don't depend on the authorities to help. You'll have to feel your way forward."

"Forward to where?" Aaron spoke from behind her, but she still didn't turn.

"There's a major hub of the Children's operations in a town called Colville, New York. That's where you need to go."

Incredulity and hopelessness rose within her. "Just the three of us? Attacking an installation with dozens, possibly hundreds, of Children?"

Saul shook his head with a jerky, frustrated gesture. *"No. You'll find help. But don't think about numbers. We're past the point where strength in numbers would have helped, if it ever would have. Now you have to rely on intelligence and stealth."*

"What do we do when we get there?"

"You'll know."

"The fuck is that supposed to mean?" Her voice rose to a shout. "Every time we ask you for concrete assistance, you respond with some kind of vague, New-Age-sounding bullshit. If you and your people are really concerned about the Earth, how about you get off your asses and do something to help us?"

A faint smile flitted across Saul's face. *"You'll have to trust me when I say that we are helping in the only way we can, and we will give as much aid to you as we are able along the way. It's at the point that I can't even fully jump forward into your time frame without alerting every Child in a hundred-mile radius, so giving you material assistance from here would cause more harm than good. But even so, we're almost out of time. The Children have undoubtedly been waiting for you to try to reestablish contact with me, so they'll be here in minutes. Go. Drive. Pick your path carefully. Stay to small towns. You'll find food and shelter when you need it. Use your intuition to tell you when someone or some place is safe. But get to Colville as fast as you can. You'll find the address of the installation in the database. You still have access to it, yes?"*

Aaron nodded. "I have my laptop. It's downloaded."

"Good. Get to Colville. I'll be in touch when I can. I—"

Saul's familiar form, and the column of light that surrounded it, suddenly flew apart into sparkling fragments that swirled in the night air for a moment, then were swallowed up by the darkness. Simultaneously, a brilliant white light shone through the pocket of Kerri's jeans, and her heart thudded painfully against her ribs.

"Get in the car! We've got company!"

As they dashed back and swung themselves into the front seats of the car, a rectangular sheet of light appeared against a rock face on the opposite side of the road. Will breathed the words, "Holy shit," as Aaron slammed the gearshift into drive and stomped the accelerator to the floor. Gravel flicked out from underneath the tires as a small, slender figure, then another, then another, stepped through the gateway.

The last thing she saw, looking over her shoulder, was three elfin faces peering up the road toward them, their expressions showing no emotion at all.

"That was way too fucking close." Aaron had a white-knuckle grip on the steering wheel.

Will leaned forward, and Kerri turned. His face was ghastly pale in the darkness. "Did you believe all that stuff about trusting we'd get food and shelter?"

"I don't disbelieve it." Kerri chose her words carefully. "Saul's guidance has been good so far."

"Didn't stop the Children from kind of waltzing in and taking over. Don't you have any concerns that he might not really be on our side? That he's secretly aiding the Children, or at best playing his own game for his own reasons?"

"I won't say the thought hasn't crossed my mind. But all I can say is that we've held out as long as we have because we've done what he's told us. And he gave me the beacon. Hard to explain that if he's not telling the truth."

"Okay, you're right. But we still need to keep our eyes open and our brains engaged."

"No argument there."

A FEW MILES SOUTH OF where they'd encountered Saul and the Children, Aaron pulled over, and slowed to a stop.

Kerri's heart sped up, and she peered into the darkness. "What's going on? What did you see?"

Aaron laughed. "Nothing. We need to get turned around. We're still heading south, and unless we want to go to Mexico, we're going the wrong way. Plus, I need to pee."

"Me, too," Will said from the back seat.

Aaron's smile vanished. "We're gonna have to stand guard, you know. Cover each other when we've got our pants down. It'd be the final indignity if the Children grabbed you while you were taking a piss."

Will's voice was earnest. "Fuck modesty. Anybody who wants to watch me can watch all they want. I'm not going off into the bushes alone."

Now Kerri and Aaron both laughed.

Aaron turned to look at the young doctor. "You're learning quickly."

"Explain to me how I have another option."

They took turns. While one took care of bodily needs, the other two stood nearby, guns drawn. But despite their concerns, there were no further appearances of the Black-eyed Children.

A few minutes later, they were retracing their path up Highway 80. Aaron slowed the car as they passed the spot where they'd spoken with Saul, but there was nothing there except for the shadowed forms of rocks and scrub, indistinct in the darkness.

"Guess we really are on our own," Kerri said, her voice solemn.

Will responded around a yawn. "What do you think our chances are?"

"At the moment, I'm putting them at about ten thousand to one against."

"But you're not giving up."

"Nope. Ten thousand to one against isn't zero. Better a slim chance than none. I won't roll over to those parasitic bastards no matter what happens. Even if we're ultimately doomed to fail, I'm going down fighting."

"Cheerful outlook." Will's voice was deadpan.

Kerri chuckled. "My dad always used to say he'd rather be an optimist who was wrong than a pessimist who was right. Wise man, my dad."

SUNRISE FOUND THEM AT A roadside stop just outside of the little town of Safford, Arizona. They breakfasted on granola bars, fresh apricots, and orange juice they'd picked up at a small grocery store south of the village, which stood wide open and unoccupied. There was a sign on the propped-open front door.

The time of the LORD is at hand, see that you call on the NAME OF JESUS before it's too late! Take all you need of food and drink, none of us will need it much longer, because soon EVERYONE will be gathered up by GOD or by SATAN. Which will it be? Choose GOD and join me in church before the Tribulation is upon you!

Will frowned at the hastily-scribbled message, as the paper that carried it fluttered in the ever-present dry wind. "Should have ended it with 'Have a nice day.' Kind of grim otherwise, don't you think?"

They stocked up on provisions, especially long-lasting, individually-packaged food, water, instant coffee, sugar, salt, and as many other necessities as they could think of. Batteries, matches, toothbrushes and toothpaste, bottles of ibuprofen and antihistamine and No-Doz. A road atlas, after Will pointed out that they couldn't count on internet connections continuing to provide maps. They did grab a few perishables, like a flat of apricots, which was a welcome addition to their breakfast.

They chose to get as far away from the store as they could after loading the car with food and supplies.

"I don't want Mister Bible Thumper to come back and find us here eating his food in the parking lot," Aaron said. "It's fifty-fifty he'd decide we're Satan's minions and get his shotgun."

So they headed a little north from the village and found a roadside stop with a covered picnic area, pulled over, and ate breakfast while they watched the sun rise over the rocky hills to the east.

Between bites, Aaron fiddled with his phone, frowning, and finally looked up. "Getting across Arizona and New Mexico is going to be a pain in the ass. We want to be heading generally east. Looks like Highway 60 is a possibility, but it'll mean heading west for a while on 70. I hate to lose time that way, but I think that's going to be the most direct. There's Highway 380, but that takes us way too close to White Sands. You know the Children have to have hit Alamogordo and Roswell."

"Wonder how the UFO nuts handled an actual alien invasion?" Kerri followed a mouthful of granola bar with a swig of orange juice.

"Don't want to get close enough to find out. But I think we're going to have to continue generally north for a while. I want to cut east at some point, though, because if we don't, we're going to end up in the Colorado Rockies, where the roads get even more twisty. If we take 60 that'll mean we'll have to be on I-25 north for a while, but then we need to keep to the secondary roads. I'd like to avoid Albuquerque."

"I hear it's easy to take a wrong turn there," Will said.

Aaron grinned at him. "Smartass. Once we get into eastern New Mexico, it should be easier. After that, it's flat as a pancake." He peered back down at his phone. "Looks like Highway 60 trends exactly the direction we want to go, at least till it hits the border of Oklahoma. Damn near all the roads in Oklahoma and Kansas run due east-west or north-south. Once we're there, there's probably going to be no direct route. We'll have to do a lot of jittering one way then the other."

"As long as it keeps the Children guessing, I'm good with it," Kerri said. "I wonder how long it'll take them to figure out we're heading for New York? If Saul was right about Colville being a major hub, if they start plotting our path, it won't be hard to figure out."

Will spat an apricot pit out onto the gravel surrounding of the picnic area. "That does bring up a question I've been wondering about, though. How do the Children know where we are? Or do they? It's obvious that they can go wherever they want, judging by that doorway thing they jumped through last night, which, I have to add, was one of the scariest fucking things I've ever seen. But you said they already knew about that place and that we'd try to go there."

"Saul said the same thing."

"Right. So it's not surprising they'd jump through there. But now, do they know where we are?"

Aaron shrugged. "No way to know for sure."

"My guess is no." Kerri looked off into the arid, rocky hills. The Children were out there, and they were powerful, but they had to have some limitations, some kind of Achilles' heel. No need to imagine them to be omnipotent. "Every time we've been attacked, it's either been in a place they knew we'd be, like my apartment, or somewhere that other people knew we were going."

"Like the road in El Paso where we found that poor bugger who had his mind erased," Aaron said.

"But who knew you were going there?" Will looked from one of them to the other. "If they don't track us using their magical alien superpowers, that would imply they're getting their information from spies."

Kerri nodded. "Yes. Exactly. It's probable that at least one of the people at the Boundary headquarters was being controlled by the Children. It would explain how they knew about our movements. It's what made us vulnerable."

"If you're right, then they have no idea where we are right now."

"Which is the first hopeful thing I've heard in days." Aaron stood and stretched. "But it also means we have to be double careful not to be seen by other collaborators. You know they're looking for the three of us. Especially now that they know we've contacted Saul. Once we're spotted, they'll have us pinned down. We've got to maintain our advantage as long as possible."

BUT THREE HOURS OF DRIVING, first northwest on Highway 70 out of Safford, then generally northeast on 60 toward the town of Show Low, then due east toward the border with New Mexico, brought them nothing in the way of resistance. In fact, few cars were heading either way on the highway, which cut directly across the Fort Apache Indian Reservation, a few small towns, and mile after mile of barren desert.

Some of the tension drained from Kerri, and she relaxed back into her seat, her muscles unknotting for the first time since seeing the news broadcast signaling that the Black-eyed Children had at long last launched their first direct attack.

Aaron reached over and rubbed her shoulder. "Hard to stay ramped up for that long, isn't it? At some point, your body says, 'Enough already.'"

She gave him a grateful glance. "Yeah. You can only take so much adrenaline."

"I think we're going to have to find somewhere tonight that we can get some actual sleep. I know it's a risk, but eventually catnaps stop cutting it." He glanced in the rearview mirror and smiled.

Kerri turned. Will was sound asleep in the back seat, his mouth hanging open, body held upright only by his shoulder belt. "I know we're having trouble processing all of this. But can you imagine what he's going through? At least we knew about the Children. Hell, we signed up to fight them. Will? A couple of weeks ago, he was the Assistant Medical Examiner in his home town in southern Louisiana. Now, the world's falling apart, there's an alien invasion, and he's fleeing across the United States with a couple of members of a secret organization that he'd never heard of in his life."

"He said he comes from a big family. He's got to be worried about his parents and siblings."

"We all are." Kerri looked out of the window at the rocky, arid hillsides slipping past under the brilliant sun and cobalt skies of the desert in summer. "I tried to text my mom and dad a couple of times. No response."

"Same."

"I don't think I've ever been this worried."

"It doesn't mean they're not okay." Aaron sounded like he was saying this as much for his own benefit as hers. "Both Saul and the news reports said that the Children were targeting military, government, and communications. Have you gotten any texts or calls on your cell at all?"

"The last one was from Asha, telling us to get out of Las Cruces."

He nodded. "I haven't gotten anything either. Part of it could be poor service—we're pretty far out in the middle of nowhere—but I'll bet it's also because the Children knocked out cell towers. Maybe even satellites. I mean, think of it. You want to take out an entire civilization? Stop them from communicating with each other, that'd be the first step. After that, you can take your time picking off whoever you want. If people can't communicate, you've stopped them from being able to plan any kind of resistance."

"Damn," Kerri said under her breath. "Do you know how hopeless that makes this sound?"

"Oh, yeah. Yeah, I do. But doesn't matter, I'm not giving up, and I wouldn't give up even if I knew I only had a few days left. I am not going to give in to those fucking mind-suckers, not without a fight. For one thing…." He put his hand on her leg, and gave it a squeeze. "This is gonna sound corny as hell, but we… you know. We've got something, you and I. I don't want it to end."

She rested her hand on top of his. "Me, either."

Aaron gave another little glance into the mirror. "You think we should clue Will in that we're, you know, involved?"

"Why would it matter to him?"

He shrugged. "Not sure it would. But in his place, I'd want to know. Make it clear what the situation is. Avoid any misunderstandings."

Kerri grinned and rolled her eyes. "Whatever you think. Have your man-to-man with him. But just remember one thing."

"What's that?"

"I don't care how Stone Age things get, keep in mind that I'm not gonna put up with you two fighting over who owns me. You and Will go all I-Hereby-Claim-the-Fair-Princess on me, I'm likely to kick you both in the balls and walk away."

Aaron snorted laughter. "Point made, your Royal Highness."

KERRI WOKE TO AARON GIVING her arm a shake. She blinked and swallowed, rubbed her eyes, and turned toward him, squinting against the bright light of midafternoon.

"Sorry to wake you."

"'S'awright. What's up?"

"I'm falling asleep at the wheel. You mind taking a turn driving?"

She stretched, her back cracking pleasantly. "Sure. No prob. Where are we?"

"We just cleared the thriving metropolis of Quemado, New Mexico. Looked like population maybe fifty."

"Have you seen anyone?" She gazed at the empty band of the highway, spooling out ahead of them, its outline rippling with heat shimmer.

"Nobody much. Couple of cars heading the opposite way. One of them was a woman in a minivan, packed to the ceiling, roof rack overloaded, looked like a couple of kids in the back seat. She gave me a terrified glance and sped up as we passed, like she thought we were gonna ram into her or block the way or something."

"Wonder where she was going?"

He shrugged. "Who knows? I guess it's natural. Your home town gets attacked, you're gonna think, 'Somewhere else has got to be safer.' Here, though—I have the feeling it's everywhere. You might actually be better off hunkering down, hoping you don't get noticed as long as possible."

"Not exactly what we're doing."

"No. But we're the ones who might actually have a chance of doing something to stop all this."

"What?" The single word sounded bleak, hopeless.

"I'm hoping we'll figure that out as we go along."

He pulled the Renault over to the side of the road.

When Kerri opened the door, the arid wind slapped her, making her wince.

Aaron walked around the front, giving a rueful look and a pat to the dent in the hood where the barrier had struck. "Sorry, baby," he muttered under his breath. But as he passed Kerri, he gave her a quick kiss on the mouth.

Which felt good. No matter how bad the situation got, there were still little things that could buoy you up, even if just for a few moments.

Aaron switched off with Will, taking the back seat, and he was asleep as soon as Kerri hit the cruise control at a comfortable seventy miles per hour. Will gave a cavernous yawn.

"How long was I out?"

"Couple of hours."

"I dreamed I was back at work in the Medical Examiner's office in Lafayette. I was supposed to autopsy all these bodies. They were all children. I kept trying to get someone on the staff to tell me what happened, how there could be all of these dead kids, but no one would tell me. And then I realized they weren't dead. They wanted me to autopsy live people."

Kerri shivered. "Did we tell you about the Black-eyed Child we saw autopsied in Tacoma?"

Will shook his head.

"We killed one of them. Or at least, we thought we had. Gunshot right through the chest. We brought it to the Boundary lab in Tacoma to be autopsied. As soon as it was opened up, you could see it wasn't human. And its head was filled with all of these green fibers, like what you saw covering Doctor Chauvin's brain."

"Holy shit."

"Yeah. But I haven't told you the worst part. The thing came back to life, kicked its way out of the locker it was stowed in, and got away."

"Jesus. They can't be killed?"

"Not that way."

"You have those tranq rifles, though, right? Some kind of magic potion that makes them melt?"

She nodded. "One of them. The one that was in Aaron's car, plus a handful of hypodermic cartridges. But that's slow and inefficient. If there were more than two or three Children attacking you, you'd be toast if that's all you had to defend yourself."

"Cheerful. We're not curled up in a fetal position crying, why?"

"I don't think the human mind works like that." She frowned, looking at the empty desert around her, and the highway that was leading them to... what? To a confrontation, certainly, and one in which they were so completely outnumbered that it was hard to imagine any outcome except horrible ones.

"You know the situation is dire, but you keep going. I know people sometimes give up, but I think it's in our nature to keep trying to survive until it's over."

He frowned and nodded. "Yeah, that's probably right. I mean, realistically speaking, we're three people against how many? But if we were surrounded by Children right now, I'd be fighting like hell."

"Saul said not to think about numbers."

"Hard not to."

"That's for damn sure." She paused. "But I guess there's no point in beating it to death, either. I don't even know what possible plans we can make, other than 'get to Colville, New York.' So maybe we should find something else to talk about."

"Like what?"

She gave him a grin. "Like the fact that Aaron wanted to make sure you knew we were in a relationship."

"Why?" Will shrugged. "It's kind of obvious, you know?"

"Obvious how?"

"The way he looks at you. And I saw when you kissed him when you switched off driving."

Kerri's cheeks warmed. "I didn't think you were looking."

He grinned at her. "Just happened to catch it. You weren't blatant or anything. It was so offhand, and kind of sweet. Not self-conscious, you know? Something you'd only do with someone you really cared about."

"Aaron wanted you to know, so there wouldn't be any misunderstandings later on."

"You mean, like me propositioning you, not realizing you two were together?"

"Something like that."

Will laughed. "Little chance of that."

She gave him a quick, questioning frown.

"No offense intended," he continued. "It's just that if anyone should be worried about being propositioned, it's him, not you."

Her frown deepened, then turned into a smile. "You... I mean, you're...."

"Yup. I'm gay." He shrugged. "Probably best y'all know that, too. But don't worry. I'm not going to go after Aaron. Y'all make a nice couple." His smile turned wicked. "But he does have a nice ass."

Kerri gave a guffaw. "That he does."

———————

HIGHWAY 60 MERGED WITH I-25 north near the town of Socorro. In Socorro itself Kerri stopped for gasoline—the tank was near empty, and there was no telling when the next gas station would be. Their luck held, however, and they weren't challenged, if indeed anyone was there in the attached mini-mart to challenge them.

Best of all, her credit card worked. It was anyone's guess how long that'd continue to be true, and she wondered briefly if Aaron had considered what they'd do if they were no longer able to fill the tank. New York was a hell of a long way on foot.

She pulled away from the station and back onto the highway. The overpass where I-25 crossed was straight up ahead. She felt more than a little apprehension as she looped onto the on-ramp. She'd seen people in Socorro, men and women who turned hostile faces toward them as they sped by. One of them had hoisted a gun and given a sweeping gesture with one hand, the meaning of which had been all too obvious.

Don't even think of stopping. Keep going, and don't make us use these guns, because we will.

They still saw only a handful of cars, most of them in the southbound lanes, heading away from Albuquerque. What would a city that size be like in a situation like this? Chaos could bring out incredible selflessness and com-passion, but it also triggered fear, anger, greed, irrationality. Aaron's insistence on avoiding cities was smart, but who knew how far the danger would spread, how quickly?

"I think we're in trouble," Will said, in a flat, quiet voice, and pointed ahead.

Made stark by the crimson light of the setting sun was a group of people standing in the middle of the road. At the noise of their approach, faces turned. The westering sunlight cast weird shadows across their faces, making them look surreal, not quite human. As she neared them, they didn't move, frozen like statues. At their feet were crumpled bodies, perhaps a half dozen, maybe more.

They were a hundred yards from the cluster of figures before one of them turned, smoothly raising a gun and aiming it right at the car. She didn't hear the report of the gun firing, but she did hear its aftermath—a sharp bang as the bullet struck the side of the car, somewhere ahead of where Will sat on the passenger side.

Kerri swerved around them, the left wheel slipping off into the rocky verge. The man fired again, this time missing the car entirely.

Will pressed the button to roll down the window, yelling toward the people as they swept past, "What the fuck, guys? Save your Neighborhood Watch bullshit for the real enemies!"

Whether they heard him or not was impossible to determine, but there were no further shots.

It was only after they'd gone a mile farther, and the cluster of vigilantes had been lost to view in the failing light of evening, that Kerri realized several of the bodies lying collapsed on the road surface had been children.

Black-eyed Children? Or some poor human children, unlucky enough to be mistaken for them? No way to be sure. She hadn't seen any blood on the asphalt, but at the speed they were traveling, she might well have missed it.

"What the hell just happened?" said a sleepy voice from the backseat. "You putting more dents in my car?"

"Not me. Some dude who thinks he's a Rambo clone took a pot shot at us."

Will shook his head. "Bound to happen. I think we're in for some serious *Lord of the Flies* shit."

"I always hated that book." Kerri gripped the steering wheel tighter. "Right now, I just want to get this piece of interstate behind us. The closer we get to Albuquerque, the more nervous I get."

"Agreed," Aaron said. "But according to the map, it's only twenty-five miles or so before Highway 60 peels off toward the east again. Then it's a straight shot across eastern New Mexico and into Texas."

"Great." Will snorted. "Texas'll be fun. Your average Texan has enough fire-power to make Rambo look like he was packing a popgun."

"Well, we're not going to get there today. Once night falls, I'd rather hole up somewhere safe and try to get a good night's sleep."

Kerri gave a quick look at Aaron in the rearview mirror. "Where's safe?"

"I don't know. We'll have to trust our gut and hope for the best."

"Hasn't that been what we've been doing all along?"

He shrugged. "I guess."

"And you know what?" Will said in a faux-cheerful voice. "All three of us are still alive! So far, flying by the seat of the pants has had a one hundred per-cent success rate!"

The sign for Highway 60 East appeared, the green reflective paint bright in the surrounding gloom. She put her turn signal on, for no particular reason, and pulled into the turn lane. "Honestly, I'm not discounting that. Like I said earlier, I plan to keep fighting until the last possible moment."

Will grunted assent, but added, "Yeah, I know. But right now, I need to take a piss, then get some food, a bottle of cold beer, and a comfortable bed, in that order. Sorry if I'm grumpy."

"You have reason," Aaron said. "We all have reason."

CHAPTER

6

FULL DARK HAD FALLEN BY the time they saw a sign that said, *CITY LIMITS. Vaughn, New Mexico. Pop. 412.*

"City?" Will said.

Kerri smiled. "By comparison to the surrounding hundred square miles, it's Manhattan." The past hour had been a drive through terrain that was flat, dusty, an unending plain carpeted with sagebrush and creosote bush and not a whole lot else. She pointed to a sign, barely visible in their headlights, that said, *Flying Z Motel,* adorned with a cartoonish depiction of a cowboy with a lariat looped around an ornate letter *Z* with wings. There was only a single light on, in what appeared to be the office.

"Chance it?" Aaron said, easing his foot onto the brakes.

"We can't keep driving rotating shifts forever. We've got to get a good night's sleep, or eventually the fatigue will stop us cold." She peered out of the window at the low, blocky row of rooms, perhaps a dozen or so. "May as well give it a try. But keep your gun handy. Even if the Children aren't here, some scared and trigger-happy humans might be. We'd be just as dead either way."

"Jesus, Kerri," Will said from the back seat. "You sure know how to encourage a guy."

Aaron pulled into a space in the otherwise empty parking lot and shut off the engine. There was no sound but the hiss of the wind. Moving as quietly as they could, all three exited the car and moved toward the lit window, which was next to a door with a faded sign that said, *Office.*

"Better not just bust in," Kerri said. "Things as they are, I know if I was out in the middle of nowhere like this, three strangers come barreling in, I'd shoot first and sort it all out later."

Aaron nodded, and gave a gentle rap on the door. "Hello the house. Can we come in? There's three of us, but we mean no harm. We need a place to sleep."

There was a clunk and a low dragging sound, like someone moving a chair across a wooden floor.

Then a low voice said, "All right. But keep your distance. I'm armed."

It was impossible to tell if the voice was male or female, young or old. What was certain is that it was rough with fear.

They exchanged wide-eyed glances, then Aaron reached for the door handle, turned it, and pushed the door open.

Standing behind a waist-high wooden counter was a tall, thin woman, perhaps forty-five, with long brown hair shot through with gray, done up in an untidy bun. Her face was tanned, and crow's feet showed in the corners of her eyes. She wore a worn dress that looked a pale canary yellow in the lamplight. She gave the three of them a darkly suspicious look, but at least the shotgun she held remained pointed toward the floor.

"Where y'all from?"

"Near Las Cruces." Kerri turned her hands toward the woman, palms upward. "We're just trying to get away from this craziness."

"The riots and such?"

Kerri nodded.

The woman shrugged. "Y'all don't know? It's everywhere. There's news from LA and Las Vegas and Dallas. Other places, too. Heard that on the TV before the signal cut out. If you're runnin', best realize what you're runnin' from is the same thing you'll likely be runnin' into."

"At the moment," Aaron said, "we're just trying to stay one step ahead and stay alive. But we've already had one sleepless night, and if we keep going, we're gonna collapse. Can you rent us a room for the night? We don't have cash, but last we checked, our credit cards still worked."

The woman gave a mirthless laugh. "Credit cards? Shit." She cleared her throat. "Y'all could sign a credit slip for ten thousand dollars, wouldn't make no difference. Don't you realize? This is it. The whole shootin' match is fallin' apart. Don't even much matter if you paid me in cash, I reckon. If it's worth anything now, won't be for long."

Kerri shook her head. "It's all we have."

The woman's shrewd brown eyes met Kerri's gaze steadily. "I'm guessin' that's a lie. You got this far, you gotta have given some thought to food and water and supplies and such. But hell, I don't blame you, if it were me I wouldn't want to give that away either. Gonna be worth its weight in gold soon." She set the shotgun on the counter with a clatter. "Anyhow. All one to me. Got no other guests, not likely to get any, now or later. Y'all want a couple o' rooms, take 'em. My treat."

"You're trusting."

"I got a good second sight about people. I can tell when they mean me harm. Hasn't failed me yet."

"You might want to be a little overcautious in the next few weeks. But thanks for not starting with us."

"It's the Christian thing to do. You're in trouble, I can tell that, a ways from home, if there's even a home for you to go back to. Way I see it, good folks gotta band together, or we're sunk."

"That's true." Kerri released a breath she hadn't realized she'd been holding. "And thanks. We'll leave first thing tomorrow. We're telling the truth that all we want is a good night's sleep."

"I'm Rose Dawson." The woman held out a brown, work-hardened hand, and each of them shook it in turn.

After introductions were made, Kerri said, "What do you know about what's happened?"

One corner of Rose's mouth twitched upwards, the first approach to a smile

Kerri had seen. "I'm gonna make a guess, here, and that's that y'all know more about this than I do." She gestured toward them. "You two have guns, and look pretty official. Betcher detectives or something. Am I right?"

"Close," Aaron said. "DHS."

Rose snorted. "You didn't keep the homeland very secure, did you?"

"There's not much we could have done." He glanced over at Kerri. "I think we owe it to her to tell her what we know."

Kerri nodded, and Aaron launched into a much-abbreviated account of the invasion, and the events of the last few days.

There was a long silence after he finished, but finally Rose spoke, in slow, measured tones. "Last week, if someone told me that, I'd'a told 'em to take their story down to Roswell. Today? Hell, it all fits with what I seen and heard. Aliens, huh?"

"That's what we think," Kerri said.

"And it's all over the world, not just the US."

She nodded.

Rose scowled at her. "And what are you trying to do about it? I got a pretty good eye, and I don't think three DHS agents driving forty-eight hours straight—or however long y'all been at it—is a coincidence. You're not just tryin' to get away. You're headin' toward something and for a particular reason." She placed both hands on the counter, and leaned toward them, lifting her shoulders and making her bony frame looked even more angular. "You tryin' to stop these sonsabitches?"

"That's what we're aiming at, yes," Aaron said. "We don't have a good plan yet, but we're heading toward New York, where there's supposedly some kind of command center of the Black-eyed Children."

"New York City?"

"No, somewhere upstate. Don't know the geography that well, but it's somewhere in the western part of the state."

"Huh." One ironic eyebrow went up. "And just the three of you, storming a command center?"

Aaron chuckled grimly. "Yeah, I know. Has 'suicide mission' written all over it, doesn't it?"

"You could say that."

"Even so, we have to try, you know?"

"Where there's life, there's hope, you mean?"

"Yeah, I suppose."

Rose shook her head. "Guess you gotta keep tryin'. Me, I'm just gonna hunker down here and take my chances. I figure I'll do okay. I got a generator, and my well's pretty reliable for this part of the world. I can defend myself if anybody stops by thinkin' they'll rob me or whatnot, or if little green men show up at my doorstep. I been preppin' for something bad going down for a while now. Figured the way things were goin' in the world, it was bound to happen sooner or later, though I gotta say I never expected something like this."

Kerri gave her a grim nod. "No one did."

"You're right about that. I got enough food socked away to keep me goin' for a while, probably at least three months or so if I'm careful with it. At that point, what you're tellin' me is true, either the powers-that-be'll have it squared away, or the aliens'll have won and it'll all be over. I gotta just sit tight until I see which it'll be." She looked down. "Anyhow. Y'all must want to get some sleep. Two rooms or three?"

Kerri gave Aaron a little smile. "Two."

Rose unhooked a pair of keys from a rack and slapped them on the counter. "One and two. Next door, and next one over. You sleep tight. I'll probably be up tomorrow morning by the time you're ready to go, but if you need to bug out and I'm not here, then… well, good luck. Y'know. With whatever damnfool thing it is you're tryin' to do. Give those bastards an extra kick for me, okay?"

Aaron laughed. "We will."

They picked up the keys and exited into the warm, still night.

"That was lucky," Kerri said in a quiet voice. "I could see that going way worse, considering some of the folks we've seen today."

"I'm not going to completely relax until we're back in the car, driving, tomorrow morning." He looked over at Will. "Let's just say I'm not as trusting of my fellow humans' good intentions as she is. Lock your door tonight."

Will yawned. "No duh."

"You need anything, pound on the wall and scream your head off. We can give you one of the guns for now—we don't need both in one room. Tomorrow, we should see about getting you armed." Aaron unholstered his gun, and held it out. Will took it, a little gingerly.

"Ever fired a gun before?"

The doctor nodded. "Did some duck hunting when I was a teenager. Haven't shot a gun in a while, though."

"Don't hesitate to use it. Someone tries to break through the door, shoot. You might not get a second chance."

Will nodded, his face white in the dim light. "This fucking sucks."

"That it does," Kerri said. "Good night."

"Y'all too."

They each unlocked their doors, and disappeared into the rooms. Kerri heard Will's door lock and the sound of a chain being fastened.

The room was clean and tidy, if a little musty-smelling, and there was a thin coating of dust on the dresser and the top of the television. She sat on the bed, which creaked slightly, but seemed comfortable enough.

"You know, it's amazing Will's doing as well as he is."

"True that." Aaron gave her a concerned frown. "How about you? How are you holding up?"

"I'm honestly not sure."

He sat down next to her and slipped his arm around her waist. "If there's one thing I've learned, it's that everything seems more hopeful after a good night's sleep."

She gave him a grateful smile. "I hope you're planning on not getting to sleep right away."

He grinned at her. "You're in the mood? I figured you'd be dead exhausted."

"I am. But I need you." She reached out a hand, let her fingertips trail down his chest. "Make love to me, Aaron. I need to be reminded that whatever is going on around us, and whatever might lie ahead for us, what we've got right now is sweet."

He leaned over and gave her a tender kiss on the mouth. "I can remind you of that whenever you want it."

She smiled as she unbuttoned his shirt. "We'll need to keep it at least a little quiet. Will's right next door."

"The bed creaks," Aaron said, running his hand along her side. "Not much we can do about that."

"He'll have to deal." She wrapped her arms around him, pulling him onto his side, pressing herself against his lean, muscular frame, and for a time there was no more conversation.

———————

KERRI WOKE IN THE MIDDLE of the night. A digital clock on the bedside stand said 3:12, too early for there to be even a hint of light in the eastern sky. She rolled over, snuggling up against the warmth of Aaron's bare skin, and put one arm around his waist. He gave a little moan of pleasure, shifted slightly, and subsided back into sleep.

What kind of chance did they have? Rose had been right—what they were planning was nothing more than a suicide mission. All of their earlier talk about fighting back, holding out until their last breaths, seemed like foolishness. Part of it was fatigue and grief speaking, horror at the memory of Asha Choudhary's last, desperate text message, that Asha and the rest of the people she'd known at headquarters were probably dead by now, or worse. Hell, she even found herself worrying about Rendell, for Chrissake, and he'd certainly never done her any favors. At a moment like this, any person, good, bad, or otherwise, was preferable to the blank-faced Children, who were lightyears removed from flesh-and-blood humanity.

She rested her cheek on Aaron's shoulder, breathing in his scent, and closed her eyes. She couldn't accept the possibility that this relationship, so newly minted, was doomed to be torn apart only days, or at the most weeks, ahead. What kind of happy ending she could expect, she had no idea, but it had to contain more than she and Aaron being food for the Children, or turned into mindless automata. And Will Daigle—the wry and quick-witted young doctor had thrown his lot in with them without a backward glance. That kind of self-lessness couldn't end in loss.

It just couldn't.

But then she remembered Danielle Tauriac, bleeding her life away next to a New Mexico highway. A pointless, empty death, one that accomplished nothing for either side except to take away one of the staunchest fighters they had. The reality was, they weren't guaranteed any kind of positive outcome. It was all in flux, all in constant motion, and anyone's guess how it would fall out.

The universe owed them nothing. Their little battles and loves and losses and wins were not so much as a blip, a shudder in the fabric of space and time, there and gone in an instant, leaving no lasting mark.

A tear streaked down her cheek and dripped onto Aaron's shoulder. Kerri wasn't someone who cried easily, but here, in the darkness in a strange town, with a thousand miles of unknown risk ahead of her, she couldn't hold it in. Aaron stirred, then rolled toward her, and his strong arms encircled her, pulling her against him as her body was wracked by sobs she couldn't contain.

"I'm sorry," she said, when the storm had mostly passed, when she could speak again.

"For what?" Aaron's voice was sleepy and warm and comforting.

"For waking you up. For losing it. For everything."

He kissed her cheek, and ran one hand through her hair. "You never have to apologize to me for feeling things."

She gave another shuddery sob. "I just don't want to lose you."

"Why do you think you're going to?"

She pressed her face against his chest. "Aren't you afraid? Of losing it all?"

"Of course I'm afraid." He stroked her back. "It comes and goes. I go through periods of the screaming horrors. I just hide it well. Yesterday, while I was driving, more than once I wanted to pull over, run off into the desert, and find a nice cave for the three of us to hide in until this is all over. But you know what? It's worth fighting for. All of it. I know humans have done some really stupid things. We've fought idiotic wars for idiotic reasons, hurt each other, let greed and ignorance and apathy run things. But I still believe it's worth saving. We're worth saving."

"We, as in humanity? Or we, as in you and me? What we have?"

"Both. Look, Kerri, this may not be the right time to tell you this, but there's no guarantee that there'll be any other time except now. I've never felt about another woman like I feel about you. Somehow knowing we could be in a battle for our lives tomorrow, with no certain outcome, brings it all into sharper focus."

His lips brushed her forehead, soft as butterfly wings.

"I love you, Kerri Elias. Whatever happens, whatever decisions we have to make, wherever we end up, the one thing I can't face is that I might miss my only opportunity of telling you that. I love you."

"I love you, too." The words came out with a hiccup of a sob. "I've been wanting to tell you, too. It's just all too much."

"See if you can get a little more sleep. For now, let it all go. I've got you. I'll hold you till morning. When the daylight shows us what new challenges we have to face, we'll decide what to do then. Right now, sleep."

She nestled up to him, drew a shuddery breath, and let it out slowly. Amazingly, she felt her body relaxing as she lay there cradled in her lover's arms. The last thing she thought, before she was overtaken by sleep, was that they wouldn't end their run captured and enslaved by the Children.

She knew, knew beyond any doubt, that whatever they were destined for, it wasn't that. She also knew that this certainty wouldn't last, and the attendant fear would return.

But for now, it was enough.

SHE WOKE TO THE HARSH light of a desert morning angling in through a gap in the curtains. Aaron still held her close, but he was deeply asleep, chest rising and falling with long, deep breaths. She let her consciousness rise slowly, not moving, for the moment simply relishing the comfort. But soon, other ideas edged that one out, and she slipped her hand across the flat skin of his belly, then farther down still.

"Careful," he said, a drowsy smile in his voice. "You'll awaken the dragon."

"Seems like he's already awake."

Aaron made a noise a little like a purr. "Not my fault if he'd like an encore after last night."

Forty-five minutes later, she swung her legs out of bed, hoping that muscles unstrung and wobbly, and a brain spinning in a dizzy, post-orgasmic fog, would carry her into the shower.

They did.

Barely.

When she returned to the room wrapped in a towel, Aaron gave her an appreciative grin and stretched luxuriously, arms behind his head, back arching.

"I wasn't sure I could stand up," she said.

"I'm still not sure I can."

She touched his face, traced his rough jawline with one finger. "Thanks. Thanks for last night."

"Which part of it?"

"All of it. Especially holding me when I lost it. I hate breaking down, losing control that way. Thanks for understanding."

He shrugged. "It happens to all of us. We're gonna have to lean on each other, you know? None of us have been in this kind of situation before."

"I wonder how Will is handling all of this?"

"I don't know. It's gotta be hard."

"I didn't tell you. He and I had a conversation about the fact that you and

I are involved. There was an opening to bring it up while you were sleeping in the car yesterday, so I mentioned it."

"Oh? How'd he respond?"

"He said not to worry about it, he's gay anyhow."

Aaron grinned. "Well, that makes it simpler."

"And he told me not to worry, that he wasn't going to proposition you, or anything."

The grin turned into a laugh. "At least we won't have to worry about friction over who's sleeping with who."

———

WHILE AARON SHOWERED, KERRI DRESSED—same clothes as yesterday, they hadn't even been able to grab a change of clothes from their apartments in their haste to get out of Las Cruces. Have to do something about that soon, or they'd be stinking the car up so bad they'd have to drive with their heads out of the windows. She went outside and found Rose Dawson pouring a pitcher of water on some potted plants that stood near the office door.

Rose shaded her eyes and squinted. "Sleep all right?"

"Well enough. Thanks for letting us stay here."

The older woman shook her head and gave a dismissive gesture with one hand. "No skin off my nose. Not like you were edging out paying customers. Where y'all heading today?"

"Into Texas. Aaron's got it plotted out, at least the next few steps. It'd be a lot harder without GPS."

"Internet still working? Mine's been out since yesterday morning."

"I haven't checked this morning," Kerri said. "But none of us were able to send or receive cellphone messages yesterday. In any case, GPS and internet are separate. As long as the satellites are transmitting, we'll have GPS. But cell service and internet—yeah, I'm not surprised those are out. The news report we heard said the first things attacked were military installations and communications centers."

"Cut people off from each other, stop them from defending themselves."

"Exactly. By the way, do you have any idea where we might be able to find a store to get a change of clothes? We left Las Cruces with nothing but what was on our backs."

Rose frowned. "If you head up 54, Santa Rosa has a coupla stores. Straight on down 60 about an hour is Fort Sumner, and there's a gift store there where y'all could get some t-shirts at least. Doubt they sell underwear, though. Another hour along, there's a Walmart and a Target in Clovis, right before you cross into Texas. That might be your best bet."

"We can stand each other for at least a little while longer, I think."

Rose gave her a solemn nod and turned back to caring for her plants.

Kerri went to the door of Room #2 and gave a quiet knock. "Will? It's Kerri."

"Oh. Okay. Hang on, let me get dressed." There was a series of rustling noises for a couple of minutes, followed by the sound of the chain being pulled back and the deadbolt unlocked. Will squinted out into the bright morning.

"G'morning, sunshine," Kerri said. "How did you sleep?"

"You mean, after y'all were done banging the headboard against the wall?"

Kerri hoped her blush didn't show too badly in the sunlight. "Sorry."

"No problem. Wouldn't want to spoil your fun. Anyhow, after that I slept like a baby. Woke up every two hours crying for my mommy."

She laughed. "We should hit the road soon. I talked to Rose. She said there was a Walmart in Clovis, two hours down the road, where we could pick up some changes of clothes, and maybe more food and water."

"You think they'll be open?"

"One way to find out."

They were ready to go a half-hour later and thanked Rose for her generosity.

She shrugged. "I didn't do nothin', not really. Let you have a place to sleep. Like I said, Christian thing to do, and besides, pretty certain I won't have other guests any time soon, way things are goin'."

"Take care of yourself," Aaron said.

"I'm good at that. Been on my own for thirty years. You get good at knowin' who's trustworthy and who's not."

"My recommendation is to be suspicious of children, especially ones in ragged clothes."

"Yeah, you made that clear enough. Good luck to y'all, I hope you succeed at whatever the hell you're tryin' to do. Still don't really understand it."

"I'm not sure we do, either," Kerri said. "We're figuring things out as we go."

Rose sighed. "Crazy old world. Still never guessed it'd come to this." She raised her hand as they got into the Renault and started it up, then leaned on the frame, and Aaron rolled down the window.

"Y'all need gas, there's a filling station a little way further along Route 60. Run by a friend of mine, Lewis Hanlon. Tell him I sent ya, that y'all are friends of mine. He'll help you out."

"Thanks," Aaron said. "You've been far more helpful than we had any right to expect."

This elicited a little smile. "Hell, we humans got to stick together, right? Any case, some advice. I got on the shortwave radio this morning. TV and radio are pickin' up nothin' but static at this point. But I raised a coupla people on the shortwave. Things are bad out there. Food's runnin' short, and gasoline's gonna be next. Once that happens, people are stuck where they are, they're gonna get desperate. And desperate people do stupid stuff."

"That's the truth."

"One guy I talked to said there're already people going around ransacking houses for food. Guess once something like this happens, it's pretty obvious what direction it's going."

"At least we know there are people like you who are willing to help out strangers. There must be others. That's a hopeful thought."

"I s'pose. Y'all take care of yourselves."

"We will," Kerri said. "You do the same."

She nodded, straightened up, and gave them another solemn wave as they backed up, turned, and pulled back out onto Highway 60 heading east toward Texas.

———————————

THEY GASSED UP AT HANLON'S E-Z Mart—Rose was right, the proprietor approached them with a scowl and drawn gun until they said they were friends of hers, then he happily let them fill the tank. The credit card reader on the pump was offline, but Hanlon let them pay by signing a credit slip against Aaron's VISA card.

Unlikely he'd ever be able to cash it in, but Kerri didn't say that.

"Sucks that we didn't think about getting money from the bank," Will said as they were pulling away from the gas pump. "Too late now."

"Why do you say that? There may still be banks out there trying to keep things together."

He shook his head. "Won't work. Remember what Rose said? Internet's down. I'll bet that's true everywhere. All the accounts are linked electronically. Even if you went to your home bank, they'd have to have a working server to see if you had money in your account, or even were a customer. Any other bank—no possibility. We missed our shot at cash."

"At some point people'll realize that cash is worthless, anyhow," Aaron said. "Food and clean water and medicine are going to be the tradable commodities really soon."

Will shrugged. "It might have bought us a few days' leeway. The real problem is going to be gasoline. I don't know how the hell we're going to deal with that one."

"Farms," Kerri said. "All farms have some sort of reserve gasoline storage, to fuel tractors and so on."

Will gave her a dubious look. "Might be our best option. But farmers are also likely to be guarding it pretty well."

The next two hours were much the same as the previous day had been.

Miles of highway unspooling ahead of them, crossing the arid plains of eastern New Mexico. Bright sunshine in a cloudless blue sky. A small town, an expanse of empty scrubland, then another town, one following another. Yeso, Fort Sumner, Taiban, Melrose. It was just outside of Melrose, as they passed a green sign that said, *CLOVIS 24 miles,* that Kerri saw in the distance a pair of figures walking by the side of the road.

"Aaron," she said, giving a little gesture with one hand.

As they got closer, she saw that one of them was a child of about twelve. The other, however, was a man, perhaps forty years old, with a crewcut, a sunburned face, and wild, desperate eyes. As soon as he saw them approaching, he began to jump up and down, flailing his arms.

At the same time, the little boy's knees buckled, and he crumpled to the side of the highway.

Aaron slowed the car.

"What the hell are you doing?" Will shouted from the back seat. "A kid. It's a *kid.* You know what that could mean."

But Aaron continued to slow, finally pulling alongside them, and used the switch in the driver's side door to roll the window down, her own heart rate accelerating. They'd trusted Rose Dawson, and it'd turned out all right. If they continued to trust the people they met, however, sooner or later it would backfire. Badly.

"I'm with Will," Kerri said in a harsh whisper. "He could be a collaborator. We can't risk it."

"We can't leave them out in the desert to die."

"You've got to help me," the man shouted, running toward the car. "My son... my son's ill. Our house was attacked by people, by people looking for food and water. They drove us out, threatened to kill us both if we didn't leave. But Jason...." He looked back at the inert figure of the little boy. "He's got type-one diabetes. They wouldn't let us take his insulin." He choked back a sob.

Aaron's voice was grim. "Tell your son to look at us."

The man's face creased with bafflement. "What?"

"If you don't back up, right now, and tell your son to open his eyes and look at us, I'm flooring the accelerator and getting right the hell out of here."

The man backed away, his face still a study in perplexity. He went to the boy, and lifted his thin frame, turned his head toward the car.

"Jason," he said, his voice gentle. "Jason, wake up. Open your eyes. Look at the people in the car."

Jason's eyes fluttered open, and he gazed around him without focusing on anything. Kerri saw smoky gray eyes, dark pupils contracted against the brilliant sunlight, surrounded by glossy whites.

"Get in," Aaron said.

CHAPTER

7

THE MAN'S NAME WAS GREG Lantz, and he was a general contractor in Melrose. Former Army, divorced, he spoke with a direct bluntness that made Kerri trust him immediately, but his no-nonsense demeanor was undercut with true fear. After he and his son had fled their house, they'd taken to the road on foot—the gang that had attacked trashed his car. It was run or fight, and he was not only outnumbered two dozen to one, but he had his son to consider. Heaven only knew what he'd have done if they hadn't happened along, walking with a sick child by the side of a desert highway in midsummer. At least now they were safe in the back seat of an air-conditioned car, Jason tucked between his father and Will Daigle. The boy seemed to be sleeping, but whether it was simple fatigue or a manifestation of his illness was impossible to tell.

"Do you have any idea what the hell is happening out there?" Greg asked, as they passed a sign saying *Melrose 3 miles*. So far they hadn't encountered any resistance, but it was becoming increasingly clear their luck would run out sooner or later.

Kerri wondered if he would take to an explanation of an alien invasion as quickly as Rose Dawson had and decided to give him a less fraught answer.

"There's been a coordinated attack on military bases, police stations, and communications centers. How extensive it is, we don't know yet."

Greg gave her a grim nod. "Terrorism. I figured something like that. Television and radio stations all went out midday yesterday. Internet an hour later. Even before that, I only got sketchy information on what was happening. It seemed bad, that's all."

"I think that'll turn out to be an understatement," Aaron said.

"What are the three of you running from? Or running to? You look like you're on a mission."

Aaron glanced at Kerri, who gave him a little shrug.

"We're in a position of trying to fight back. We're DHS."

A new measure of respect came into the man's voice. The military obey-your-superiors instinct was evidently still there. "What can I do to help?"

Aaron shook his head. "Your son comes first. We have to see if we can get him his meds. But in any case, we're trying to get across the country, following intelligence that a hub of operations for the enemy is in western New York state. Some town called Colville. I think it's close to Rochester."

"And the three of you are planning on an attack? You have backup, right?" He looked from one of them to the other.

No one spoke.

"I see. I guess you do what you have to." His tone of resignation was obvious.

"We've been given a slim ray of hope," Aaron finally said. "We're going to give it what we can. Better than curling up into a fetal position."

"Absolutely. And I appreciate the fact that you stopped. But I gotta ask—what was the thing about having Jason look at you? Why was that important?"

So much for avoiding the truth.

"Look, this may be hard to believe."

"Okay."

"It's not terrorism. At least not like what you're probably thinking of. We weren't attacked by foreign agents. We were attacked by something on another level entirely."

"Some... *thing?*" Greg looked from one of them to the other.

"It's a group of... I don't know what to call them other than 'aliens.' They're certainly not from the Earth. They masquerade as children, but you can tell by the eyes. Their eyes are solid black. No irises, no whites."

"Aliens," Greg repeated. He spoke in a flat voice that communicated neither belief nor disbelief.

"It's the best descriptor we've got," Aaron said. "I know it sounds like science fiction."

"That's the truth." He paused. "But hell, I got no better explanation. And I remember from the news reports, what few I was able to listen to, that someone mentioned being attacked by kids. I heard that more than once, reports from several different cities. LA for sure, and Phoenix, and I think I remember one from Seattle. I assumed they meant, you know. Teenagers. Gangs. Kids who were taking advantage of the chaos to loot and riot."

"No. These children are something else entirely. And they were the cause of the attacks, not opportunists trying to profit from them."

"I don't even know how to respond to that."

"I've been caught up in this for a couple of weeks, and I still don't, either," Will said.

Greg pointed. "Take the next left."

Aaron turned onto Brownhorn Street, then gave Greg a questioning look.

"Six blocks up. Right on Wisconsin. We're the third house on the left."

They'd only gone two blocks when Greg said, in a low growl, "That's them. The sonsabitches who broke into my house."

A group of perhaps a dozen, all males, all armed, turned in unison to look at them as they drove past. The leader seemed to be a blond man with a mustache and goatee, shirtless except for an unbuttoned Confederate-flag-emblazoned jean jacket that did nothing to hide a paunch that flopped over his belt. The man spoke a quick command, shook his head, and put out a meaty hand to hold back one of his friends. But his steely eyes followed them as they drove up the road until they were lost to sight.

"That guy," Greg said, his voice taut with fury. "He's the bastard who wouldn't even let me get Jason's meds from the fridge." He stroked his son's hair, and the boy stirred and moaned softly, but his eyes didn't open. "He said he'd shoot him for me, that it was better than letting a sickly kid live. Can you believe it? I knew there were people like that, but right here, you know? In your own home town."

Kerri pictured Rose Dawson's unsmiling face, offering them a place to stay the night and asking nothing in return. "Extreme situations bring out the best and worst in people."

They passed other ransacked houses. Doors stood open, windows broken. One had a screen door torn right off its hinges, lying bent and useless against the low stone wall of a rock garden.

The worst was a low ranch-style house. There were bullet holes in the door, showing splintered wood and what looked like blood stains. A woman in a flower-print dress lay face down, collapsed in the driveway in a pool of her own blood.

From the back seat, Will breathed the word, "Jesus."

Kerri swallowed hard and forced herself to look away.

Aaron turned onto Wisconsin Street and pulled into the driveway of the third house on the left. It was a small cottage, modest but well-kept, although like most of the homes they'd passed, the lawn had crisped to a dismal brown in the summer sun.

And like the others, its front door was wide open, and one of the windows had been shattered.

Aaron turned off the engine, and slowly, quietly, they got out of the car.

Greg shook his son's shoulder gently. "Jason, buddy? Time to wake up. We're back home."

The boy looked up at his father, winced a little, and cleared his throat. "Dad, I'm thirsty."

"We'll get you a glass of water when we're inside. And your meds. That'll help you to feel better. All right, sport?"

Jason gave a little nod and struggled to his feet.

Aaron and Kerri drew their guns as they approached the door. Their quiet footfalls scrunched on shards of broken glass from the window. Aaron stepped through first, turning quickly to look behind the door, but no one was there.

He motioned for the others to follow.

The living room was a shambles. Sofa cushions were slashed. A rocking chair lay on its side, its delicate woodwork splintered by a kick of a booted foot. Bookshelves were emptied, the books and framed photographs they'd held lying in piles on the floor.

"Why?" Greg said in a stricken voice. "Why would they do this? It must have been obvious I didn't have much worth stealing. It's just destroying for the sake of destroying."

There wasn't any good response to that. Kerri gave the man a sympathetic look, then followed Aaron into the kitchen.

If the living room had been trashed, the kitchen was worse. Every cabinet stood open and empty. The fridge and freezer doors were twisted almost off their hinges. What little they'd left behind—all Kerri saw at a quick glance was a mostly-empty jar of mustard, a ratty-looking head of lettuce, and a carton of milk that lay on its side, its contents dripping from the shelves—was hardly worth stealing.

Greg gave an inarticulate cry, and knelt on the floor, pawing through the detritus. Scattered around were about a dozen small glass bottles, each one smashed with what must have been a deliberate intent to leave not a single one unbroken.

He looked up, oblivious to the cuts on his hands from handling the broken glass. Tears wet his cheeks, incongruous on a face as tough as his.

"Why?" He looked down, his chest rising and falling spasmodically.

"Are any intact?" Kerri asked.

He shook his head.

Aaron put a hand on the man's shoulder. "Then get what you need from the house. There's no reason to stay here. We've got to find a pharmacy."

At least Greg was able to get his son a glass of water before they left, which the boy guzzled gratefully. Then they made their way out of the ruined kitchen, through the living room, and onto the front step. There was still no sign of the raiders. All of the houses in sight stood with doors open. No need to stick around once anything of value had been taken.

"Where the hell are the police?" Greg said, as they climbed back into Aaron's car. "What's my tax money paying for?"

Kerri buckled herself in. "What we heard is that police, military, and communications were targeted first. It might be that there are no police left around here."

"God." Greg dragged the back of his hand across his wet cheek. At the moment, he sounded more furious than sad. "It didn't take the lowlifes long to figure out that they had free rein."

"It usually doesn't," Aaron said as he backed his car out onto the street.

They turned back down Brownhorn toward Route 60, and at the same spot was the heavyset blond man and his cohort. The gang had known what they'd find in the house, and were waiting for them to return, for one more chance to gloat.

And sure enough, as they passed, the blond man grinned at them, raised one hand with the middle finger extended, and with the other grabbed his crotch.

Aaron slammed on the brakes, snarling out an obscenity.

"No!" Kerri shouted. "No. It won't accomplish anything. We have to get Jason's meds first. They're not worth the ammunition."

Aaron swallowed and nodded. The blond man, his smile gone in an instant, was striding toward the car, reaching for his gun, and his friends had surged forward as well.

Aaron floored the accelerator, and the gang's ugly faces were obscured in a cloud of dust and flying gravel. His jaw clenched. "Makes me sick to let trash like that get away with ruining people's lives."

"Shit," Greg said from the back seat. He sounded near tears again. "What turns people like that? I don't get it. I just don't get it. I could be starving, and I wouldn't do that to someone."

Aaron shook his head. "Look at how conquerors treat the people in the countries they've invaded. If you're trying to establish dominance, you do what it takes to make people lose the will to fight back. If you destroy people's stuff, it has a profound psychological effect. They feel afraid. Most of all, they feel unsafe. If you can get rid of someone's sense of security, their sense of being in control of their own lives, they're halfway defeated already."

"What I don't understand is why someone wants that kind of dominance in the first place. Over who? A retired Army guy with a bad back and his sick son? You saw that woman they'd shot down in her front yard? That was Mary Hamelin. She baked cookies for people. No reason, just because she liked doing it. What did they accomplish by killing Mary? What did they gain? There's nobody here that's worth destroying. I just don't get it."

And once again, there was no good response to that. They turned left onto Route 60 toward Clovis.

"The woman we stayed with last night said there's a Walmart in Clovis," Aaron said, as they cleared the last cross streets and left Melrose receding in the rearview mirror. "They'll have a pharmacy."

"The Walgreens in Clovis has the prescription. I just filled it last week, I don't know if they'll refill it again so soon."

"Maybe if they know it's an emergency." Kerri turned toward the boy in the back seat. He was tall for his age, on the thin side, but looked like he'd have his dad's powerful build when he was an adult. His hair was sandy brown and needed a cut. "Hey, Jason," she said in a soft voice. "How are you feeling?"

"Lousy." It sounded as if it were an effort to speak. "This sucks. What if they won't give us insulin in Clovis?"

"Then we'll try somewhere else. Until then, try to keep your mind on other stuff."

"Like what?"

"Do you play sports?"

He nodded. "I'm on the middle school soccer and track teams."

"That's cool. I ran track in school, too. What are your events?"

"I'm a sprinter. I won regional last year in the fifty and the one hundred. I suck at distance, though. The longer the race is, the worse I do."

She laughed. "I'm the opposite. I'm not fast, but I can keep going. My teammates called me the Energizer Bunny."

That got a smile, but it was followed by a wince.

"What do you want to be when you grow up?"

Dusky gray eyes met hers. They were filled with undisguised fear. "Am I gonna get the chance?"

Kerri regarded him solemnly. "If I have anything to do with it, yes."

"I like messing with electronic stuff. A couple months ago I repaired an old radio my grandpa gave me. I downloaded some circuit diagrams from online and figured out what was wrong with it. All it took was a piece of wire and a solder gun. I'd like to learn how to build or repair computers."

For the first time, Greg Lantz's face relaxed into a smile. "He's got an incredible knack for it. If he pursues that, he'll make a hell of a lot more money than I do."

The twenty-five-mile drive from Melrose to Clovis proceeded largely in silence. Jason had evidently exhausted whatever energy he had and dozed against his dad's side. Will looked shaken by what he'd seen, Aaron still angry at their helplessness, their inability even to exact revenge on the people who'd acted with such mindless malice.

Kerri herself felt sullied by contact with the vigilantes. She knew that people like that existed. There'd been a handful of them in her high school, bullies who took pleasure in hurting others, who only obeyed the rules when the teachers were looking. She was only rarely a target. She'd established early that she could take care of herself both physically and emotionally, and such people always prey on the weak.

But the idea that a town had so quickly fallen to this sort of evil was sickening. Just from the way the man had looked at them—the cocky insolence, the smirk that said, "There's nothing you can do, I can hurt you if I want to," made her feel like she needed to take a shower.

Things could get back on an even keel. She had to believe that. If they could drive back the Children, regain the upper hand, maybe even defeat the

Children completely. And then civilization would reestablish itself. Saul had hinted it was possible.

But right now, that goal seemed more and more like a pipe dream.

———————————

CLOVIS, NEW MEXICO WAS A considerably larger town than Melrose, but as they drove past the city limits, what they saw looked oddly depopulated. There were few cars on the road, and the ones they passed had drivers that looked at them with wide, frightened eyes. Almost all of these seemed to be headed out of town.

That primal instinct to flee danger. Even though in this case, there was nowhere safe to flee to.

At Greg's prompting, they turned left onto North Prince Street. They were on what appeared to be auto row, but all of the businesses they saw were dark, the parking lots empty. A few had smashed-in windows. A Mexican restaurant stood with its door wide open, showing a shadowed interior and what looked like a man in a white apron collapsed in a heap in the entryway.

"Holy mother of God," Will said under his breath. "It didn't take long for it all to fall apart."

Greg nodded. "As soon as the police are gone, it goes to hell. Clovis was kind of a rough place to start with. A lot of poverty. The only thing keeping the town going is Cannon Air Force Base."

"There's a military base nearby?" Aaron said, alarm registering in his voice.

"Yeah," Greg responded. "South of town. But I'm guessing they have their own problems. I don't think they'd be much help."

"That's not it. Military bases were primary targets of the attack. We're trying to avoid them, because the Children might be using them as a base of operations."

Greg absorbed this in silence.

"Walgreens," Kerri said, pointing at a blocky building on the corner of Prince and 21st.

Aaron turned into the parking lot, and said, "Uh-oh."

Greg pulled up in his seat and peered past him, and said, "Oh, shit."

There was a crowd in the lot. All, so far as they could see, armed. At least they looked a less disreputable lot than the gang in Melrose, but there was not a friendly face in the crowd.

Aaron braked to a stop, about twenty yards from the nearest. "You all stay in the car. I'm going to see if I can reason with them."

"No one seems to be listening to reason anymore," Kerri said quietly, as Aaron got out and walked toward the people, hands raised in a conciliatory gesture.

"We need help," he said in a loud voice. "We've got a sick kid here. He needs insulin."

A man in a plaid work shirt and jeans, wearing heavy plastic-framed glasses with thick lenses, said, "That's none of our concern."

"He'll die without it."

"We're protecting what we've got. There's no police, no sheriff's department. Hell, the highway troopers and military have disappeared, too. No one's seen anyone from Cannon since yesterday morning. It's up to us."

There was a murmur of assent.

"Look, all we want is a bottle of insulin. One. Then we'll leave."

The man shook his head. "The people of Clovis are taking care of ourselves. Outsiders can find their own way. And if you had any idea of trying to force your way in…." The man pointed to a light post at the far corner of the building. A young man with a swatch of black hair, his hands and feet tied, hung from a rope by his neck. His head was tilted at a grotesque angle. A sign on his chest said, *LOOTER*.

There was the sound of a car door opening, and Aaron half turned. Greg Lantz had gotten out of the back seat, his face twisted in anger. "C'mon!" he shouted, his voice desperate and shrill. "You're going to let my son die?"

"Greg, get back in the car!" Aaron shouted, but the man either didn't hear or didn't want to hear.

It was too late in any case. The spark had been set to the tinder. Someone in the crowd fired a gun, and it took Greg high in the chest, just under the collarbone. He grunted from the impact, spun around, and fell to his knees.

Jason clambered out of the car, crying out, "Dad!"

Aaron pulled his gun and backed away. Three more shots were fired, one of them taking out the Renault's driver's side headlight. "Get back in the car!" Aaron shouted again. More shots, a scream, and a cry of, "God, no! No!"

Aaron turned and leapt into the front seat. Will was helping, half dragging Greg into the back seat of the car.

Jason. Where the hell was Jason? Kerri vaulted out into the parking lot. The boy was collapsed on the pavement. She scooped him up, carried him into the passenger seat of the car, and slammed the door shut with a hand she only then noticed was sticky with blood.

Aaron slammed the shift into reverse and stomped on the accelerator, just as the nearest of the vigilantes was within arm's reach of the car. He hit the brake, heeling over the steering wheel, and spun almost a hundred and eighty degrees. He rammed the shift into drive and floored it again, as several more shots rang out from the crowd, none of which hit their target.

They zoomed down Prince Street toward the highway at more than twice the legal limit. Least of their worries, at the moment. There was a moan from the back seat, and Kerri turned to see Greg's face white and twisted with pain. Will had turned away and was looking out of the window, trying to hide the fact that he was weeping.

"Jason," Greg said, in a strained voice. "Is my boy okay?"

Kerri looked down at the thin face of the boy who had hoped to be an electrical engineer. His eyes were still half open. Her own tears spilled over, dripped down onto Jason's t-shirt to merge with the wetness of blood surrounding a dark hole in the middle of his chest.

"Oh, Greg, I'm so sorry, I'm so sorry…."

The only sound from the back seat was the raw, terrible noise of grief, rage, and loss, of a tragedy that would never be put right even if they succeeded in their insane plan of crossing the United States and taking on the Black-eyed Children.

Ironic that this one wasn't even directly the fault of the Children.

Kerri felt herself dropping into a dark miasma of thought. This was only the beginning. If things had gone this far awry in only a couple of days, what would the United States be like a week, a month, a year from now? It was ironic. Humanity now had a common cause, a vital reason to band together to defeat a real enemy, and they responded to it by finding new ways to hurt and kill each other.

CHAPTER

8

THIRTY MILES INTO THE STATE of Texas, it became clear they weren't going to get any farther that day.

Greg Lantz's sobs had quieted, but he gave a moan and a wince of pain every time the car hit an uneven spot in the road.

Finally, Will let out a long breath. "Guys, we have to stop."

"Where?"

There was a desperate tone in Aaron's voice Kerri hadn't heard before. She suspected it was because of Jason's death. Aaron had to be blaming himself. He'd tried to resolve the situation, but it would take an iron will not to blame himself for stopping, for getting out of the car, for trying to reason with the people in front of the pharmacy—all of which led to one death and one injury of unknown severity.

And worse still, the death was a *child*. Even though they'd known the boy only for a few short hours, Jason's shooting had brought their situation home in a horrible fashion. They'd known they weren't safe, but the idea that, in only a couple of days, they were living in a nation where a little boy could be shot down in a pharmacy parking lot and they had no recourse whatsoever, was a shock.

Will looked up, the worry clear in his face. "Where? Doesn't matter. Anywhere there's shelter. I've got to take a look at Greg's wound. Not that I can do that fucking much, but it'll be better than nothing."

They found a barn near a wheat field, a few miles outside of the town of Friona, that looked like it was far enough away from houses to afford them at least a possibility of going unnoticed. Aaron pulled the car over, shut off the engine, and for a moment they all just sat there, dazed.

Kerri was the first to recover, but she felt stunned, disembodied, as if what she'd just been through wasn't quite real. "We have a first aid kit. I'm not sure what good it'll be. It wasn't meant to treat gunshot wounds."

"Better than nothing," Will said again, and exited the car. He went around the back and helped Greg out. Kerri, still carrying Jason's body, followed, and Aaron brought up the rear, gun drawn, eyes scanning every shadow and corner.

The barn was empty except for some equipment of uncertain purpose that had definitely seen better days. Kerri's family had been dairy farmers, and she had grown up around hay bales and feed troughs and milking machines. These contraptions, with their prongs and gears and blades and rotors, looked more like medieval torture devices than farm equipment. All were dented, with chipped paint and rust spots, but if the owners were anything like her dad and her uncles, they were still in fine working condition despite their appearance—whatever their purpose was.

They helped Greg into the barn, then to a low bench along one wall, and he sat with a groan. Kerri laid Jason's body on the ground, and his head lolled to one side, face slack. This elicited another bout of helpless sobs from Greg, who looked at his son's face as if nothing else in the world existed.

"Greg," Will said gently. "I need to check out your wound. We've got to get your shirt off."

Greg dashed away his tears with the back of his right hand. His left, the side of the injury, lay limp against his leg. Aaron and Will maneuvered the man out of the bloody mess of his shirt, and more than once he gasped in pain, face twisted and teeth clenched so he wouldn't cry out.

Finally, the wound was exposed. Kerri grimaced as she watched. The bullet had hit him lower than she'd thought. She'd hoped it might have gone through the meat of his shoulder or upper arm and out the other side. But it was quickly apparent that the gunshot had penetrated his upper chest just below the clavicle—and that the bullet was still embedded in his flesh.

Will probed the injury as gently as he could, his face grave.

"I'm not sure what I can do. I think the bullet kept going until it hit the inside curve of his scapula. It's in there too deep for me to get out."

"There's no way for you to remove it?" Aaron's voice sounded accusatory, but Kerri knew it was out of anguish, not any disparagement of Will's skill as a doctor.

Will glanced over at them, face pale in the dim light, then gave a jerk of his head, and they moved a little away from the wounded man.

"I'm not a surgeon." He kept his voice low. "I've got a medical degree, but my area is forensic pathology. I don't just want to start digging around in there and hope for the best. Plus, without anesthetic?" He snorted. "All of those old Westerns, where they're always giving people a slug of whiskey and then prying bullets out of their bodies, are bullshit. You'd have to strap someone down, and you'd still have to deal with them straining their muscles and moving involuntarily. No fucking way could you hold still while someone's sticking their fingers into a bullet hole."

"Not meaning to criticize you," Aaron said. "I'm just trying to figure out what to do, here."

Will shook his head. "No, I get you. But shit, this is bad. I mean, he's not going to bleed to death. It looks like it missed major arteries. Otherwise he'd be dead already. But my worry is infection."

"Do we have antiseptics?" Kerri opened the first aid kit and rummaged around. "There's a tube of Neosporin."

"I guess. But guys. We can slather the stuff on the parts of the injury we can reach, but it goes too deep to…." He stopped, swallowed. "I suppose we can try it. There's not a hell of a lot else we can do."

Greg bore Will's dressing of the wound stoically, only giving a hissing intake of breath as he smeared the antibiotic gel into the wound itself. They tore his shirt into strips and used it to bind his shoulder, winding it underneath his armpit and across the injury, then over the top of his shoulder. It didn't look terribly secure—all they had to hold it in place were safety pins—but there was no other option.

Aaron motioned Kerri over to another corner of the barn, while Will cleaned the blood off his hands with one of their bottles of water.

"You know we're going to have to leave the boy's body here," Aaron said in a near whisper.

Kerri closed her eyes and took a deep breath. "Yeah. That thought occurred to me, too."

"There's no way for us to bury him. Nothing to dig with, and even if there were, we shouldn't take the time. I hate to do it—and I don't know how Greg will react."

"I'm sure he'll react like you'd expect. Jason's the man's only son."

Aaron nodded. "I know. But we don't have a choice. In this heat…."

"I agree with you. It just sucks. It just really fucking sucks."

"No argument there."

For now, however, the only thing they could do was get Greg comfortable, see if they could induce him to eat and drink, and wait out the hottest part of the afternoon before trying to figure out what to do next.

As the sun was sinking below the ruler-straight horizon in the west, they offered Greg some of their provisions. He gladly took water but refused any food.

"Don't think I could swallow it." His voice was hoarse. "I'd probably just puke it back up. I don't know if it's the pain or…." He looked back over at Jason with longing in his eyes, then forced himself to turn away. "I just can't eat. I hurt too bad."

Aaron moved the car around to the back of the barn, so at least it wouldn't be visible from the road. But that whole afternoon, they didn't hear a single car pass by.

"No planes, either," Will said, as they were eating a makeshift meal of protein bars, chips, and what was left of the flat of apricots.

Kerri shrugged. "I hadn't noticed."

"Sky's completely clear. No contrails. And no distant sound of jets. We're not far from that Air Force base the guy in the pharmacy parking lot mentioned. But still nothing."

"This has stopped civilization in its tracks."

"From everything but killing each other." Greg had been dozing, but when Kerri looked over, he regarded them with a fierce intensity, and when he spoke, his voice was equally harsh. "We've always been good at that, haven't we? Didn't need any aliens to get us to kill each other."

He shifted, winced. The bandage across his bare chest was crimson with blood. Evidently the bleeding from the wound hadn't stopped, after all.

"I should change your dressing," Will said, finishing his bottle of water and rising.

Greg shrugged, as if he didn't care much one way or the other.

As Will was using what was left of Greg's t-shirt to rebind the wound, Aaron looked over at Kerri. "We don't have time for this."

"I was thinking the same thing."

Aaron shook his head. "I know it makes me sound like a heartless bastard. But Jesus, Kerri, what do we do? Saul made it sound like getting to this base in New York was essential, and that it needed to be done soon. We could be well into Oklahoma by now, and here we sit."

"We can't leave him."

"I'm not saying we should. God, that's the kind of thing the people in Clovis were doing, you know? 'We have what we need, we know what we should be doing, to hell with everyone and everything else.' I don't want to be that. Hell, I went into this job because I wanted to help save people, not abandon them when they're hurt."

Kerri gave another glance over at Greg, and there was a pang in her stomach at his drawn, pale face. "I wish I knew what to say. We might have to pack him up and move tomorrow, however much pain he's in."

"That's what I'm thinking. I wonder if we should try tomorrow morning to go down into that town we just passed, what's it called?"

"Friona."

"Give another shot at finding a pharmacy. Get some antibiotics. Also some heavy-duty painkillers. Right now the best we have is ibuprofen."

"Worth a try." She caught his gaze, held it. "But Aaron. No heroics, okay? We all have to promise that. However horrible today was, it could have been a hell of a lot worse. What if they'd killed or wounded more of us? What if they'd shot through the radiator and taken out your car? I don't want to see Greg suffer any more than you do, but we have to give thought to putting some miles behind us."

He nodded. "I promise. Will and I will go. He'll know which antibiotic is the best. Me, I'd be just as likely to accidentally grab some medication for erectile dysfunction or something."

Kerri laughed, and some of the tension relaxed from her. She hadn't been aware of how taut she was holding her muscles, as if preparing for an attack. "You don't need any help in that regard."

Aaron's smile flashed out at her, there and gone in an instant. "Not with you around, sexy."

———————————

THEY BEDDED DOWN ON THE dirt floor, which was lumpy and uncomfortable, but Kerri was so exhausted she fell asleep in minutes. She awoke twice, the first time when Aaron turned toward her in his sleep and put an arm around her. She gave a sigh and snuggled into his warmth. His touch was comforting, tender, reassuring, and she was able to let go of the memories of the previous day that surged upward in her brain, threatening her repose.

But the second time, she woke to the sound of Greg crying softly, and moaning in what sounded like agony. She extricated herself from Aaron's arms—he didn't stir—and felt her way forward in the pitch dark toward where Greg lay.

"Greg. What can I do?"

There was a catch in his breathing, and he answered in a voice tight with pain. "Nothing. You can't bring my son back. I know you tried to help, and it's not your fault." He shifted, which elicited another groan of pain. "My shoulder feels like hell. Hurts worse than yesterday. Much worse. And I'm chilled. I think I'm spiking a fever."

"We're going back to that town we passed a few miles back. See if they have a pharmacy. Try to get some good pain meds, and antibiotics."

"I guess." His voice sounded despondent. "What I need is surgery. The bullet's still in there."

"Don't lose hope. Back in the day, people with injuries like this healed, without surgery or modern medicine."

"Back in the day, lots of people died."

There was no arguing with that. "We'll do the best we can."

"That's all you can do. I appreciate it. The whole country's just gone to shit, and you can't fix that." He coughed, and it ended in another groan. "You really think this—this invasion, or whatever it is—is worldwide?"

"We think so. Before all the internet connections went out, Will saw references on Twitter to attacks happening in a lot of different countries. This thing is huge."

"We're fucked, then. Pardon my language."

"No need to apologize. Sometimes the situation calls for it. But as far as our being fucked, I'm not giving up yet. We're going to keep fighting as long as we have strength."

"I'm glad. And I hope you beat the bastards. But c'mon, Kerri, be realistic. You think I'm going to be here to see it? With nothing more than some Neosporin and a cloth bandage? You need to leave me here. Seriously. Best case scenario, I'm going to slow you down. Worst case, the wound gets infected, and I linger for days and die. Either way, I'm hampering you."

A shudder ran up Kerri's spine. It wasn't that she hadn't thought of all of that, but the matter-of-fact way he spoke of his own life chilled her.

"Leave you here? No food or water? You'd die for sure."

"Maybe drive me back to Friona, see if there's anywhere I could at least be left where there's other people. There'll be shelter and food and water, at least for a little while. I'll take my chances. Just like the three of you are doing."

"That's pretty brutal."

"It's realistic. Look, Kerri, I served in Afghanistan. I've seen men and women die. You always have to decide when to be heroic and when to cut your losses."

"Even when cutting your losses is referring to human lives?"

"Yes."

"Our direct supervisor was Army, too. Did duty in Iraq. Carried an injured buddy out under live fire, saved his life. I'm gonna use her as a model."

"Where is your supervisor now?"

Kerri didn't answer for a moment. Should have known he'd ask that. "She was killed during an attack by the Children a month ago."

There was silence. He didn't say, "My point," but it was as clear as if he'd spoken the words.

"In any case," she continued, "we're not ready to abandon you yet. Give us a shot at getting some medications. They'll leave as soon as it's a reasonable time for the pharmacy to be open."

"Okay." His voice sounded resigned. "I appreciate it."

Kerri got up, felt her way to the open door of the barn. The eastern sky had just the faintest trace of pearl. Probably about four a.m. It would be a long wait until day. Greg was right—they had to be willing to make decisions that in what she was already coming to think of as the former world would have been brutal, heartless, out of the question.

The situation had changed completely, upending all of their civilized behavior in only a few days.

She still held out some hope that things would work out, that the Children could be defeated, that they could rebuild what had been lost.

But here, in a barn in the middle of nowhere in northern Texas, that thought seemed as remote as the far-off hints of sunrise on the distant horizon.

———————————

THE SUN'S RAYS WERE SLANTING in through a hole in the side of the barn when Aaron and Will roused. They went outside to take care of their bodily needs in pairs—Aaron with Kerri, Will helping Greg. The injured man hadn't even wanted to stand up, and when he did, his teeth were chattering, and once again his makeshift bandage was saturated with bright red blood.

As Aaron and Kerri retrieved food for breakfast from the car, Will took off the fouled dressing, and his face creased with worry. He motioned them over.

Even in the dim light, the red streaks from the bullet hole—up and underneath his arm, down his chest, and, most alarmingly, along the side of his neck—were obvious. His face was flushed, and there was a light sheen of sweat on his skin.

"Infection?" Kerri asked, even though she knew what the answer would be.

Will nodded. "It was kind of inevitable. There are so many bacteria on our skin and clothing, ones that are harmless enough if you keep them out of your body, but can turn serious if they get into your bloodstream. We need to get antibiotics. Fast."

"How long?" Greg rasped out. His voice sounded worse even than a few hours earlier, when he'd spoken to Kerri in the dark.

"We'll leave as soon as we've had something to eat—"

"No." Greg's good hand lifted, and caught Will's sleeve. "How long?"

"I hope a lot of years."

Greg made a dismissive noise. "C'mon, Will. It's blood sepsis, isn't it?"

The doctor nodded. "I think so, yes."

"So how long?" He shivered, despite the warmth in the still air of the barn.

"Unless we can get some broad-spectrum, fast-acting antibiotics into you, maybe two or three days."

Greg nodded, his expression showing satisfaction. "Thanks for not pussy-footing around, Doc. I want to know the truth. I may not like it, but I want to know."

"We're still going to do what we can to get you meds." He looked up. "Aaron, are you ready?"

"Let's go." Aaron gave Kerri a quick kiss. "We'll be back as fast as we can." He turned toward Will. "Let's do this."

The sound of the car doors opening and shutting was loud in the eerie silence that had engulfed the world. Kerri watched the car drive away, turning west, then went back and sat on the ground next to Greg.

"It shouldn't take very long. I think the town's only about five miles back."

Greg nodded, leaning his head back against the wall of the barn. "You'd all be within your rights to leave me here, you know."

"I know. But that lowers us to the level of the Children, killing without any regard, without compassion, without necessity."

"How do you know there's no necessity?"

"We can take you along. Leaving you isn't something we have to do."

"No, that's not what I'm talking about."

"Okay, then what do you mean?"

He coughed, winced, cleared his throat. "How do you know what's necessary to the Children? I mean, think about it. I love fishing. I always make sure to eat what I catch—I hate the whole fishing and hunting for sport thing. But even so. Think about it from the fish's perspective. You get hooked, pulled out of the water, and slowly suffocate, to provide food for a different species you don't understand. How is this any different?"

Kerri didn't answer for a moment. "I don't know. But I do think the fish would be in their rights to fight back, don't you?"

He gave her a fleeting smile. "Yeah, I suppose you're right. I wonder if the Children are evil, like you consider them, or whether they're just doing what they have to in order to survive."

"Like everyone else."

He nodded.

"I honestly never considered that."

"It doesn't change what you have to do. But me, I always want to know the whole picture."

"This whole picture sucks."

"That it does." He shifted a little, took an uneven, halting breath, then turned his head back toward her. "You got any family?"

She nodded. "My parents live in Nebraska. I'm the middle of three siblings, an older sister and younger brother."

"Heard anything from them since all this started?"

"No." The word sounded bleak, an admission of tragedy.

"I got two brothers, myself. One in Albuquerque. Other's in the Marine Corps, and he was overseas in Okinawa."

"Was?"

He lifted an eyebrow. "Maybe still is. Hard not thinking of everyone in past tense, you know?"

"I know."

"You mind telling me what you three are planning to do once you get to New York?"

She snorted. "Right now, the only plan we've got is 'improvise.' We know this place is a hub of operations, but other than that, we know nothing about it. How well guarded it is, what exactly they're doing there, even why it's so important."

"So this informant dude of yours, he didn't tell you much in the way of useful information?"

"I got the feeling he told us what he could."

A shrewd expression came into Greg's eyes. "How sure are you that he's on our side?"

"Believe me, we had the same question about him at first. All I can say is, what he told us bore out, and a couple of his tips saved our lives more than once. I think we have to take what he told us and run with it. I mean, if we don't, what other option is there? Hole up somewhere, hope it all blows over? I don't think this is going to blow over, at least not by itself."

"I think you're right about that. And I'm not saying you shouldn't trust him, just to look at all sides of the situation."

"We're trying to do that."

"I'm sure. You know, the craziest thing about all this is how fast it happened. What, a week ago? We were all doing our usual stuff, buying groceries and cooking dinner and going to work, and now it's all falling apart." He looked over at his son's body, the paleness of the boy's narrow face making him look younger than his twelve years. "All of it. You don't think about it, not until it happens."

"No one could have anticipated this." She stopped just short of correcting herself. They could have anticipated it. Saul had warned them, warned them weeks ago, that an invasion was imminent. Duke Rendell, and even Aaron's mysterious bosses higher up in the chain of command, had done nothing to prevent it, or even to prepare.

But what could have been done? The Children were more than ever looking invincible. They had to have some kind of weakness, but God alone knew what it was.

She looked back at Greg, who was watching her intently. "All we can do is try and deal with what we've got in front of us."

He nodded. "That's all we can ever do."

"That, and help each other. Resist the temptation to slip back into tribalism. You heard what the people in Clovis said? The medications in the pharmacy were for the people of Clovis, not outsiders. In three days, we've already gotten to the place where people from the next town over aren't part of our tribe."

"Built into the human brain, I think. Protect the clan."

"It's time to resist instinct, then. You should drink some water, and try to eat something. Aaron and Will won't be long. With luck, they'll have some good drugs."

"I hope so." He gave a convulsive shudder. "I feel like shit. And I'm chilled to the bone. I think my fever is worse. Feels like when I had the flu a couple of years ago."

"We've got Tylenol. That'll at least make you feel better for a while."

"With luck." He winced and closed his eyes.

But as she went to get medicine, food, and a bottle of water for the wounded man, she couldn't help the thought that as of yesterday, their luck had run out.

WHEN AARON AND WILL RETURNED, Kerri knelt next to Greg, her hand on his forehead. He was shivering uncontrollably. The red streaks had spread, like evil fingers gradually wrapping themselves around his body. When the car door slammed, he didn't jump, only turned slowly toward the sound with unfocused eyes.

Kerri looked up as the two men entered the barn. "How did it go?" But one look at Aaron's face and both men's empty hands gave her all the answer she needed.

"Friona is a ghost town," Aaron said. "It looks like most of the people bugged out, reason unknown. At least we didn't run into armed resistance again."

"Did you find a pharmacy, or a clinic, or anything?"

He nodded. "Somebody got there ahead of us. Cleared out anything they could find that could be useful. There's a little pharmacy on Main Street—'Bi-Wize,' or some such stupid name—but the door was wide open, and the whole place emptied. Whoever did it knew what they were doing. There wasn't a bottle of painkillers or antibiotics to be found. We had a little more luck with the grocery store and resupplied at least some of the food and water. But the meds were a bust." He nodded toward Greg's prone form. "How is he?"

"Worse," Kerri said in a low voice. "He's burning up. He's gone downhill just since you've been gone."

Will dropped to his knees and touched the side of his face. Concern filled his eyes. "What did you give him, Tylenol or aspirin?"

"Tylenol."

"When?"

"About forty-five minutes or so."

Will shook his head. "It's not touching it. This is bad, guys."

"More Tylenol?"

Will stood and gave a little jerk of the head for them to follow him a few feet away from the stricken man. When he spoke, it was in a low voice. "I don't think it'll do much good. He's definitely got sepsis. That's a dicey condition if you're in a good hospital. People die of sepsis even with the best of care. Here?" He gestured at the dim interior of the barn. "There's not a lot we can do."

"Dammit." Kerri could almost taste the bitterness in her voice. "This is not right. How can we just let him die?"

"We're not. We couldn't have prevented this." Will's voice dropped further. "And we can't prevent his death. Not at this point, unless a miracle occurs." He glanced over at the prone man, who hadn't moved, but was regarding them with a glassy stare. "And we've been pretty fucking short of miracles lately."

"And we need to get moving again." Aaron gave a helpless shrug. "Do we bring him along? Or wait here with him until…."

"Until I die," Greg's voice was weak but clear. All three of them turned toward him. "You can say it."

"Goddammit," Kerri said. "I am just so sorry."

A shiver wracked his whole body. "Not your fault. Any chance we have is up to you. You have a job to do. Do it."

"But—"

"No. No buts. Just do one thing before you leave."

None of them spoke.

"One of you. End this." He gathered his breath, and a trickle of sweat rolled from his forehead. "I'm pleading with you. One bullet. The end will be the same in either case. Merciful. My son is waiting for me." He shivered again and closed his eyes.

Kerri looked from Aaron to Will. Both men were wide-eyed.

Aaron spoke first. "For fuck's sake. We can't do that. Can we?"

"We would do it for a dog that's suffering," Will said.

"He's not a goddamn dog! He's a human being!"

"So we should treat a human with less mercy than a dog?" Will shook his head. "C'mon, Aaron. Think if it was you. You'd want this. You know you would, dammit."

Aaron stared at the doctor in silence, and finally, slowly, nodded his head.

"You're right. I know you're right. But it's different, with a living man here…." He seemed near tears. "I never thought it'd come to this."

"Which one of us does it?" Kerri had to force the words out. It sounded so callous, so cold… and so final.

There was silence for a moment, then Will said, "I think that's obvious, don't you? I'm the doctor. I was trained to care for people. If this is all I can do to respect his wishes and prevent his suffering, I have to do it."

"Oh, God, Will—" Kerri started, but he shook his head.

"Look. We have no reason to put it off. You know we need to get back on the road. He's right. Time is running out. There is no other option."

"So he couldn't recover… fight off the infection…." Kerri knew she was grasping at straws, but she couldn't stop herself.

"Honestly? I think his chance of surviving this without intravenous antibiotics is near zero. I saw this kind of thing once when I was an intern. A girl got a puncture wound on her foot playing on a playground, and it went septic. She looked like Greg does—feverish, sweating, streaks radiating every which way from the injury. They treated her with heavy-duty antibiotics, intravenous, and an induced coma."

"Did she survive?"

Will nodded. "Barely. And they had to amputate her leg at the knee."

"Jesus," Aaron said under his breath.

"I thought it would come to this as soon as I saw the streaks yesterday. I was hoping I was wrong. But I was pretty sure I knew what was going to happen, and what we would have to do. What I would have to do."

Greg took a wheezing breath. "Please. Just do it. There's nothing to be gained by waiting. Nothing. Let me go to my son. That's all I need."

Will met Aaron's eyes, and the two men's gazes locked for a long moment. Then Will held out his hand.

Aaron handed Will his gun, then closed his eyes. Now tears did spill over onto his cheeks. "Fuck this whole situation."

"Agreed, my friend." Will looked from Aaron to Kerri, and Kerri saw a strange serenity come into his expression, a calm wisdom that surprised her. She'd seen Will joking around, she'd seen him scared, angry, appreciated his wry sense of humor and his quick intelligence. But at that moment she perceived a depth in him that she had not yet seen.

"You'll be all right, Will?"

He nodded. "You two should go. You don't want to see this." He went to Greg and knelt next to him. He stroked the man's sweat-soaked hair.

"Thank you," Greg said, in a weak but steady voice. He managed a feeble smile. "Bless you." To Kerri and Aaron he said, "Good luck." He took a deep, uneven breath, let it out slowly, then closed his eyes. "Okay. I'm ready. Do it."

Aaron took Kerri by the shoulder and turned her, and led her out of the barn toward the car. Once outside she stopped, and he tightened his arm around her.

When the gunshot came, she shied like a frightened horse, even though she'd been expecting it, waiting for it. She sobbed, but was able to force back her tears. She pressed her face into Aaron's chest, and they held each other for a moment.

Will came out of the barn, a ghastly expression on his face, mouth in a twisted grimace. He got only a few feet before he fell to his knees and vomited up his breakfast, retching until there was nothing more left to bring up. Kerri ran to him and put her hand on his back, feeling the spasms strike him again and again. Finally, he straightened up, shuddered, and wiped his mouth with the back of his hand.

"Guess I'm not as tough as I thought I was," he said in a hoarse voice.

Aaron put one hand on Will's shoulder. "Dude. That took brass balls. Seriously. You did the right thing. Of the three of us, you were the one who took charge and did the right thing."

"Merciful Jesus." Will shook his head. "I hope that's true. And I hope it's a right thing I never have to do again."

CHAPTER

9

WHAT DO YOU THINK HAPPENED to everyone in Friona?" Will gave a quick glance over to Kerri, who was riding shotgun while Aaron snoozed in the back seat. They had bypassed the town of Amarillo, continuing along Route 60 into the flat expanse of northeastern Texas. The road went from a four-lane divided highway to two lanes, and signs of habitation were becoming sparser. "The place was seriously a ghost town. It looked like there should be a shop sign hanging from a post, squeaking in the wind, and a tumbleweed rolling down the street."

"They may have been in hiding. Think about what that roving gang did in Melrose. They may have seen that you were armed and decided to get out of sight."

"I dunno. It really did feel emptied. Deserted. Like the entire population had upped stakes and taken off." Will frowned. "You think the Children could have captured them? All of them? I mean, that's what their ultimate goal is, right? Depopulating the Earth."

Kerri shrugged. "Could be. I wouldn't think they'd begin with a little town in the middle of nowhere like Friona, though."

"Gotta start somewhere."

"I guess. But honestly, I think it's more likely that the residents heard about the riots and attacks, then when the Internet and television and radio went offline, they got spooked. Maybe there's a hideout somewhere nearby. Somewhere that a lot of people could hole up for a while."

"Like where?"

"Like an airport. Remember that movie *Warm Bodies?*"

Will gave her a tired grin. "Yeah. That was a fun one. Plus, the lead zombie was kind of cute."

"Their home base was an airport. Big, spacious, generally no trees or other obstructions for a long way. You can see who's coming, long before they can do any damage. Plus, there's cafés and snack bars and so on. It'd be a smart place to run to." She paused. "I'm not saying that's what they did, only that it's a possibility. I know small-town folk tend to be pretty tight. Something happens, they band together and protect their own."

"Honestly, that's what the people in Clovis were doing," Will said. "I think if we'd just gotten back in the car and driven away, they'd have left us alone. But pressed, when they thought we might try to force our way in, they struck first."

"We're seeing the gamut of reactions, aren't we? A calamity happens, and some people will hunker down, like Rose Dawson is doing, hope it all settles and that people'll just leave her alone until then. Then you have your amoral opportunists, like the gang in Melrose, taking advantage of the situation to rob and steal and whatever else they want to do. Then there are the ones in Clovis—and maybe the ones in Friona, too—banding together to keep their friends and relatives safe, to hell with everyone else."

Will looked thoughtful. "There's a fourth option, you know."

"Which is?"

"Fight back. Like we're trying to do."

Kerri didn't answer for a moment. The impossible weight of what they were planning was heavy on her shoulders.

Finally, she just said, "Yeah."

"What's waiting for us up there in New York? What's the town, Colberg or something?"

"Colville, I think."

"Do you think we have a chance?"

"If I didn't, I wouldn't be heading there."

Will gave her a raised eyebrow. "Are you saying that to reassure me, or convince yourself?"

"Both. I can't tell you what our likelihood is of succeeding, or even surviving. I do trust Saul, and I think if it really was a forlorn hope, he wouldn't have told us to go there. There's something there we're supposed to do, something that could tip the balance in our favor."

"I guess it's just as well I came along, then."

She looked over at the doctor, who was facing forward with a serious expression. "You feeling a little more confident in your ability to help?"

"Nah, not really. I figure one more person is good, no matter who they are. It's like if you and a friend are being chased by a bear. You don't need to run faster than the bear, you just need to run faster than your friend."

Kerri laughed. "Oh, c'mon, you're not just cannon fodder, for God's sake." Her smile faded, and she gave Will's shoulder a gentle squeeze. "You proved that back there in the barn."

A long pause. "I never knew it was possible to be absolutely convinced you'd done the right thing and completely horrified at what you'd done at the same time."

"We better get used to it. I don't mean situations exactly like that, but the fact of things being different. It's completely changed the moral compass, you know? All these things we took for granted, or assumed we'd never have to think about—well, all I'm saying is that it's not the same world we lived in a week ago. You do what you have to in order to look after yourself and the people you care about, because chances are, no one else is going to."

Will was silent for a long while, and when he spoke, it was in a quiet, hesitant voice, as if he didn't want to speak the words aloud. "I have this feeling I'll never see my family again, whatever happens."

How could you respond to that? All the optimistic replies she could think of sounded hollow. Finally, she said, "There's no guarantee of anything. Never has been. That's one of the myths we created, with all our civilization and high-tech gadgets—that we could take charge of things and control the outcome."

"If that ever was true, it certainly isn't now."

Kerri nodded. "So I think we need to keep moving forward, and let the future take care of itself."

———————

SMALL TOWNS SLIPPED PAST AS the highway stretched out ahead of them, crossing from Texas into southern Oklahoma. Arnett, Seiling, Waynoka, Cherokee. They stopped for a quick lunch in Great Salt Plains State Park, which had a picnic area under some trees, looking out over a surreal chalk-white expanse of salt. The air was hot, the wind carrying a briny smell, and they ate quickly and got back on the road.

Kerri's observation about the three reactions people had to the invasion proved eerily correct, and they saw one example after another. The turnoff from the highway toward Medicine Lodge, Kansas, had wooden barriers with a large, hand-painted plywood sign saying, *NO ENTRY We will use deadly force to stop anyone passing this point NO EXCEPTIONS.* Only a few miles farther north they passed a farm that had a large fuel storage tank near the highway. There was no car in the driveway, no sign of anyone around, so they stopped to gas up. Will pumped the gas while Aaron and Kerri stood, guns drawn, casting a wary eye over their surroundings. Past the fuel tank and a barn containing a tractor and various other equipment hidden in the dim shadows, was a small white house with a front porch and an immaculate flower garden filled with the brilliant colors of zinnias and marigolds.

As Will rehung the nozzle on a hook and closed up the Renault's gas tank, Kerri gestured, and said, "Look."

Standing at the front window of the house was a woman whose face seemed to be all eyes, holding a baby close to her. At first, her expression was hopeful, but then her gaze met Kerri's, and for a moment, the woman was frozen in place. Then she dropped the lace curtain she was holding aside, and retreated back into the house, every movement radiating terror.

They climbed back into the car, Kerri into the driver's seat to take a shift at the wheel. "I really wish we could have reassured her that we didn't mean her any harm."

Aaron closed the door behind him. "More work and risk than it's worth."

"You're probably right. I guess it's better just to get away from her as quickly as possible. But I hate that all of this has made us suspect each other."

Almost immediately after they turned back north on Highway 281 toward Pratt, Will pointed ahead of them. "With good reason, though. Look."

Two wrecked cars were angled across the road, with a shot out windshield. As they slowed to make their way around the obstacle, they saw that the shot-up vehicle still contained the body of the driver, slumped toward the door, one bloodied arm dangling outside.

"Jesus," Aaron said softly.

"Wonder if he's who the woman in the cottage was waiting for?" Kerri maneuvered her way past the second wrecked car, which had gunshots pocking the side and one flat tire, and pressed the accelerator toward the floor.

"It sucks, but we can't stop to find out. He's not the only body that's going to be left behind for someone else to deal with."

"Like Greg and Jason Lantz." Will's voice was somber, and that ended the conversation for some time.

PRATT, KANSAS LOOKED LIKE THE aftermath of a battle. The sidewalk along the downtown's row of quaint brick-sided businesses glittered with shards of glass from shop windows. Five bodies lay in the lawn of the First National Bank, one of them slumped against a planter filled with daisies. A little farther along was evidence of an even larger shootout in the parking lot of Southwest Truck Parts, where at least two dozen men and women were fallen along a barrier of metal shelves flanked by a pair of semis. The pools of blood on the cement were already blackening under the heat of the late August sun.

"What were they trying to do?" Will's mouth was twisted with nausea. "Why would they defend an auto parts store with their lives?"

"No way to tell," Aaron said. "Showdown between business owners and looters, maybe?"

"Looks like the looters won."

"Which means they're probably still around," Kerri said. "Best to clear this place as soon as possible."

As if to prove her correct, two shots rang out as they passed a McDonald's and a Day's Inn, only a quarter of a mile farther. Kerri floored the accelerator, her heart thudding in her ears.

Will shouted out of the open window, "Fuck you! We're leaving!"

Their assailant never showed himself, but it wasn't until they were several miles down Highway 61, and back out into flat, unbroken stretches of wheat fields, that her pulse slowed back down.

"I THINK WE SHOULD AVOID Hutchinson." Will looked up from the road atlas, which he'd been studying in silence ever since leaving Pratt and the unseen shooter behind. "It looks like it's a good bit bigger than Pratt. We were lucky that the road itself wasn't blocked back there. What if the people in the parking lot had put those barriers across the road? We couldn't have just driven through it like we did back in Las Cruces. It'd have left us trying to find a detour in a town none of us know, so we'd end up derping around trying to find our way. Any snipers who wanted to could pick us off, no problem. Far as I'm concerned, the farther we can stay out of cities of any size, the better."

"Agreed," Kerri said. "Any other roads to get around it?"

"Yeah, there are some back roads we could take. North to a town called Nickerson, then cut east again and rejoin the highway farther along. We're going to have to make a decision after that, though, and that's risk versus speed. There's I-135 ahead, and then the Kansas Turnpike. Better time than on country roads but more likely to run into other people, for good or ill. And if we head due north, we get awful close to Fort Riley Military Reservation. East, though, and we run into Topeka and then Kansas City." He frowned. "I'm not sure there's a smart way to do this, since we don't know what the risks are."

"My vote is stay right the hell away from Fort Riley," Aaron said. "If those news broadcasts were right, the Children attacked military installations first. Chances are, they didn't just hit them and leave. My intuition is that anywhere near a military base is likely to be unsafe."

"We might have trouble before that," Kerri said.

Ahead of them was the gleam of reflected westering sunlight from a car windshield, moving toward them. Behind it was another, and another—a line stretching off into the heat-shimmery distance. Kerri took a hasty left turn onto a fortunate side road, crossing only a hundred yards in front of the lead vehicle, and once again pressing the accelerator toward the floor.

Will turned, gazing back through the rear windshield, and Kerri took a quick look in the rear-view mirror herself, afraid they'd turn toward them, eager to do battle, but the first of the convoy passed the intersection without slowing. The lead was a pickup truck, moving slowly, with two men armed with what looked like machine guns standing in the bed, elbows braced on the cab. More trucks followed, then cars, most with bundles and luggage tied to roof racks, and armed men leaning out of windows, scanning the fields with grim expressions.

The long line of the convoy was quickly lost to view as they sped forward. What would have happened if they'd met head on? Perhaps they were only armed to defend themselves, but all it would take is one trigger-happy guy, and the whole thing could have ended very, very badly. She recalled the fallen defenders in the parking lot of Southwest Truck Parts. The man slumped in the driver's seat of the wrecked car near the farm north of Medicine Lodge. The roving gang that had destroyed Greg Lantz's house, and ultimately, been responsible for his death and that of his son. It was all too easy to picture the three of them, riddled with bullets, in the remains of Aaron's blue Renault, angled off the road into a wheat field, where their bodies would stay until someone restored order and cleaned up the remains of the disaster.

If, indeed, anyone ever would. Maybe this really was it, this spasm of violence was the last gasp of humanity, its nerve centers cut, flailing and injuring itself like an animal in its death throes. Who would be left after this to restore order?

No one, if the Children succeeded.

She edged the accelerator downward, and the Renault zoomed along the narrow, dusty road. Out here, in the middle of nowhere in Kansas, with the increasingly populated eastern half of the United States still to cross, the idea that they would ever get to Colville, New York, much less accomplish whatever it was they needed to do there, seemed more and more an impossibility.

———————————

BY SEVEN IN THE EVENING, the sun was angling down toward the western horizon, and Kerri's back ached from sitting all day behind the steering wheel. Will dozed in the back seat while Aaron gazed out of the passenger window watching the wheat fields roll past, his expression looking as if his mind were far, far away. They continued their effort to stay off main roads, and for a while paralleled I-35 North, finally cutting across just north of McPherson, Kansas. Kerri turned off at a sign that said, *Maxwell Wildlife Refuge/McPherson State Park.*

To Aaron's questioning look, she said, "I need to pee. And eat. And either rest, or else switch drivers."

Aaron nodded, and they drove down a narrow road cutting across a grassy expanse that was hilly, at least by comparison to the rest of Kansas. The road turned from pavement into light, dusty gravel, but there were patches of trees, which had also been in short supply.

Finally, the road curved north and then east around a shallow lake, which

119

a sign proclaimed to be McPherson State Fishing Lake. They passed signboards and turnoffs to cabins, and a restroom building that all three took advantage of.

"I'm falling asleep at the wheel," Kerri said. "My vote is to stop for the night. I can't imagine there'll be much competition for cabins. We've barely seen anyone since that convoy coming out of Hutchinson."

"You won't get any argument out of me," Will said around a yawn. "I'm also famished."

Aaron nodded. "It'll also give us some time to plan strategy. We're getting to the point that we have to make some decisions about how to proceed. Take bigger roads and risk big cities, or jitter around on back roads and take way more time."

"Danger either way," Will said.

"No question. But I'd like to make as good a decision as we can, using the information we have." He pointed. "Take this right. There are a couple of cabins down that way, right by the lake shore. We could also go for a swim and wash away some of the grime. Maybe even give our clothes a rinse the old-fashioned way."

They pulled into a gravel strip beside one of the cabins, and Kerri braked to a stop and turned off the engine. They exited into silence, broken only by all three of them stretching and groaning as stiff muscles loosened up. The cabin was locked, but it took only moments for Will to knock out one of the panes in the single window, unlock and pull up the sash, and climb in.

"Wouldn't have thought you were the breaking-and-entering type," Kerri observed as he let them in.

Will shrugged. "New world, new rules. I'm allowed to reinvent myself, right?"

The cabin was clean, with two single beds and not a whole lot else. It had a dry, musty smell, as if it hadn't been inhabited for a while.

"Gonna be tight quarters tonight," Kerri said.

Will shrugged. "There are other cabins. I broke in once, I can do it again. I'm happy to give y'all some privacy."

"Is that really a good idea? At least when we were in the motel a couple of nights ago, we had adjoining rooms. Here, we'd be separated by a hundred yards, if not more."

Aaron plunked down on one of the beds. "She's right."

"Suit yourselves. I mean, I don't want to get complacent or anything, but we haven't seen hide nor hair of the Children since we left Arizona. If they haven't tracked us down yet, hard to see how they'd do it now."

"It's not only the Children I'm worried about," Aaron said. "At the moment, our fellow humans are as much of a threat as the Children are."

They made a meager dinner off dried fruit, beef jerky, bread, and the last of a package of sliced cheese that was much the worse for wear and lack of refrigeration. By this time, stars were appearing in an ultramarine sky, and the fatigue reasserted itself now that Kerri had a full stomach.

"Lord, I'm exhausted," she said. "Let's get some of the stuff from the car, and turn in before I faceplant right where I sit. I—" She stopped, her ears pricking, and turned toward the door. "What's that?"

A low buzzing growl in the distance. It was steady at first but soon was clearly approaching. A small plane? A truck? It had the sound of a motor, but it was impossible to tell what sort. They exited the cabin silently, standing on the front porch in a tight cluster, and Kerri couldn't stop the despondent thought of Dammit, what now? from zinging through her mind.

A mosquito whined near her ear, and she slapped it away. The sound was louder now, still getting steadily closer, and what had seemed the rumble of a single engine could be heard as at least three. Aaron had already drawn his gun, and Kerri did the same, but still they stood frozen, uncertain whether to hide, flee, or prepare to defend themselves.

"Maybe they'll pass us by," Will said in a near-whisper. "Maybe they're just trying to find a place to spend the night, like we were."

"Plenty of cabins," Aaron said. "Don't see why we'd need to fight over one."

They'd already seen all too much fighting over things that, two weeks ago, they'd never have considered as worth killing for. But Kerri remained silent as the engines continued to approach.

In a cloud of white dust that swirled up into the clear evening sky, three motorcycles came around the curve in the road that led past the cabin. The one in the lead was a huge beast of a machine, jet black with sleek chrome trim. When the driver saw them, he gave a gesture with one gloved hand, and all three of them simultaneously braked, coasting up toward the cabin alongside Aaron's blue Renault.

The engines fell silent. The lead driver swung his leg over the seat and stood for a moment looking at Kerri, Aaron, and Will, then pulled off his helmet, freeing a wild mass of long, black hair shot through with gray. The man fit the machine he'd ridden—a tower of muscle, a good five inches taller than Aaron, with a heavy midriff, thick arms, and a broad face whose lower half was hidden by a tangle of beard. His two companions, neither of which matched his girth or presence, stood a little behind him, and for a moment both triangles faced each other, still and silent.

The lead rider spoke first, in a low, rough voice that matched his appearance, but what he said was so unexpected that for a moment, Kerri was unconvinced that she'd heard him correctly.

"I'm looking for Kerri Elias and Aaron Vincent."

"What the actual fuck?" Will said it under his breath, then fell silent, regarding the man with a dumbfounded expression.

Aaron recovered his composure first. "You've found them." His voice, though level, betrayed shock.

The man gave them an unsmiling nod. "Thought so. We saw you drive into the park. Wasn't sure you'd stick around, thought you was maybe just passing through. Had to convince my boys it was worth the trouble to come check you out."

"Okay." Kerri took a deep breath, trying to dispel the feeling she was dreaming. "What do you want with us? And… how the hell did you know we'd be here?"

"The Prophet told us," one of the other men said.

"The *Prophet?* What Prophet?"

"It ain't what he calls himself," the leader said. "But it's accurate enough. You're here, right? Just like he said you'd be. He knows things. Don't ask me how, but he does."

"And who is he?"

"He said you'd recognize the name if I told you. Said you was real close to his sister." He cleared his throat, fixed Kerri with intense, dark eyes. "His name's Kyle. Kyle Tauriac."

CHAPTER
10

THERE WAS NEARLY A MINUTE of dead silence.

Aaron was the first to speak. It sounded like he was keeping complete incredulity out of his voice only with an effort. "Danielle's brother?"

"That's right," the leader answered.

"But how did he…?" Kerri trailed off.

"I told you. He knows things. Me and the boys been talking to him for about six months, at first on the Ham radio. I don't remember now how it got started, but you could tell right away he's a persistent cuss. He kept at us, saying it was important. Things was gonna fall apart, and we had to prepare. And he was right."

"But why did he want you to meet us?" Kerri's voice sounded surreal in her own ears, as if she were dreaming, as if she were disembodied.

"He told us the invasion was gonna happen, you were gonna be the ones to stop it. He knew his sister was gonna die, told us about it—said there wasn't nothing he could do to stop it."

"He *knew* she was going to die? Why didn't he warn her, at least?"

"You'll have to ask him about that. Far as how he knew it was going to happen, he said the Pleiadians told him."

"Wait—" A jolt like an electric shock ran through Kerri's body. "Saul? He knows *Saul?*"

The leader frowned. "I don't know about Saul. He talks to them as he calls Pleiadians every day, seems like. They keep him informed. But some of the stuff he just seems to come up with his own self, like tonight when he said you were down in one of the cabins on McPherson Lake. He said we was to come get you."

"Get us?" Aaron said. "Why?"

A shrug. "He said it was important. This point, we know to take it serious when he says something's important. We're from just out of Topeka, and when all this shit went down, we'd'a been screwed if we stayed there. But the Prophet, he warned us in time, and we came out here to where Roan's pa had a farm. The old man'd died a few months ago, and the house was empty. The Prophet said we was to go out where the dead man's fields were. That's how he said it and how we knew."

Kerri shook her head in an attempt to clear it. "He's there right now?"

The leader nodded. "Yeah, he joined us there a couple weeks ago. Said he'd best get up here while he could, 'cause soon it'd be too late, and he'd be stuck down there in Louisiana. So he come up here, and today he told us we was to go find you and bring you back."

"Look." Aaron's brows drew together into a scowl. "I don't know how to say this nicely. And maybe the time for nice speech is past in any case. But how do we know we can trust you? We've almost gotten ourselves killed by people who'd turned collaborator, not to mention by regular humans who decided the time was right for some good old-fashioned raping, looting, and pillaging. You're expecting us to get in our car and follow you back to your home base without asking any questions?"

A faint hint of a smile crossed the man's face. "Seems to me you been asking questions just fine."

"Well, let me put it this way. What we've been through in the last few days has made me reluctant to trust anyone if I don't know whose side they're on."

"The Prophet said you might say something like that. He said if you did, to give you this." The leader reached into the pocket of his leather jacket.

Aaron tensed, and Kerri knew he was waiting for the man to pull a weapon. But his hand came out with a clenched fist—no gun, no knife. He held it out toward Kerri.

Kerri took a cautious step forward and held out her own hand, palm upward. And the man dropped into it something lightweight, something that glinted a little in the light of a nearly-full moon that was still near the horizon.

A slender chain, with a little twist of a gold loop, in the middle of which was a tiny jewel that glittered green.

The necklace that Danielle always wore, that she'd been wearing the day she died.

"My God." Kerri felt like she'd been punched in the solar plexus.

Another fleeting smile. "Yeah, he said that's probably how you'd react. And that it'd tell you that we ain't here to harm you. We want the same thing you three do, same thing the Prophet does, same things his pals the Pleiadians do. To clear the Black-eyed Children right the hell outta here."

Kerri nodded mutely.

"What is it?" Will said in a near whisper. "You recognize it?"

"It's Danielle's necklace. I don't know what its significance was to her, but she always wore it. He must have realized—Kyle must have realized—that I'd know it immediately. That it'd mean they were telling the truth."

Aaron didn't look convinced. "Kerri, you're sure…."

"I'm sure. I think we have to do this. If Kyle and his friends can help us, I don't think we can afford to get spooked and say no."

Aaron didn't respond, but his face still registered suspicion.

The leader nodded. "Good. You made the right decision. Follow us. It's only about five miles." He paused. "I'm called Brace." He held out a meaty hand, which all three shook.

The tension in the air seemed to evaporate. One of the other two men stepped forward, grinning. His blond hair had a bleached look, and a handlebar mustache was an obvious hommage to Hulk Hogan. He jerked a thumb toward the leader.

"He goes by Brace because he doesn't want people to know his real name is Marvin. I'm Joe, but call me Skids."

The third man, a muscular African American with a shaved head, regarded them with an unsmiling expression, and just said, "Barker" as he shook their hands.

"Guess you already know who we are," Kerri said.

"Only the two of you," Brace said. "The Prophet said it'd be you and Aaron traveling together."

"I'm Will. Will Daigle." His voice still sounded as if he didn't quite believe what had happened. "They picked me up in Lafayette, Louisiana. Sorry I don't have a cool nickname, so Will'll have to do."

"Pleased to meet you. Any other talking we want to do, we should wait till we get to Roan's pa's farm. No use standing here jawin' and getting mosquito-bit."

———————————

BY THE TIME THEY GOT to the farmhouse, it was full dark. There were over a dozen motorcycles parked at the side of the house that faced away from the road, presumably so they'd be hidden if anyone drove past.

As they approached the front door, Brace yelled, "It's us. We got 'em."

The way he phrased it gave Kerri a momentary jolt of fear that they were walking into a trap, but the door was opened by a red-haired woman who gave the three of them a satisfied nod.

"The Prophet said to bring 'em right in."

"Anything happen while we were gone, Roan?"

She shook her head. "All quiet."

Candles and lanterns lit in the living room cast a fitful, wavering glow on the group as they walked down a hall and into a broad room that looked like it had served as a den. There were six more bikers there, two women and four men, all of whom gazed at Kerri, Aaron, and Will in obvious curiosity, and some other emotion—fear? Reverence? It was apparent that they, too, were astonished by what Kyle Tauriac knew. At the back of the room, in a recliner against the wall, was a slender, fragile-looking young man with dark skin and eyes that were nearly black, whom Kerri had last seen at his sister's funeral, only a month ago. A metal cane leaned against the chair. His posture and the positions of the others in the room gave the appearance of a king attended by his courtiers.

"Thank you for coming," the young man said in a quiet, musical voice. "It was a significant act of trust for you to believe my friends and do what they asked."

"Kyle," Kerri said, as if the word affirmed what she still could not quite believe was true.

He nodded, a ghost of a smile flitting around his mouth. "My sister thought very highly of the two of you. As do the Pleiadians." He nodded toward Will. "And you, Doctor. You threw your lot in with them as well. Good. I wasn't certain of that, but I hoped it was so."

Will swallowed and nodded, obviously at a loss for words.

Kerri stepped forward, Danielle's necklace hanging from her fingers. "I'm sure you'll want this back. If you thought it would prove to me that Brace was telling the truth, you were right."

Kyle nodded again but held up one hand. "Keep it. I think my sister would have wanted you to have it." He looked at two of the leather-clad men. "Torn, Del, if you'll bring us some food and drink? Then we can begin to plan our strategy."

To Kerri's amazement, the two men, one of whom had a jagged scar up the side of his face, simply turned and left the room.

However Kyle had done it, these tough, bike-riding men and women had accepted him as their leader.

But before she could look ahead, even think about strategy, there was something she had to know first. "Kyle, Brace said you knew Danielle was going to die."

For the first time, a hint of unease came into the young man's face. "I did."

"How long did you know before… before it happened?"

"Only a day."

She couldn't keep the accusatory tone out of her voice. "Then why the hell didn't you warn her? You could have saved her life."

He shifted in his seat, and a brief frown crossed his brow. "It is often unwise to use knowledge of the future to attempt to change it."

"Then it's not much fucking good, is it? For God's sake, Kyle, this is your sister we're talking about. Her death accomplished nothing."

"How do you know that?"

That question stopped Kerri in her tracks, and she merely stared at him, trying to calm the white-hot anger burning in her chest. But she kept picturing Danielle's face, hearing her last words, not of regret or fear over her own death, but apologizing for not trusting Aaron at first, admonishing them to take care of each other—and it was an effort not to lash out at her brother, sitting here in safety with his unlikely set of court attendants and bodyguards. But he spoke before she could put together her words well enough to articulate what she wanted to say.

"It's why the Pleiadians are exceedingly cautious about how they interfere. If you tell someone about the future, then you lose control over what they might do to try to alter it."

"I'd think those scruples wouldn't apply if it was your sister's life they were talking about," Kerri choked out.

"That's when it's especially important—when feelings are involved. What if Danielle's death wasn't meaningless, as you claim? What if her death set in motion events that would lead to the defeat of the Children? You only see what's in front of you, what's happening now. The Pleiadians can look forward, backward, see how everything weaves together."

"What about you?" Will said. "Can you see into the future?"

"Me?" Kyle smiled. "No. I'm an ordinary human. My own connection to the Pleiadians happened more or less because of an accident—if there are such things as accidents."

The two men Kyle had addressed as Del and Torn came in with a platter with bowls of chips, salsa, dried fruit, and what looked like refried beans. One carried a pitcher of beer.

"I hope the food makes up in quantity what it lacks in quality," Kyle said. "We have yet to solve the problem of no refrigeration, so perishables are out of the question for the foreseeable future."

All three were famished, and even Kerri, despite the anger that still formed a tight knot in her chest, ate gratefully.

So Kyle claimed to be an ordinary human, but his followers called him "The Prophet" and said that he "knew things." Which, she wondered, was closer to the truth? Was he simply being modest about some esoteric talent of his own—or was he taking advantage of the Pleiadians' foreknowledge?

In the end, it didn't matter. She had trusted Saul and his pronouncements before and accepted that he could, in some fashion, know the future. Or at least a part of it. It hadn't occurred to her that this meant he'd foreseen Danielle's death. What else did he know that he hadn't revealed? Perhaps Kerri's own death. The idea that Saul sent them on this mission knowing that she was going to die— worse, knowing Aaron was going to die—struck her as being as coldly calculating as the machinations of the Children.

"How did you meet the Pleiadians?" Aaron asked Kyle through a mouthful of chips and salsa.

"I don't know how much my sister told you about me, but I've had an interest in arcane matters since I was little."

That much, Kerri knew. In fact, Danielle had alluded to the fact that Kyle was widely regarded by those who knew him as being odd, and in fact that she had left Louisiana in part to get away from the reputation of "Kooky Kyle."

"I became a licensed Ham radio operator when I was fourteen years old. It allowed me to talk to people all over the world. It also, as I found out, beamed my signal out to space. Ham radio makes use of satellite transmission, so there was no way to avoid it. Because of this, anyone out there listening could pick up my signal."

"And the Pleiadians did."

He nodded. "I had joined a group of people scattered across the globe who were interested in the possibility of extraterrestrial intelligence. In communicating with them, I found out about the threat of the Black-eyed Children, and was in discussion about how the people on Earth might counter this threat. I knew Danielle was involved in the effort as well—"

"You knew about the Boundary?" Kerri interjected.

"Yes. She'd told me shortly after she joined, saying she felt obliged to admit I'd been right about the threat of alien invasion. There was much she could not tell me—you need have no fear that she betrayed classified information to me—but she wanted me to know I'd been on the right track all along. In fact, she urged me to join the Boundary myself."

"You didn't," Aaron said.

"No. For one thing, I am not physically strong enough to do what you do. Danielle suggested that there might be capacities in which I could serve even so, but I had my doubts that the Boundary would accept me considering my condition and decided that it was better that I continued as I was doing."

"What condition do you have?" Will asked. "If I'm not being too nosy."

"Not at all. As a doctor, I would expect you to be curious." Kyle stirred in his chair, and his face betrayed a quick wince of pain, there and gone in a moment. "Even in childhood I wasn't able to keep up, but at the time we didn't know why. I was diagnosed two years ago with Friedreich's ataxia. It is progressive and incurable and has robbed me of much of my mobility, which I only mention to explain why I sent my friends to bring you back rather than going myself. In any case, joining the Boundary was out of the question, so I looked into other ways I could participate in the war against the Children. I was contacted a year ago by a representative of the Pleiadians."

"Saul?" Kerri asked.

Kyle shook his head. "A woman who called herself Ahinoam. But surely you must realize that those are neither their real names nor real appearances."

Truthfully, that had never occurred to her. Saul's behavior in her presence had been so peculiar that figuring out what she was actually seeing and hearing was enough without speculating that his very appearance might be a disguise.

"What did she tell you?" Will asked.

"That my role was to create a network of people who knew what was going on and would function to keep humanity together and informed when the inevitable invasion occurred. She also gave me enough information to know whom to contact and when. It was on her suggestion that I contacted Brace and warned him and his friends of what was to come. I didn't expect to be believed, but Ahinoam assured me that it would not be a problem."

"Something about what he said made sense." Brace had stood behind them in reverent silence the entire time—odd in a man who exuded such an air of physical power. "I can't explain why. But when he talked to me and Roan and all on the ham radio, it was like—I dunno. Like I'd been waiting all my life to hear it. Like it was an urgent message that I better listen to, if I knew what was good for me, that I'd regret if I ignored or laughed at." He paused. "Like what a born-again must feel when he hears the Word of God for the first time."

Kyle gave Brace an embarrassed smile. "I have tried to assure Brace and the others that I am just an ordinary man, only one who was lucky enough to make contact with entities who wish to help us, that I have no special powers."

"Pardon," Brace said, "but that'll take a hell of a lot of convincing."

"It's of no matter either way, I suppose." Kyle gave him another smile and shook his head slightly. "We were in touch for some months by ham radio, and I urged Brace to let as many people know as he trusted, warn them to be ready. When Ahinoam told me the invasion was imminent, I made arrangements to meet Brace in Topeka, because otherwise I would have been stranded in southern Louisiana, which as you know is a center of activity for the Children and their human slaves. And she told me you'd be fleeing across the country, and crossing through Kansas, and that I was to meet you."

"Now that we have, what next?" Aaron said. "I mean, this history is all well and good, and I guess we need to know how the pieces fit together. But now that we know this, what do we do? We've already had delays, and I know the farther east we go, the more we'll hit. That's not even counting any trouble we'll run into once the Children catch up with us. So far, we've lucked out in that respect, but we can't count on that luck to hold."

"No. You're right. And you're also correct that it is urgent. I have merely the vaguest notion of what you're being expected to do—only that getting to Colville, New York is of paramount importance. Ahinoam made that clear, and in response to my questions said only that she could not tell me more. My role, she said, was to steer you correctly so that you would arrive there as quickly as possible. What outcome we can expect after you arrive—indeed, what exactly you'll find there or how you should respond to it—I have no idea."

"So we're still whistling in the dark." Kerri could hear the bitterness in her own voice.

"Not completely. I do have some information about which route across the Midwest and into the northeast will be the safest. There are areas that are already being cleared by the Children—cities that have been largely depopulated. Others are battle zones, and others yet still largely untouched, although as you've found out, that doesn't mean they're safe. The dangers from our fellow humans can be as serious as the ones from the invaders."

"True that," Will said.

"The Children are moving fast. Once they mount their invasion, they do not waste time. Therefore you should not, either. We should discuss your plans tonight and give you a good night's sleep here. Tomorrow morning, you should leave as early as possible."

"How will we avoid them?" From Aaron's tone of voice, he sounded as if the thought *As if that's possible* was floating just beneath the surface.

Kyle's dark eyes passed from one of them to the other, his languid glance seeming as if it were taking in far more than an ordinary man's. Kerri found herself understanding why these men and women had come in only a short time to revere Kyle Tauriac as a prophet. Despite his repeated denial that there was anything special about him, there was some ineffable quality in his manner that gave Kerri the impression he was not quite human.

Such magnetism in a more ruthless person would result in a cult leader, a high priest, a demagogue. Was it Kyle's physical condition that kept him from seeking to use his personal power for his own advancement? Or simply morality? But just as his demeanor separated himself from the rest of them, it made that part of him inaccessible. Whatever he told them, whatever part of himself he showed them, it would be a deliberate, calculated choice.

"Topeka will be safe," he was saying, as her attention was brought back to the room. "For a terrible reason, but it works in your favor. Topeka was one of the first cities in the Midwest to be attacked, and the Children have cleared it."

"They killed *everyone?*" Will's voice was high, tight with anger, his face showing a combination of disbelief and horror.

Kyle shrugged. "Killed or removed. You know they can jump through space."

"We've seen it happen more than once," Aaron said.

"Then you might recognize that they can also jump great distances, not just from one place to another on Earth. It's been known for a while that some of their victims are drained of their neural energy and their bodies left as an empty shell—"

"We've seen that, too," Aaron's mouth twisted in disgust.

"And some simply vanish. We believe that those are taken elsewhere to be used for food. Another group are, to put it bluntly, parasitized and returned to their homes, where they act as informants or assistants—effectively, as slaves."

"We think those are the ones the Children terminated last week," Kerri said.

"Do not assume that all of the men and women parasitized by the Children were terminated. They no doubt want you to think that. Our suspicion is that they were selective about which ones died, and that there are many more out there. I believe that they will only terminate the last few when—if—the Children have won, and the Earth is cleared of sentient life."

"Jesus Christ," Will said softly.

"I know you have been careful which humans you trust. You will need to be more careful. What I would suggest—well, do you recall the old television series, *The X-Files?*"

"The Truth Is Out There," Will said.

"Yes. But that is not the phrase I would have you recall. The salient one here is 'Trust No One.'"

"Good thing we didn't decide on this before tonight," Aaron said, a trace of irony in his tone.

Kyle gave them a fleeting smile. "Indeed. I have been anticipating this meeting for some time, and I believe it is critical to the success of your mission. I… I believe…." His voice, already slurred because of his disease, trailed off and finally stopped. His mouth hung open a little, head tilted to one side like a dog waiting for a command, eyes focused on no one.

A shudder ran down Kerri's backbone. Was the young man having a seizure? She'd never heard of the disorder he had, and in fact now couldn't even recall the name he'd told them earlier. Was this one of its symptoms?

But none of his attendants rushed to his side. In fact, they were all suddenly more attentive, alert, eyes intent on the limp figure in the oversized recliner.

The tough-looking, red-haired woman who had met them at the door, the one Brace had called Roan, said in a low voice, "Listen. It's starting."

And Kyle began to speak again. His voice was different than before, more forceful, more authoritative, the voice of a man in command. Watching his lips move, and a voice not Kyle's own come out, was as eerie as anything Kerri had ever seen.

"Safe and quick. Across the flatlands and into the hills. Eyes open, face forward. See what's in the cover of darkness, watch each other's backs when they come."

"The Children?" Will said in a low voice, and one of Kyle's followers shushed him.

"Their speech is as the hissing of snakes, their fangs dripping with poison. Be steadfast, and you will come through blood and rain and iron, on to where the purifying fires burn. You will know who speaks with the voice of God by their actions. Find help where you seek it. You will know him by a pillar of smoke, a heat and light that cleanses. You will search for your blood but not find it, but do not let that deflect your arrow shot straight toward the heart of the enemy. Find the one who was captured, then save the one who was lost. There you will find a door, which all of you must step through without question. If the door closes, you will be trapped. That is all. Do all of these things, and you will complete the circle. I will say nothing more."

Silence fell. Kerri had the sense of what it must have been like for the ancient Greeks to sit at the feet of the Oracle of Delphi, listening to her words, trying to parse the sense of what seemed like random babbling. As she watched Kyle, his eyes fluttered, and he licked his lips. He raised his head, wincing a little, flexing fingers that had been gripping his own knees. He turned and let his gaze pass over them again.

"I… forgive me. I have lately been prone to these episodes. Do not dismay yourself. I recover from them quickly enough." His voice was back to the slow, slightly slurred speech of Kyle Tauriac.

Kerri stared at him in incredulity. Did he not recall what he had said, only seconds before? She looked at Kyle, and began, "What did you mean…." but stopped when she caught out of the corner of her eye Brace giving her a little frown and a shake of the head.

"I fear," Kyle continued, "that when these fits take me, it leaves me quite exhausted. I apologize to you, but I must rest. My friends will show you where you can sleep. We will complete our discussion of your plans for crossing the plains into New York tomorrow morning, after we have all passed what will be hopefully a quiet night."

With the help of his metal cane he stood, straightening legs thin enough to look as if they might not support him. Roan and the scar-cheeked man who had brought Kerri and the others food—the one Kyle had called Torn—went to his side and assisted him in walking from the room.

Kerri gave a questioning look at Brace, who returned her gaze levelly.

"I'll explain," he finally said, in a low voice. "Much as I can, anyhow. Honestly, I probably don't understand this any more than you do."

C H A P T E R
11

"WHAT THE FUCK WAS THAT?" Will's voice contained equal amounts of awe and fear. "If that was a seizure, it's not like anything I ever heard about in medical school."

"Wasn't a seizure," Brace said. "It's like there's somebody else in the Prophet's body, and sometimes that other person pops out. Can happen any time. What he says when that other person, or whatever it is, talks—well, it's always important. Honest to God, that's how I knew he was something different, that I made the right choice when I agreed to help him. He told me things…." A look almost of embarrassment crossed his face, looking out of place on that rugged countenance. "Well, lemme just say I wasn't in doubt after that."

"And he really doesn't know what he said afterward?" Kerri said.

Roan shook her head, then pushed back her long red hair with one hand. "We don't think he does, no. He knows some odd thing's happened. Always seems a little ashamed, you know? Like you would if you pissed your pants in public, or something like that. At first, we tried talking to him about it, asking him what he meant, but he always got frustrated, almost angry, when we did that. Far as we can tell, he doesn't know anything about what goes on when he's out. Like Brace said, it's like there's two people in the same body, and they both suspect each other's there but don't want to think about it. Then they kind of elbow each other out of the way to be the one at the microphone."

"But what did all that mean?" Aaron said. "I'm having a hard time even remembering it. It made no sense."

"That's what we all thought at first, too," the blond Hulk Hogan lookalike they'd met at the State Park—the one who had introduced himself as Skids—said. "Till we started paying attention and found out it all really means something. Something important. If I was you, I'd try writing down what you remember. You wait very long, it'll all slip away, and you'll only find out later what you lost."

There was a commotion in the back of the room, and a door opened to let in the taciturn African American man who'd been the third, with Brace and Skids, to come to the park to bring them back. But before he went more than two steps into the room, he was pushed aside by a muscular brindle pit bull, who charged Kerri. She backed up but in two steps was against a wall.

Afterwards, she wondered why the hell she hadn't drawn her gun but was glad she hadn't. The dog jumped up on her, planting both paws solidly in her solar plexus, slamming her hard against the wall, and gave her an enthusiastic lick across the face.

Roan scowled at the man. "Barker, control your damn dog! About scared the life out of her."

"Sorry." Barker crossed the room in three strides, grabbed the dog by the collar, and said, in a deep voice, "No."

The pit bull looked at him with a goofy expression of love, and wagging furiously, sat down with a plunk.

"His name is Bongo," Roan said, her voice still disapproving. "He's harmless but stupid. Barker takes him everywhere. He'd have brought him along when he went to pick you up if the Prophet hadn't said no. He's even got a sidecar on his 'cycle for the silly mutt. Sorry, hun, did he hurt you?"

Kerri shook her head. She was still trying to get her breath back. "It's okay," she wheezed. "I love dogs."

Barker gave her a look of approval and let go of Bongo's collar. He raised one finger in front of the dog's face, and said, "Gentle."

Bongo loped over to Kerri again, more sedately this time, and sat down next to her for an ear scratch.

Roan rolled her eyes. "Well, now you know why he's called 'Barker.' His dog talks more than he does. Anyhow, lemme show you where you'll be sleeping. You're together, right?" She wagged a finger between Aaron and Kerri.

"It's that obvious?" Kerri smiled.

"Yeah." Roan's face was deadpan. "Yeah, it is. Okay, you two can have the back bedroom. Me and Del can sleeping bag it tonight. You need a comfortable night's sleep way more than we do." She paused, and a sympathetic, almost sorrowful, look crossed her face. "You got a hell of a long way still to go."

MORNING CAME FAR TOO SOON. Kerri's consciousness returned slowly, and for a while she simply relished being in a soft bed, in clean sheets—and having her body clean. Before sleep, Roan had shown them an improvised shower they'd put together from a gravity-fed cistern on poles out behind the barn. At this point, even a cold shower was wonderful.

But bliss—that was waking up with Aaron spooned up behind her, skin on skin, his arm encircling her waist. She pushed aside thoughts of the day's journey, what dangers it might bring, and simply let herself relax into the warm comfort of a blanket, a comfortable mattress, and a gentle embrace.

An hour later, after making love—Aaron was a morning lover, she had discovered, a tendency that suited her just fine—they got out of bed, took a quick face wash from a metal basin in the corner of the room, and dressed. It looked like another fine day was in the making. Good traveling weather, although it'd be hot again.

Was it still August, or already September? Kerri tried counting backwards and each time got a different answer. It was odd how quickly what day of the week or month it was ceased to have any meaning at all. Within only a week, they were back to survival mode, only looking toward the next meal, the next place to sleep, with the ever-present question "friend or foe?" popping up every time they saw another human being.

Kyle was already up when they went into the den. He sat in his recliner, cane propped in exactly the same place as it had been the night before. He had a plate of dried fruit and crackers on his lap, same fare as they'd had for dinner. Banding together, apparently, hadn't solved the food problem, which was bad now and only going to get worse.

"I was telling you about your path when I had one of my unfortunate episodes," he said, once they were settled with their own meager ration. "I believe I told you that Topeka would be a relatively safe choice."

"It was cleared, you said," Aaron said around a mouthful of crackers.

"Largely. We do not know how thoroughly, but Brace, Roan, Del, and the others are all from the Topeka area, and they saw it happening. Torn barely escaped in time. He said people were being rounded up like animals, and then pushed along until they… until they simply vanished."

"Through a portal," Kerri said grimly.

"Torn had to weave through a crowd of Children who were trying to snatch him right out of his motorcycle seat. He said that during much of his passage through Topeka, he saw no one except Children."

Kerri shuddered. The memory of her narrow escape from a group of Children who were chasing her at night through the streets of Las Cruces was all too fresh in her mind.

"It is terrible," Kyle said, "but it works in your favor. Our surmise is that once a city is largely cleared, they move on. I expect, based on Torn's experience, that by now Topeka is more or less a ghost town."

No one responded.

"I have spoken with the Pleiadians, specifically with my contact Ahinoam, about your path beyond Topeka. She is in agreement that driving northeast from there, and making the river crossing at Saint Joseph, is safer at this point than going straight east and crossing in Kansas City. After you're in Missouri, go straight east. Most of the towns you cross will be small."

"What kind of resistance can we count on?" Aaron asked.

"That is unknown. Ahinoam has information, but she and her people are not omnipotent. Also, conditions change. In a situation like this, they can change hour to hour. All we can tell you is what would be the prudent choice now. Day after tomorrow, it may well be that these towns will be impossible to cross."

"Cheerful guy," Will mumbled.

"Realistic." Kyle turned his slow gaze on the young doctor. "In any case, from there, you have a choice. My only caution is to detour around the large cities along the lakes, or avoid them by taking another path altogether. Ahinoam told me that much of Chicago is, as we speak, on fire."

"God help us," Will said.

"Will we be anywhere near Findlay, Ohio?" Kerri tried to make the words sound offhand, but Aaron was watching her closely. He knew her well enough at this point not to be fooled.

"I do not know this town, but you will be crossing central Ohio, so I would expect that it is unlikely to be far off your path no matter where it is. Why?"

She looked down, suddenly uncomfortable. "My brother Jake lives there."

Kyle looked at her, his face inscrutable. "You wish to see him?"

"Of course."

"It might…." He stopped, looked upward for a moment, choosing his words. "It might not lead to the ending you are wishing for."

"I know that. I have to try."

"I understand. If you choose to go that way, I would only press you not to take long about it. Ahinoam said her people are in agreement that the window for accomplishing your task is closing. Do not let yourself be delayed."

"But what *is* our task?" Kerri tried to keep the frustration out of her voice, with little success. "If Ahinoam is like Saul, all we get when we ask questions is some vague-sounding New Age bullshit about trusting our intuition and knowing what to do when we arrive. Well, I'm sorry, I'm having a hard time accepting that right now. I don't know what possible harm can come from giving us specific instructions."

Brace, sitting a little apart from them, gave her a disapproving frown but said nothing.

"I do not know how to answer that," Kyle said. "Myself, I trust Ahinoam and her people implicitly. I cannot force you to that trust. I believe if they are withholding information from us, it is for a good reason. They are cautious with their exercise of power."

"I'd think caution would take second seat to having us succeed." Kerri's voice still sounded sullen in her own ears.

Kyle was apparently unperturbed by her irritation, and when he responded, his face and voice were still placid. "If they were mutually exclusive, Ahinoam would have told me more. In any case, I cannot enlighten you further on this point, because I simply do not know the answer. I believe that you must decide whether to continue your journey on Ahinoam's advice, or abandon it. There is no alternative."

Kerri couldn't come up with a good response to that. Indeed, they'd come this far because of belief in Saul's message. If she abandoned it now, then everything they'd been through had been to no purpose at all.

"I'll keep going," she finally said. "I have no idea why I'm saying that. None of this makes any sense."

"Then perhaps you should leave that judgment until afterwards. Some things only make sense in retrospect." He gave her a faint smile. "Of course, that is easy for me to say, as I am not the one undertaking a dangerous and risky voyage toward an uncertain end."

"Damn straight," Will said under his breath.

"We have foreseen a few things you may need along the way, however. You have no doubt given some thought to the difficulty of fueling your car."

"Yeah," Aaron said. "We've lucked out and stumbled on a couple of farms that had gasoline tanks for their tractors and gotten away with pilfering enough to fill the tank. But I can't expect that luck to hold out."

"No. And as they are equipped with electric pumps, you cannot obtain gasoline from filling stations in the ordinary way. However, when I was told we were going to meet you here, I was also told to give you this." He gave a little come-hither gesture to Brace, who brought forward something in an unopened cardboard box that had an illustration on the front that looked a little like a bicycle air pump.

"It's a hand-cranked suction pump," Brace said, plopping the box down in front of Aaron. "You can get gasoline from a filling station that way. You have to do it through the fill spout, though. Look around, you'll find something that looks like a manhole cover. Undo the set screws, and right underneath should be the tank fill spout. Most of 'em have a screw-on lid like on a car's gas tank, but bigger. Drop the end of the intake hose down into the tank, put the end of the flow hose into your tank, and pump as much as you need."

"That's fantastic," Aaron said. "I kept wondering if at some point we were going to simply run out of gas and be stuck out in the middle of nowhere."

"We also chucked a couple of five-gallon plastic gas cans into the back seat of your car. When you can, fill those, too. It'll give you a reserve in case there's trouble. But be careful, you know? I'm guessing people have figured out pretty quick to guard the gasoline they got, because there's no more coming. You gotta expect some people'll be willing to shoot you if you're seen pumping gas into your car. Keep alert, and move as quick as you can. While one of you operates the pump, the other two should keep 'em covered."

"Thanks, Brace." Aaron gave the man a grateful smile. "That's another thing, though. Only two of us are armed. Do you know anywhere we can get a gun for Will? I'd feel better if all three of us had weapons."

"Way ahead of you, dude." He went back to the chair where he had been sitting and picked up something off the floor, handed it to Will with some reluctance. It was a small but deadly-looking handgun and a holster to go with it. "You ever shot a gun before, Doctor?"

Will took it, a little gingerly, and nodded. "My dad and I used to go duck hunting. But the first time I used a handgun was yesterday morning." He gave a quick glance at Kerri and Aaron and seemed relieved when Brace didn't ask for any elaboration.

"Be careful, then. Keep the safety on until you're ready to shoot." He gave Will a dubious look. "I gotta say, sometimes a gun in the hands of a noob is more dangerous than being unarmed."

Will drew himself up with a frown, even though the result was that Brace still towered over him by at least a foot. "Hey, bro, don't make assumptions. I can handle myself."

Brace snorted but didn't respond.

"We will have to trust that you will all do what you need to do," Kyle said, his expression still mild. "But I fear it is time to say farewell. As I said, speed is of the utmost importance. While I am glad to have given you a brief respite, it is time to end it."

"We appreciate your help." Kerri thought back to the bizarre message they'd received from him the previous evening, that she had jotted down—as much of it as she could remember—on a scrap of paper before going to bed. What help would that be? Even if it was prophecy, it was couched in such mysterious verbiage that it was hard to see what possible guidance it could provide.

Deciphering that would have to wait. Brace had made it clear that Kyle Tauriac was not going to cast any light on what he said in one of his trance states. If, indeed, he even could. If he was unaware of what he was saying, or—frightening thought—the information was coming from some unknown source outside of him—there was no way he could tell them more.

A half-hour later, they stood next to Aaron's Renault, the once spotless car much the worse for wear, in the relative morning coolness of what looked like being another hot day. When Aaron took the empty gas cans out of the back seat to move them to the trunk, she saw that they had also included a bag of food and three bottles of water.

"Sorry we can't give you more," Roan said. "We'd like to. But we're short on provisions, too. The Prophet didn't want you to leave with nothing, so we spared what we could."

"It's kind of you," Kerri said. "Everything you did. I wish we could repay it somehow."

"Just do what you can to get rid of these bastards," Brace said. "That'll be plenty payment enough." He frowned. "Oh, and listen. Pay attention to what the Prophet told you. You don't seem like the believing type, and that's fine. I got no quarrel with what other people think. But I can tell you the Prophet's words—well, there's something in them. He don't say things unless they're real. You'll see, whether or not you choose to believe 'em. But you'd be better off believing, letting 'em guide you."

Kerri thought about the slip of scrap paper in her pocket with the cryptic words on it—*You will know who speaks with the voice of God by their actions… the purifying fires… You will know him by a pillar of smoke, a heat and light that cleanses. You will search for your blood but not find it… Find the one who was captured, then save the one who was lost. There you will find a door, which all of you must step through without question. If the door closes, you will be trapped… Do all of these things, and you will complete the circle.*

But she was no closer to understanding what it meant.

Will took the first driving shift, with Aaron in the back seat and Kerri riding shotgun. They said a brief goodbye to Brace and his friends—even the taciturn Barker, holding his dog by the collar, raised one hand in farewell. Kyle had remained inside the house, saying he could not easily manage the front steps, but that he would be "watching them from afar."

As they pulled out of the gravel driveway and back onto Kansas Route 56, the thought crossed her mind that if anyone could do that, it was Kyle Tauriac.

THE MORNING'S DRIVE WAS QUIET. They stopped at a filling station in Cottonwood Falls, Kansas that looked abandoned, and after driving a slow loop around the place, pulled up to the spot near the pumps where a metal plate covered the gasoline reserve tank.

Will offered to pump the gas, but Aaron said, "You should get used to having your gun in your hand. I hate to admit it, but Brace was right. If most of your experience of firing a gun is with a hunting rifle, you have to learn how to handle a handgun. I hope you don't have to use it, and there's no time for any real training, but at least you should get used to the feel of it."

So Will and Kerri covered Aaron while he pumped gas into the car's tank, and also filled the three plastic gas cans Brace had given them. But they saw no one, heard nothing but the ever-present prairie wind hissing in the grass, pushing along dead leaves, a gum wrapper, a Styrofoam coffee cup.

Humanity's legacy, right there. Empty buildings and trash.

But that thought was so depressing Kerri pushed it out of her mind. They loaded the gas cans into the trunk, got back in the car, and drove away.

Once they left the rural highway and got onto the Kansas Turnpike at Emporia, they began to see more signs of humanity's footprint—abandoned cars, and more than one car with corpses draped on the steering wheel or lolling against the windows. They drove through the tollbooths without slowing—there was no one there to question them, and if the camera with its black glass eye made note of their license plate number, they had bigger worries to face.

In any case, with the electrical grid failing, perhaps already out completely, it was doubtful the camera worked anyway.

They saw houses near the Turnpike as they approached Topeka—and no signs of life. If Kyle was right that Topeka and the surrounding area had been cleared, the Children had done a damn thorough job. Even the armed gangs they had to contend with in Melrose and Clovis, New Mexico would have been better than this preternatural silence. But if the Children achieved their goal—destroying humanity by using it as a food source—that's what they would achieve everywhere. A landscape scoured clean of every last human, an Earth where the whole human species was used up, gone forever.

They angled off the Turnpike south of Topeka onto an interchange that took them toward Highway 4, cutting upward toward Saint Joseph and the Missouri River crossing. Tall buildings appeared on the skyline, but it was apparent their route was going to bypass them around most of the city proper.

Fortunately. The emptiness in the farmland and countryside was eerie enough. To see a whole city depopulated was the stuff of nightmares.

Kyle's advice, at least this far, had been good. The only slowdown they had involved working their way around an overturned semi shortly after getting onto Highway 4 North. It required some maneuvering, and the loss of a little more paint scraped from the Renault's side, but soon they were driving all alone down the abandoned highway toward Valley Falls.

At least the scenery was improving. Central Kansas had been board-flat, with no trees except for the omnipresent poplar windbreaks that sheltered farmhouses from the prevailing winds. Here, there were trees, giving the eye something green other than cornfields. The terrain began to undulate a little as well. Not the craggy mountains and canyons of New Mexico, but at least something other than dead straight roads running endlessly through mile after mile of agricultural land.

Kerri didn't realize that she had been dreading passing through a city until she felt her body relax as they left Topeka behind. With luck, the other cities they'd have to drive through would be equally easy. The speed with which the Children had moved in clearing the towns of people was terrifying, but at least it made their voyage toward their ultimate goal easier, whatever it was they were being expected to do when they got there.

She found out in short order that her relief was premature. They had gone only a few miles on Highway 4 when they passed a Presto Mart and saw what they dreaded. Three small, slim figures standing in the shade of the awning, all three peering through sunglasses that looked black in the glare, faces turned toward the unexpected appearance of a car.

"Oh, Jesus," Will said. "It's them."

One of them raised a skinny arm clad in a ragged sleeve and pointed directly at them.

Will hit the accelerator. It was unnecessary. The Children couldn't have caught up with them, and in any case made no attempt to, merely following the car with their eyes—mercifully hidden behind the dark lenses—until they were lost to view.

It was Aaron who asked the question Kerri didn't even want to put into words.

"Do you think they recognized us?"

"It looked like it," Will said. "They were gunning for us pretty hard more than once. They're smart enough to know what your car looks like. It doesn't take a rocket scientist. But what do we do about it?"

"What can we do?" Aaron said. "It would be stupid to go back and try to kill them. If they saw us driving up, they'd call for reinforcements damn quick."

Kerri couldn't help looking in the side mirror, checking for pursuit. There was none, or at least none that was evident. "The most important question is, could they figure out where we're going?"

Neither man responded for a moment. Then Aaron said, his voice thoughtful, "That depends."

"On what?"

"On how many command centers they have. If Colville, New York is the only one—or, at least, the main one—yeah, they should be able to figure out what we're doing pretty quick. But if they have outposts scattered all over the world, there's no reason for them to know which one we're planning on attacking." He snorted. "Especially considering that we don't know why we're attacking this one."

Will frowned. "So it all depends on whether we're talking about a central nervous system or a neural net."

"Yeah," Aaron said. "I mean, you're the biology expert. But if I understand you correctly, that's it exactly. If Colville's the brain, they'll know immediately. If they are acting through some kind of decentralized network, we should be okay."

"Which is it, do you think?" Kerri asked.

"I'd place my money on the latter," Aaron said. "And I don't think that's just optimism speaking. From everything we've seen about the Children, they don't seem to have any kind of leadership hierarchy. We've never gotten any evidence they have commanders and underlings. So they act almost like one single organism, communicating by telepathy or however the hell they do it. If I'm right, then there's no reason they'd think of creating some kind of central node. They'd be much more likely to have an interconnected array of strongholds from which to work, not one command center that's calling the shots for the whole invasion."

Will took a deep breath. "I hope like hell you're right. Because if they radioed ahead and we're walking into a trap, I'm gonna be pissed."

——————————

THEY CROSSED INTO THE STATE of Missouri at a little before noon on a long, steel-braced bridge that arched over the wide, placid Missouri River. The white puffy clouds that had been in the sky were drawing together into a gray cloud bank on the western horizon, but with any luck they'd outrun the bad weather. They bypassed most of the city of Saint Joseph, once again seeing little but scattered accidents, abandoned automobiles, and a row of silhouetted buildings on the skyline. Soon even that was left behind as they drove steadily east on the ruler-straight lanes of Highway 36. They switched drivers just before Cameron, Missouri, with Kerri taking over and Will moving to the back seat to take a nap, but not before giving wide berth to another threatening, hand-painted sign blocking a turnoff, like the one they'd seen near Medicine Lodge, Kansas. This one said, *KEEP OUT THIS MEANS YOU. This road is closed. We are armed and on guard. AMERICA STILL STANDS.*

"For now," was all Will said.

Once the doctor was asleep, his body held up only by his shoulder harness, head tilted to one side and his mouth open slightly, Kerri said in a soft voice, "I don't know if you're right about the whole command center thing, Aaron."

"Oh?"

"I mean, I hope you're right. It'd work in our favor, although it does bring up the question of why we're being sent to this particular one. But think of your analogy of the Children acting like a single organism. Okay, maybe that's true. But what if they're more like the cells in a human body? We have all these independently operating tissues, made of blood cells, bone cells, skin cells. If you looked closely at any one cell, you wouldn't see its connection to the others. More importantly, you wouldn't see that there was a master organ calling the shots. You wouldn't infer the existence of a brain."

Aaron didn't respond for a moment. "If you're right, what is their brain? And where is it?"

"Beats me. And I don't know if I'm right. But if the Children are like worker ants, carrying out the will of the whole, where does that will come from? There has to be something instructing them on what to do, when to act. What's moving the ants themselves?"

"Like Will said, we'll find out when we see if they've anticipated our going to New York."

"I'm not sure we should wait that long. Whatever the source of their intelligence is, there's no doubt of how smart they are. If they have the ability to anticipate what we're doing, we're doomed."

"How do we tell?"

"I think we have to be on the lookout for more Children. You know we're going to see them, especially given the higher population density in the East. It makes sense that the Children's presence would be more spread out in the West. But we need to step up our vigilance, and especially, watch how they act. See if they're laying strategy by predicting our next move."

"That's pretty terrifying to think about."

"Yeah, no shit. I've been in a state of high terror pretty much since the invasion began."

Aaron didn't answer for a moment, just looked out of the window at the farm fields and occasional trees flying past. "I know what you mean. If we get out of this, I think I'm going to need to sleep for about a week straight just to purge my body of all the adrenaline."

But the rest of the day passed without their seeing any other Children, nor, in fact, any humans. If there were any survivors they were, understandably, laying low. In this situation, no one in their right mind would come out of hiding at the sound of a car. Too much chance of being spotted by the

Children—or by humans who were taking advantage of the chaos for their own malign purposes.

They did, however, see results of the invasion. More wrecked cars. The aftermath of a massacre in the town of Chillicothe, requiring a detour to avoid running over dead bodies on the street, many of whom were apparently hacked to death. No sign of who, if anyone, had survived the riot, nor what had caused it. The marauders had either fled, were in hiding, or else had been captured themselves by the Children after they were finished with their brutal work against their own kind.

Over and over the pattern repeated. Depopulated towns, the leavings of a civilization being destroyed, evidence of humanity's determination to contribute to the tailspin rather than fighting against their common enemy. Once they saw a herd of cattle that had been turned loose, the gate for their pasture wide open, and a huge sloppily-painted sign standing in front of it that said, *SEE TO YOUR AFFAIRS THE END OF THE WORLD IS UPON US*. The cattle, apparently having no affairs that needed seeing to, took advantage of their newfound freedom by grazing in a neighboring wheat field, and raised placid, content faces to watch them as they drove past.

"What's going to happen to them?" Will's voice sounded heavy with grief, and Kerri gave him a curious glance.

"The cows?"

"Yeah. Cows. And dogs and cats. And even things like corn and wheat. Look at all the corn fields and wheat fields we've passed. What will those be in a year, five years, ten years? I remember one of my college biology profs saying that corn had been artificially selected for so long that it has become lousy at reproducing myself. The seeds are so tightly packed they don't let go of the cob, and the whole thing just falls to the ground and rots. Without humans planting it, corn would go extinct."

"I suppose the cats will do well enough. Feral cats have gotten by for years."

He nodded. "But if the Children win—if humanity does vanish—it's not going to take long for the entire planet's face to change. Trees will take over farmland again. Buildings will weather and fall apart, bridges rust, subways and tunnels collapse. We've only kept nature at bay, we haven't really beaten it. Once we're gone, it comes roaring back with a vengeance."

"Rats and cockroaches inherit the Earth." Aaron's voice was somber.

"I dunno," Will said. "I think the rats and cockroaches are pretty tied to humans. Without us, their stock in trade—living off our refuse—is gone. It'll cause evolution to veer off in a whole new direction."

"Might not be a bad thing."

"I'm not in favor of it," Kerri said. "If that happens, it'll mean we've failed."

"Whatever happens," Will said, "humanity won't be what it has been. Those people who've been taken, towns that have been cleared, like Topeka was. Those aren't coming back, I don't think."

THEY DECIDED TO SPEND THE night in the town of Hannibal, Missouri, after Will recommended stopping once it was dark enough that headlights were necessary.

"I'm sure they can hear us coming," he said. "But they can see headlights from a hell of a lot farther away. I'd rather not give the Children, or anyone else for that matter, any more advance notice of our arrival than we can possibly help."

They found a motel near the city limits that appeared to be deserted. It looked like a hundred other low-rent motels scattered across the United States, with a low flat roof, a scraggly foundation planting of poorly-maintained yews and junipers, a couple of run-down excuses for raised-bed gardens, doors with scarred paint and tarnished room numbers.

"I wonder how many Starlite Motels there are in the world?" Aaron pointed to a dingy sign as they got out of the car, guns drawn, scanning the area around them for any movement, human or otherwise.

"At least it's not the Dewdrop Inn," Will said.

Leaving Aaron to guard the car, Kerri and Will made a slow circuit of the building. All they saw was a dog, a border collie from the look of it, that eyed them warily and dashed off into the cornfield when they got too close.

When they came back into the parking lot, Aaron was standing still, gun ready, facing the highway and doing a slow back-and-forth scan.

"Anything?"

Kerri shook her head. "Just a dog. No people, no Children, not even any dead bodies. The place looks abandoned."

"I'm not counting on it until we make as sure as possible. It may sound like overkill, but we need to search every room before we settle in. Think about it. You're hiding because you're scared, three strange people drive up, you're not going to open the door and say, 'Howdy.' You're gonna hide, hope they go away—or wait till they let their guard down and strike out."

Kerri nodded. Thinking that way sucked, but Aaron was right. Being incautious in this new and dangerous world was a short voyage to getting captured or killed.

After calling out in front of the room that said Office, assuring anyone inside that they meant no harm, and getting no response, Aaron used the butt end of the tire iron from his car's trunk to break the window. He reached through and unlatched it, stepped across the sill, and after a quick look around the shadowed room and seeing nothing but worn furniture and a wilted house plant, unlocked the door and let the others in.

Kerri walked across the dingy carpeting toward the front desk, stepped around it, checked underneath and in a little alcove that apparently served as a coat closet and storage for a vacuum, two brooms, and a mop.

No sign of anyone.

"I think we're okay." She gestured toward the key rack. "We gonna split up, like we did in Rose Dawson's place? Or cozy up as a threesome?"

"I'd be more comfortable if we were all together," Aaron said. "In fact, I think we should post a guard and sleep in shifts. The farther along we get, the fewer risks I want to take."

"Agreed," Will said. "But you and Kerri start getting frisky under the covers with me in the room, I'm gonna leave."

Kerri laughed. "No worries. I'm so tired I don't think I'd be ready for any nighttime activities anyhow."

They pulled a handful of keys from a rack, and went back outside. It was nearly full dark. The car was hardly visible, but as a precaution, Aaron moved it around to the side of the motel where it would be less noticeable from the road, while Kerri and Will used flashlights to search one room after another. Behind shower curtains, inside cabinets, under beds.

Nothing. All eight rooms of the Starlite Motel were completely empty of life.

They locked up the rooms again and returned the keys to the office with the exception of the one for Room One. Will gave her a questioning look.

"Maybe we're not the only ones fighting the Children and needing a place to spend the night. May as well leave things as we found them, as much as we're able."

They met Aaron and brought their few necessities into their room, bolting the door behind them. The room had two beds, clean if not especially comfortable, and Aaron agreed to take the first guard shift.

Kerri was asleep nearly as soon as her head hit the pillow, and Will was already snoring as she drifted off. She was barely aware when Aaron turned guard duty over to Will, slipped his body under the sheets, spooned up behind her with a sigh, and encircled her middle with one gentle arm.

Some undetermined amount of time later, she snapped back to consciousness for no reason she could identify, all of her senses on high alert. Aaron was still snuggled up to her, his breathing slow and steady. Slowly, warily, she tilted her head upward, and opened her eyes.

The door to the room was wide open. She saw a rectangle of stars, and a bit of the parking lot glowing silver in moonlight, felt a light breeze brush her face.

And at the foot of the bed stood two slight figures, looking at the sleepers with tilted heads, like a predator trying to decide when to strike.

The Children had found them after all.

CHAPTER
12

KERRI WAS FROZEN, STARING AT the silhouetted faces. Did she have time to grab for her gun? Unlikely. It was on the nightstand, and chances were, if she moved, they'd pounce. On the other hand, they were trapped. What did she have to lose?

And where the *hell* was Will?

She made her move with hardly any conscious thought, rolling toward the nightstand and reaching out blindly with her right hand for the gun. Aaron jolted awake, giving an inarticulate noise of alarm, and the two Children jumped forward.

But suddenly one of them was knocked sideways, landing on the floor with a thud. The other turned in time to catch the backhand swing of some heavy object in the middle of its face, crushing its features with a ruinous noise. Then it, too, toppled over, and for a moment, all was still except for her gasps for breath.

Then Will's frightened voice from the center of the room, nearly an octave higher than normal. "Holy fuck, are y'all okay?"

"Yes." Kerri shuddered, pulling herself out from under the blanket, and sat up. "But we've got to get out of here. However they found us, it's likely others aren't far behind."

A desperate scramble to collect their meager belongings, and five minutes later, they were again driving east toward the steel-girdered span of the Mark Twain Memorial Bridge across the Mississippi River, Will behind the wheel.

It was only after a few minutes had passed with no sign of pursuit that Kerri said, "What the hell happened? How did those Children suddenly appear?"

"I'm not sure where they came from," Will said. "I didn't see a portal, so they might just have been in the area. Everything was quiet, and y'all were both sound asleep. I had to take a piss. So I opened the door as silently as I could, looked around, didn't see anyone. I went outside to find a tree."

"What is it with guys peeing on trees?" Kerri asked.

"Guy Code of Conduct," Aaron contributed. "Walls also work."

"And you're allowed to piss off bridges," Will said in a completely serious tone. "Required to, in fact."

Kerri shook her head. "Men are weird. Anyhow, what happened then?"

"So I finished up and was heading back to the room. I'd only gone like twenty feet away, but when I looked back at the room, the door was wide open. I knew I'd pulled it to when I left—not latched, but mostly closed. At first I thought the wind had blown it, but something set my spidey-senses tingling. I didn't bring my gun—stupid, I know, but I just didn't think of it. But fortunately, there was a loose board on the raised-bed garden below our window. I don't know how I saw it in the dark. Maybe the Good Lord was looking out for me—my mom always said he protected fools and drunks. So I picked it up and came in to find two Children standing by your bed, ready to grab you. I walloped them."

"I know it's ridiculous, but I keep thinking, "What if they weren't Black-eyed Children?"" There was reluctance in Aaron's voice. "There's no way real kids would be there and act like they did, but by now I'm second-guessing every damn thing we do."

Will didn't answer for a moment. "I hope like hell they were Black-eyed Children. If I just cracked the skulls of two human children, I don't want to think about it."

Kerri shook her head. "They were Black-eyed Children. I'm certain. I was reaching for my gun just as you hit the first one. They were ready to grab me. Why they didn't do it right away, I'm not sure."

"I think they'd just gone in. I couldn't have been gone from the room more than a minute. Less, probably."

Aaron was riding shotgun and turned to look at Kerri in the back seat. "But you know what this means."

She nodded. "They were waiting for us."

Will frowned. "How do you know that?"

"No portal. Kerri's beacon didn't light up. That means they were already here. All they had to do was wait until they had a chance to get into our room, which came when Will left the door open. Once he did, they didn't waste any time."

"They may not have known it was us." Kerri's voice sounded doubtful in her own ears. "They're going to go after any human they see."

"I don't think this was opportunistic. They weren't taking advantage of a couple of stray humans they missed. They were here ahead of us, waiting."

"Jesus," Will said under his breath. "Do you know how absolutely terrifying that is? If I hadn't just caused this whole incident by taking a piss at the wrong time, I'd be wetting myself right now."

Aaron shook his head. "You didn't cause it, dude. You prevented our getting captured. Thank your bladder for that."

"Okay," Kerri said. "So if you're right, what do we do?"

Neither man answered.

She gave a mirthless chuckle. "So it doesn't make a hell of a lot of difference, does it? We're going to keep heading east as long as it's in our power to do so. We're still trusting Saul that the goal is the Children's command center in Colville, New York. If they don't know we're coming, good. If they do, too bad. Any guesses about their motives won't change our actions."

"I dunno," Aaron said. "If we know we've got stealth on our side, it might change how we approach the attack itself."

"Sneak in and get killed, rather than rush in screaming and get killed?"

"God damn, Kerri, you sure know how to cheer the troops." Will glanced over at her. "You should design inspirational posters."

"Sorry. I still haven't recovered from two Children popping up at the foot of my bed like some evil fucking jack-in-the-box." She gave Will a sidelong grin. "I gotta say, though, that you got a good batting arm. You play baseball in school?"

"Nah. What you saw was raw, unadorned desperation at work. I knew I'd only get one good hit in for each of them, so I made them count."

———————

TWO HOURS LATER, THE EASTERN horizon was tinted rose and orange with the approaching sunrise. The dark clouds they'd seen the previous day were clustered on the southern horizon, but the sky ahead was clear. They crossed into the state of Illinois at a little after five a.m. and pulled over for a hurried breakfast at a roadside stop on I-172 just south of the town of Quincy. It was a beautiful morning—dew on every leaf and pearling the nearly invisible threads of spider webs, birds singing in the trees, a cool breeze brushing their faces. But nothing could remedy the overpowering sense of dread Kerri felt, that the Children were now watching their every move, just waiting for another opportunity to strike.

And even with their guard up constantly, how could they be vigilant 24/7? They had to sleep sometimes. She doubted the Children did. Hell, they'd taken advantage of the fact that humans have bladders that have to be emptied every so often to time their attack the previous evening.

So far, they had found one Achilles' heel—a susceptibility to an obscure poison. And how much good would that do them in the long run? They had only a few hypodermic cartridges left, and about three-quarters left of the bottle of colchicine. Once they'd used all the cartridges, the tranq rifle would be effectively useless, as would the poison.

What would they do then? The Children, at this point, seemed to have every advantage.

But she didn't say any of that to Aaron and Will. Will's comment about her pessimism earlier had stung a little. She'd always thought of herself as someone who tried to look at the positive side, who worked to fix things instead of whining about why they were broken. But here, there didn't seem to be a lot they could do, other than keep driving.

So that's what they did.

Midmorning, Kerri took over behind the wheel. Within minutes, Aaron and Will were both asleep. The night's disturbance had cheated them of a solid block of rest.

At the moment, Kerri was pretty sure that was what pissed her off the most about the attack. Odd how quickly they'd returned to the state of their ancestors, where food, rest, and protection from enemies were the top priorities.

She first noticed a problem when they were about twenty miles west of Astoria, Illinois. The crossroads, any possible exit from Highway 24, were blocked—not by threatening signs this time, but by impassable barriers of stone, cinder block, and heavy timbers. Someone had gone to a great deal of trouble to prevent people from turning off the highway.

Or was it to prevent them from escaping—by getting on the highway?

No way to tell.

She counted five such blocked intersections before, with some reluctance, she woke Aaron.

"I don't know what to make of this." She pointed as they passed another one, a turn to the left barricaded by a small mountain of debris.

Aaron blinked sleepily at the roadblock as it swept past. "Have you seen any people?"

She shook her head. "Not a soul."

"Could be now they've blocked the exits, they've retreated into their hidey-holes. Trying to wait the Children out."

"You'd think they'd be a little less obvious about it. These barricades are like a sign saying, 'Nothing to see here, just keep on moving.'"

"I didn't say it made sense."

Kerri pointed. "There's another one."

This pile was supplemented by chunks of torn-up asphalt, but the road surface itself looked undamaged.

"Whatever it is they're trying to do," Aaron said, "they were willing to put a lot of work into it."

"This is giving me the creeps. It doesn't feel like something the Children would do, though, you know? I'll lay odds that people are behind this."

"Of course, that's assuming the Children haven't taken care of the barricade-builders. Like you said, they pretty much announced their presence. It wouldn't be like the Children to ignore it." Suddenly Aaron frowned, and pointed ahead. "What the hell is *that?*"

They were driving along a straight stretch of highway, trees lining both sides, and ahead was a small sign saying *Sugar Creek*. But beyond that was—

"Slow down!" Aaron shouted. "Slow down! The bridge is out!"

Kerri jammed her foot on the brake, jolting Will out of sleep with a cry of "What? What happened?"

There was a small gravel pull-off to the left of the highway, leading a little way into a small hill with a grove of trees, and Kerri turned the car, scrunching to a halt.

She smacked the steering wheel with both hands. "Well, shit."

"Backtrack and find a way around it?" Will blinked and peered groggily at the ruined bridge.

"That may not be easy. Someone blocked the exits for maybe the last eight, ten miles."

"Why?"

"Beats the hell out of me. But we'd have to go a long way back to find any loop around this."

"Now we know where they got the chunks of blacktop," Aaron said. "But it still doesn't tell us what they were trying to do."

Will pointed toward the crest of the little hill. "Um, guys? I think we might be about to find out."

Walking down the hill toward them, like a procession of monks from the Middle Ages, was a line of men, women, and children wearing white robes. All were bare-headed and barefoot, and stared at the car with a feverish intensity. Kerri put the shift into reverse, and looked into the rearview mirror—but another group of solemn, robed figures had come up from behind them. There was no way to go backward or forward without hitting them.

She watched the nearest group of the robed men and women split and walk around each side of the car, flanking them. All of them wore beatific smiles.

It would have been better, she thought desperately, if they'd been angry. There was something unearthly about the still, placid countenances, like they were in a trance state.

Kerri reflexively locked her door, and the men did the same a moment later. One of the women, a tall, slim blonde whose hair was tied in an untidy bun, leaned over, and for the first time Kerri saw a momentary frown of annoyance. But it was swallowed up by the eerie tranquility as if it had never been, like a pebble slipping beneath the surface of a still lake, leaving hardly a ripple.

"Come, now," the woman said, in an authoritative voice. "We mean you no harm. But you must come with us. You see that you can't escape."

Kerri pulled her gun and aimed it at the woman. "Get your people away from our car."

To Kerri's shock, the woman started to laugh. "The sinful cannot harm the anointed ones. Your threats do not frighten me."

Aaron said in a hissing whisper, "We need to get out of here. Quickly."

"I'll have to back over them." Which she was scared enough to consider doing. But however freaked out she was, she wasn't at the point that she could coldly, callously run over another human being.

Was she?

The woman repeated her command. "Please get out of the car. We'd like to talk with you."

Will snorted. "Not too fucking likely, lady."

Her smile didn't waver. "Trust me when I say that when you accept God into your hearts, you will understand. Many things that were shadowed to you will become crystal clear."

"Get away from our car," Kerri said. "We've got no quarrel with you. You need to back off and let us go our way. No harm, no foul."

The woman tilted her head a little. "The Lord hath commanded us to do this work. Your worldly concerns are not ours. But it is not uncommon for the sinful to need some incentive. I will ask you one more time to get out of the car."

"And we will tell you one more time to go to hell," Aaron snarled.

The entire time, the woman's expression never changed. Their angry words bounced off her without any noticeable effect, or even any sign that she'd heard them. She turned away, and Kerri had a momentary hope that she'd given up and was going to call her people away, but then she turned back toward them, with her arm around the shoulders of a boy of perhaps ten.

And the woman drew a long, thin knife from the pocket of her robe, and laid it across the boy's neck.

"Get out of the car. I will sacrifice Micah here and now if you do not."

To Kerri's amazement, the boy's face was perfectly still. He looked afraid but steadfast, the kind of expression you'd expect in a child who was about to get a tetanus shot, not one facing having his throat cut.

The woman used her free hand to stroke Micah's sandy brown hair. "He is ready, aren't you, Micah? Because you know if you are sacrificed, you will in minutes be in the lap of Jesus Christ."

The boy gave a little nod, and said, in a light, high voice, "Yes, Priestess. I am ready."

"So I give you one final chance. Get out of the car. There are others who are willing to die for their Savior. We will baptize your car in a river of blood if you do not cooperate."

Kerri flashed a quick look over at Aaron. "I think… we have to…."

Aaron nodded. "Agreed. We'll figure a way out of this later."

And Kerri unlocked and opened her door.

The woman did not move the knife from Micah's throat, and her bland smile never wavered. "Come on." She sounded as if she were encouraging a frightened dog. "All of you."

The two men opened their doors and stepped out.

The woman Micah had called the Priestess moved the knife away from the boy's throat and slipped it back into her pocket. "You see? You must always remember this—that any of us is ready to die, at any time, to assure that the Lord's will is done. This is why a threat of violence against us will not work. If a person is ready to die at a moment's notice, why would he be afraid of anything you could do? We know we die sanctified and a moment later will be in the Field of Lilies, to reap forever the reward of our faithfulness." As she spoke, her silent followers came closer, moving around them, making any thought of escape a forlorn hope.

And that was even if she wouldn't retaliate by slaughtering a child.

"Now come, all of you, and let us celebrate," she said, giving a broad come-hither gesture with one arm. "The Lord has won three more souls this day."

The woman turned and led the way into the woods and up a gentle hill. The creepiest thing about the entire procession, Kerri thought, was their utter silence. They walked quietly, their bare feet making hardly a sound on the carpet of leaves. No one spoke. None of them deviated from the path, attempted to escape, did anything other than calmly putting one foot in front of the other.

And the Priestess never turned, never looked back to see if her orders were being followed. It was clear—when she gave a command, her followers carried it out without question. She didn't have to monitor them. She could assume obedience.

They crested the hill, and the woods opened out into a little clearing where a circle of tents and lean-tos stood around a central campfire that was at the moment barely smoldering. And that was when Kerri saw that the cult members' silence was not the most frightening thing about them.

On the periphery of the clearing were four roughly-hewn wooden poles with heavy crosspieces. Hanging from them were four human bodies, two men and two women. One of the men looked as if he couldn't have been more than seventeen years old. Their arms were pinioned by nails driven through the wrists, their ankles similarly secured to the upright. Blood, now dried and blackened, streamed from the wounds, which were buzzing with fat, black flies.

"Holy fucking Christ," Will said. "You crucify people?"

The leader turned, and in one swift movement, slapped Will hard across the face. Then she gave him a sweet smile. "You will not take the Lord's name in vain in my presence."

Will took a step back, mouth open a little, raising his hand to the reddening handprint on his left cheek.

She turned and addressed the three of them. Her followers stopped, turning their bodies to face her, gazing at her as if she were dispensing wisdom obtained directly from the Almighty.

"We have three new souls to bring into the fold." She gave a slow gesture of one hand toward Kerri, Aaron, and Will. "You will make them feel welcome." Then she addressed them directly. "You will turn over your weapons to us now. While we are unafraid to die, we do not trust people who are not yet members. Until you give yourself to the sacred, your hands could be guided by Satan. And the penalty for lack of cooperation is the one I mentioned earlier—I will personally sacrifice one of our children for each transgression. You have one day to make your decision to join us, or you will join… them."

She pointed at the crucified bodies, hanging limply from the crossbeams.

"The first week of the new world, we have already tried and failed to convince the minister of the local church and his family to join us. You see that they preferred to suffer the ultimate punishment rather than doing so. And if they considered their bodily torment before their deaths agonizing, consider that they are right now crying in desperate pain in the fiery lake of sulfur, under the whips of the demons of hell, where they will remain for all eternity. But I realize you may not believe, not yet, and so my words may not dissuade you from trying to escape. Therefore we will bind your wrists and ankles at times they are not needed for feeding yourself or our observances. You need to realize—the Lord brought you to us. It is our job to make certain you follow through on joining his ranks."

Kerri looked at her two companions. None spoke.

"Your weapons, please. Do not hesitate, it will be counted as a transgression."

Aaron reached for his holster, and in a flash, he whipped his gun out and aimed it at the Priestess's head.

But her followers were faster than he was. The man to his right grabbed his arm and pulled it backwards, and when he squeezed the trigger the shot went wild. Seconds later, all three of them were pinioned, their weapons taken. Aaron writhed in their grip like a bear in a trap.

This was the first thing that shook the Priestess's perpetual calm. Her smile vanished, and she took a step back, smoothing her clothing with one hand. "Yes. I did not realize how sunk in the powers of hell you are. Just recall that you brought this to pass."

She turned toward her followers, who were watching her with blank expressions. None seemed in the least afraid.

"No!" Aaron screamed. "Not a child! Don't kill a child!"

She looked back at him. "Why not? They are as ready to die as the rest of us."

His fierce green eyes fixed on her mild blue ones. "Don't do it. I swear, I'll kill you if you do. Believe that."

"I do not think you are in the position to make threats." She looked over her people, musing, as if she were selecting which apple to pick. "Very well. You are new to us. Perhaps a full sacrifice is unnecessary, but we must still show you the price of transgression." Her gaze traveled over the crowd and then seemed to come to a decision. "Judah. You are chosen for the sacrifice."

A well-built young man of perhaps twenty stepped forward. To Kerri's amazement, like the child earlier, he didn't look at all afraid. In fact, his expression was blissful, transcendent.

"What is the sacrifice to be, Priestess?" His calm, steady words were the first spoken by anyone but the Priestess.

"Do you recall what Our Savior said to us, in the Book of Matthew, chapter five, verse thirty?"

The young man frowned in thought for a moment, and a flicker of apprehension crossed his face, quickly submerged. "Yes, Priestess. 'And if thy right hand offend thee, cut it off, and cast it from thee: for it is profitable for thee that one of thy members should perish, and not that thy whole body should be cast into hell.'"

"Yes. And are you willing to sacrifice your hand in exchange for your eternal salvation?"

He swallowed. "Yes, Priestess."

"Then kneel and prepare yourself."

He knelt and closed his eyes. The Priestess put both hands on him, smoothing his hair much as she'd done with the child, and they both bowed their heads and closed their eyes.

A minute passed, and no one moved. Aaron was stiff, jaw clenched, the tendons standing out in his neck. Kerri knew him well enough to know that if it'd been within his power, he would have attacked the Priestess with his bare hands.

Judah raised his head, and stood. "I am ready, Priestess."

"Bless you. The Lord will help you through this. Either that, or you will be at his feet soon." She turned her gaze on the people who were guarding Kerri, Aaron, and Will, and said, "Make certain they witness this, that they do not turn away. Especially him" —she pointed at Aaron— "who has brought this to pass."

A stout, grim-looking man with a grizzled beard stepped from the crowd, and brought Judah to the stump of a tree. By this time, the young man was visibly shaking, and his face was sickly white. A woman brought rope, and his forearm was bound to the stump. His fingers flexed convulsively.

And another man, looking shaken himself, brought up a broad-bladed axe, and leaned it against the stump. Judah stared at it, wide-eyed, and gave a shuddering intake of breath.

Kerri tried to force back the nausea rising in her belly. Was no one going to stop this?

That was when she saw the blackened stains on the stump of the tree. No, there would be no stopping this—Judah was not the first one to suffer this fate.

Plus, these were people who crucified any they captured who did not cooperate. Someone who was willing to cut off a man's hand to make a point with three prisoners was beyond mercy, beyond any human kind of compassion.

The grizzled man picked up the axe, and looked over at the Priestess with a questioning expression.

And she said, in a calm voice, "You may carry out the sacrifice."

Heavily muscled arms lifted the axe.

Kerri shouted, almost involuntarily, "God, no, don't!"

Without any hesitation, the blade came down on Judah's wrist.

The young man's drilling shrieks rang through the clearing, swirling together with Will's shouts of, "Oh, God! Oh, my God! How could you do that? What the fuck is wrong with you people?"

Judah's body writhed, blood spurting from his severed wrist and cascading in a crimson flow down the stump to which his arm was still tied. Then as they watched in horror, his screams and struggles both faded, and he slumped forward, his eyes rolling upward in their sockets as he lost consciousness.

The Priestess walked slowly up to Kerri, Will, and Aaron, and while she spoke, her placid gaze passed from one of them to the other. "You see how transgressions are repaid. Perhaps you do not fear pain yourself, but are you willing to visit it upon another? And you see how willingly he faced the axe. Any of the Lord's people would sacrifice a hand, an eye, or their life if I asked it of them. You cried out piteously to witness Judah's ordeal. If you would not see such a thing again, I caution you to follow our precepts and respect my authority."

Aaron stared at her with an intensity of fury that Kerri had never seen in him before. But the Priestess was unassailable, and his anger broke against her like waves against a cliff face, thrown back without any discernible effect.

"Priestess?" The man who'd wielded the axe came up to her, his face troubled.

"Yes, Elishua?"

"It is Judah, Priestess. He has passed to the other side."

Aaron closed his eyes tight, his entire body shaking with emotion.

"Praise the Lord," the Priestess said. "One of our number has left the travails of the world and joined our Savior today. His suffering is ended, he is with Jesus. Unbind him, Elishua. We must see to our fallen brother."

Elishua untied Judah from the tree stump. The young man's body slipped to the ground, his maimed arm flopping across his chest, smearing his white robe with scarlet. Elishua gave a gesture to another man, and they carried his body away. Kerri, Aaron, and Will already had their ankles tied, and now their wrists were secured as well. They were left sitting on the ground, attended by only two of the cult members, while the Priestess and the others followed the men who had borne Judah's body out of the clearing. Moments later, the unearthly sound of singing came to them.

They were chanting hymns to the Lord in praise of their dead comrade.

Kerri turned toward one of their guards, a stocky man of perhaps forty with wire-rim glasses.

"What's your name?" she asked, trying to keep her voice steady, although her heart was still hammering.

"Abijah. When I was reborn, I was given that name."

"What were you called before?"

His eyes narrowed with suspicion, but then his face relaxed back into the expression of serenity that all of the cult members wore. "That doesn't matter. The person who went by that name is dead. All that matters is right here, right now, serving the Lord."

"Why do you think she's the one you should be listening to?" Aaron's hands, secured at the wrists with rope, were tightly clenched, and Kerri knew he was keeping his temper only with an effort.

"She speaks with the voice of God."

And Kerri was suddenly transported back to standing in the den of an abandoned farmhouse, with Kyle Tauriac intoning the words in his strange, foreign voice, so unlike his own—*You will know the ones who speak with the voice of God by their actions.*

If so, these men and women surely were agents of hell.

But Abijah was still speaking. "We followed her already—well, most of us did—but then she gathered us together when the End Times began last week, told us the human-made structures were going to crumble, the time of Tribulation was upon us. We gathered here to await the word. And just as she said, it came to pass. We heard it on the radio. The cities are collapsing, the Four Horsemen are abroad in the world striking men and women and children down. The only answer is to stay steadfast and believe in the word of the Lord, as it is brought to us by the Priestess."

"And you think it's okay to do that?" Will nodded toward the row of crosses with their gruesome burdens. "To crucify your fellow humans? To watch another bleed to death after having his hand lopped off? Is the Lord really commanding all this?"

For the first time, the man looked uneasy. "It is not for me to question."

"Yes, it is!" Will shouted. "It's what you have to do! You need to question the hell out of this, not just follow along. What if you're the next one to lose a hand? Or an eye? Or your life?"

His eyes darted to the side, toward where Judah had just suffered and died, then back at Will, and his gaze dropped. "I will gladly give my body to the ordeal, in the name of God."

"You don't sound all that certain."

"I am weak and sinful," Abijah said. "I hope I would have the strength to endure to the end, as Judah did."

"What if you're wrong?"

"I'm not."

"No, I'm serious. What if you're wrong? What if you've given your life—all your lives—for nothing?"

"You speak with the voice of Satan."

"I speak with the voice of reality."

Abijah's voice became desperate. "It's the same thing. So the Priestess says. Everything that is of the world is fallen, sinful, depraved. And now you need to shut up. I've had enough of your devil's talk." He moved a little away, forehead creased with anger.

"Maybe you made some headway," Kerri whispered.

Will shook his head, and struggled futilely for a moment against the ropes that bound him. "Unlikely. These people are completely insulated from rationality. They've given their minds to that woman and let her call the shots."

"You have to wonder how many of them would keep the faith if she was gone." Aaron's voice was still tight with anger. "I'm sure she has a few loyal supporters who carry out her will faithfully, probably so they can maintain a position as part of the inner circle. That's the way these cults always work. She made the choice of who to torture look random, but my guess is that she would never choose one of her confidants to lose a hand in order to make a point. The others obey out of fear, not just of her but of the eternal consequences if they don't." He paused. "I remember a guy I went to school with who was like that. Total Holy Roller type. He used to give a lot of the rest of us guff for being "sinful." So one day me and another guy kind of pinned him down and started asking him about morality in the Bible. One of us brought up the story of Abraham and Isaac, and asked the dude, 'So, if God told you to, would you kill your own child?' And he said, without hesitation, 'Of course.'"

"Holy shit," Kerri said under her breath.

"Don't say that too loud," Will said. "They don't like that kind of talk. My cheek still hurts from where she socked me for taking the Lord's name in vain."

"The point is," Aaron continued, "this isn't actually against a lot of what the Bible says. It's more like carrying it to its logical conclusion. Hell, they stoned people to death for damn near anything back then. This is like returning to the Old Testament days."

"But how do we get away?" Will said. "I bet if all three of us escaped, she wouldn't follow through with sacrifices. There'd be no one there to impress who wasn't already impressed to the point of brainwashing."

Kerri nodded. "We have to watch and wait for an opportunity. It'll be hard to do anything with no weapons and with our wrists and ankles tied."

But the afternoon progressed, and night fell, and no such opportunity presented itself.

They had their hands freed briefly so they could feed themselves on coarse fare that tasted like some form of oatmeal. But as soon as their bowls and spoons were taken, their wrists were bound again, this time behind them, so they couldn't use their fingers to work at the knots binding their ankles. A loop of rope was passed between their hands, and then tied securely to a tree. There was to be no escape, even by crawling.

But more disturbing still was the sound of hand saws and hammers.

Not far away, men were working on the construction of three more crosses.

As darkness was falling, one of their guards came over to check their bindings, and Will nodded toward the crosses. "Not too confident of our giving in, I guess?"

The man shrugged. "The Priestess says she's doubtful you'll join us. But if we don't use these for you, there will be others. There are always others. That's why we built the trap five days ago."

"The trap?"

"We blocked the exits and blew up the bridge. It was the last time the Priestess sanctioned the use of machines from the old world. We blew up the bridge over Sugar Creek and used the rubble to block the roads, so cars'd keep moving down the highway till they couldn't go no further. It's like fishermen using a funnel net. The fish swim in, and by the time they realize they're caught, there's no way out."

When night fell, Kerri scooted herself over to where Aaron was sitting, and leaned against his warm body.

"Of all the things we've been through, I can't believe this is what's going to stop us," she said quietly. "Crucified by a crazy holy woman and her brainwashed followers."

"I'm not giving up yet."

"Me, neither. They want to nail me up there, they're going to have to fight for the privilege"

Aaron sighed. The sound caused a welter of despair to rise in Kerri's chest. "There are a lot more of them than there are of us. And you know they'll deal with us one at a time while the others are tied."

"Should we pretend to give in?" Will said from a short distance away in the darkness. "Let her think she's won?"

"You think she'd believe it?" Aaron's voice was dubious. "She may be crazy, but I think she'll be hard to fool."

"Hey, I'm willing to try it. Anything to avoid nails through the wrists and ankles. You know how much that'd hurt? I'd agree to damn near anything if I was faced with that."

"Can't argue with you there."

"But then what?" Kerri said. "We still have to escape. And get our guns back. Not to mention the car keys."

"If we're taken into the fold, maybe they'll trust us enough not to watch us every second," Aaron said. "So maybe we could get away. And even if we can't use the car, I'm willing to take my chances with fleeing on foot. We'll deal with transportation once we're safely away."

But the night passed, with fitful sleep at best, and Kerri couldn't think of any likely ending for this than their hanging from crosspieces, bleeding their lives away.

Which was doubly horrible, because it meant that their mission to reach Colville, and accomplish something that would cripple the invasion of the Black-eyed Children, would end here, in a forested glade in central Illinois. Whatever they were intended to do would never happen.

And, if Saul was right, that meant the Children would win.

With that terrible thought flitting through her mind, Kerri must have slept, because the next thing she knew, she was being shaken awake by a hand clutching her upper arm. She gave an alarmed intake of breath, but whatever she was going to say was cut off by a hissed whisper of, "Quiet! Do you want them to hear you?"

She opened her eyes to pitch blackness. Clouds had rolled in, obscuring the moon, and a light drizzle prickled her face. The campfire had died down to embers, and illuminated nothing.

"What do you want?" Kerri said.

"I'm Keziah. I want to help you."

A surge of hope rose in Kerri's heart. At least one of the Priestess's followers was not a mindless automaton. "Untie us."

"I'll try. I can't see the knots." Hands fumbled for the ropes binding Kerri's wrists. "You've got to get out of here. She'll crucify you if you don't. She makes it sound like it's something you can get out of, that you could agree to join us and she'll let you live. That's a lie. She'll have you put to death regardless of what you say."

"Why are you doing this? Aren't you afraid of what she'll do if she finds out?"

"She mustn't find out. You have to take me with you. As for why I'm doing this—I'm Micah's mother."

Micah. The child whose throat the Priestess had threatened to slit if they didn't leave their car. Evidently watching strangers executed was one thing, but seeing the knife at your own child's throat was another.

More ineffectual fiddling with the knots. "But don't call us that. Before we… before all of this, we were Allison and Aidan. I want us to go back. I want to be back to—" She stifled a sob.

Trying to keep her voice calm, Kerri said, "You need to focus. If you don't get these ropes loose, we won't be able to help you."

"I know. I know." Her voice sounded increasingly desperate. "But I can't see anything. I shouldn't have… I shouldn't have tried. It's impossible."

"Don't give up!" Kerri tried to keep the urgency out of her own voice. "If you can just get my hands free—"

That was when there was a blaze of light, as someone struck a match to a torch. The flames illuminated the rough, unsmiling face of Elishua, the man who had cut off Judah's hand. Standing next to him, the flickering torch casting odd shadows across her face, was the Priestess, for once wearing an unambiguous expression of triumph. Two women stepped out of the shadows and caught Keziah as she jumped up, preparing to flee, and pinioned her arms behind her. She struggled like a wild thing, but only for a moment, and then her body went limp when she knew there was no escape.

"You thought the prisoners wouldn't be watched?" She smiled. "I have been keeping my eye on you for some time, Keziah. I questioned your loyalty from the beginning, but others vouched for your steadfastness, said you were a true believer. I see that my suspicions were correct. The Lord prompted me to keep vigil tonight, and now I understand why."

From behind Kerri, Aaron's voice, strong and steady. "I don't know what voice you're listening to, but it isn't God's. Most likely it's some voice in your own head, prompting you to act out the evil that's in your heart. You may kill us tomorrow. Hell, you may decide to kill us now. It doesn't matter. Those who rule by fear, even when they claim to be speaking with the divine will eventually fail. Their followers turn on them. Think of that when you are riding the crosspiece of your own crucifix."

The Priestess looked down on them, and once again, it was obvious the words had no effect. Whatever belief, whatever faith, formed her worldview, it insulated her completely, and when she spoke, it was as if she didn't even consider Aaron's words worth a response.

"When the dawn comes, we will need to make a fourth cross. And when Keziah is nailed to it, let her son watch." She paused. "Ordinarily, we excuse the young ones from witnessing these proceedings. Perhaps that was a mistake. It is time the children learn the price of disobedience as well."

Keziah was dragged away into the darkness, and gave only a thin whimper when she heard that she was to be put to death in only a few hours.

The Priestess had evidently said everything she intended to say, and after Elishua checked the security of the knots binding Kerri's wrists—Keziah's fumbling attempts to untie them had accomplished very little—they turned and walked off into the night, leaving Aaron, Kerri, and Will once again in total darkness.

"Why the fuck don't they fight back?" Will said. "She's only one person. Okay, the guy with the axe is on her side, and he looks pretty tough. But don't tell me that the rest of them are all thrilled to watch four people get nailed to posts. If they all rebelled, there'd be nothing she could do about it."

"It's not just numbers," Aaron said. "Once you've convinced someone that obedience is the road to salvation, you've got them. Okay, maybe most of them don't like watching executions, or watching some poor guy get his hand lopped off. They probably are fully aware that if they step wrong, they could be next. If that was all it was, they'd have overthrown her already. But it sounds like they were under her thumb long before the Black-eyed Children invaded and civilization collapsed. She already had them convinced she was God's spokesperson, and they had to listen to her or be damned forever. If you believed, truly believed, that if you fought back, you'd spend eternity in the fiery furnace, you'd do anything you had to in order to avoid that fate."

"That's fucked up."

"No doubt. But don't expect the others to help. If we can't find a way out of this on our own, we're dead."

———————————

THE DRIZZLE HAD TURNED TO rain by the time the cold gray of dawn was spreading across the eastern horizon. As soon as it was light enough, the sound of sawing and hammering told Kerri that a fourth cross was being fashioned. Keziah, however, was nowhere to be seen.

No. Not Keziah. Allison. If they were going to die, at least let the poor woman die with people thinking of her by her correct name.

It was only an hour later that a group of a half-dozen men, led by the dour Elishua, came up to them, grim expressions on their faces, and untied their ankles and loosened the rope that bound them to the tree.

"It's time," was all Elishua said, with a finality like the tolling of a bell.

Will's face was pale and terrified, Aaron's still fierce with anger. When one of the men hoisted Kerri to her feet, she was so weak-kneed from a combination of hunger and fear that her legs almost buckled.

She had never been so afraid in her life.

When she'd joined the Boundary, over three years earlier, she knew the risks. Even then, before the invasion, she knew that every time she went out on a mission she might die and was able to accept that. A fight against a powerful foe, no holds barred, but in some sense a fair fight.

But this death—hanging by her wrists from nails until she starved or died of shock and blood loss—facing that was a different matter. Especially knowing that the ones doing it were not humanity's common enemy, but humanity itself.

She and the others were taken to the central clearing, each of them flanked by two men—in Aaron's case, three—with firm hands on the upper arm to prevent any attempt to escape. Soon they were in view of the four other crosses erected on the periphery, each with its horrible burden. But now four new crosses lay on the ground, and next to them, metal spikes that looked as big as tent pegs, and a heavy, short-handled metal hammer.

The world began to vanish into a swirling curtain of silver, and she felt herself slipping downward again. The man at her left clutched her to keep her from falling, and she steadied herself with an effort.

No. Don't faint. Don't make it easy for them.

There was a commotion from the left, and Allison was dragged into the clearing, kicking and clawing and screaming. Evidently she had some fight left—the previous night, Kerri had wondered if she'd given up completely. The Priestess followed the distraught woman, and true to her word, she was personally leading Allison's son forward to watch his mother die. The little boy was crying, tears mixing with rainwater on his cheeks, but there was a guard clutching his arm in case he thought to rush forward in an attempt to save her.

Elishua, who seemed to be in charge of the proceedings as he was with the severing of Judah's hand, looked at the Priestess, who stood in the center of the clearing. Her blonde hair was soaking wet and had fallen from its untidy bun, her white robe drenched, its hem muddy and stained. Before, she had looked like some sort of worker of magic, a High Priestess of an ancient cult. Now she simply looked mad, an Ophelia, a Lucia di Lammermoor, a Medea, someone possessed by a spirit of true evil.

"Who first?" Elishua said.

She thought for a moment, then pointed at Aaron. "Let him suffer first. He presumed to fire his gun at me. Let him find out what happens to those who are guided by the Evil One. The others can watch and contemplate their fate."

Elishua and another man dragged Aaron toward one of the crosses. Aaron struggled, dug his heels into the muddy earth, fighting back as well as he could with his hands tied. Another man, and another, joined in to subdue him, and he was forced to his knees next to the rough-hewn wooden cross, the rope binding his hands cut, and after a moment he was wrestled to the ground and dragged until he was spread-eagled on the cross.

Kerri screamed, "No! No! God damn you, don't hurt him! Don't you dare!" And then, for no reason she could identify, she began to shout, "Help! Help! Please, somebody help us!"

Elishua picked up one of the spikes and the hammer, and knelt on Aaron's arm to hold it still, the bare wrist exposed and ready. He looked up at the Priestess calmly, although Aaron still struggled to get away, his whole body writhing.

She gave a slow, smiling gaze around the clearing, her eyes radiating triumph and supreme confidence. "You may proceed with the—"

There was a sharp report, and the Priestess's body lurched forward. Her victorious expression changed to surprise, then shock. She looked down at a slowly-spreading red stain in the middle of her chest, then fell to her knees and toppled face-first into the mud with a wet *splat*.

Elishua jumped up, still holding the hammer and one of the wicked metal spikes, and uttered a strangled noise of alarm, looking around wildly to see where the shot had come from. Then there was a second report, from somewhere nearer, and a hole appeared in the middle of his forehead. The hammer and spike fell from nerveless fingers, and he crumpled.

Chaos.

White-robed men and women running, screaming words of terror or anger or incomprehension. More gunshots, and other bodies landed on the wet earth and did not move again. Aaron jerked an arm free and drove the base of his hand into the nose of one of his remaining captors. Even over the sound of the rain, Kerri heard the man's nose break. Aaron scrambled to his feet, ran to Kerri, and after a moment's working at the knots, untied her ankles, then did the same for Will.

"What…." Will panted. "What the fuck just happened?"

"I think," Aaron said, "this is what the people in the Old Testament called a Miracle of the Lord."

Kerri looked around the clearing, now empty except for a half-dozen bodies, their robes darkened with mud, rainwater, and blood. Allison and her son were nowhere to be seen. It made sense—she had to know that there was no reason to hang around and ask questions, the priority was putting as much distance between them and those hideous crosses and spikes as they could.

But as for Kerri, Aaron, and Will, how could they do that? They still had no weapons—and, more importantly, no car keys.

"You folks all right?" Kerri whirled around to see a heavyset man wearing a plaid shirt and overalls, with rainwater dripping from the brim of a dark green John Deere baseball cap, stride into the clearing. He held a rifle tucked under one arm.

Here, apparently, was their Miracle of the Lord, as unlikely to fill that role as he looked.

"Yeah," Kerri said, her voice sounding unreal and dreamlike in her own ears.

"I came runnin' when I heard you yellin'. Glad I got here in time. I knew them damn loonies were campin' out here, but I didn't know what they'd got up to. Last few days, ever since everything went to hell, I kept thinkin' I should drive out here and check up on 'em, figured they weren't up to no good, but I didn't make time to do it. Then I come up, and there's dead bodies hangin' on crosses, and damned if that crazy leader of theirs isn't about to nail someone to another one. Couldn't let that happen, no matter what. Sorry I didn't show up sooner, but I've had my hands kinda full, you know?"

"With what?" Will said.

"With pickin' off them black-eyed bastards," the man said. "You ain't run into them yet?"

CHAPTER
13

N AME'S LESTER POOLE," THE MAN said, shaking hands with each
of them in turn. They were a sorry-looking group, especially Aaron,
who had mud streaking his cheeks like war paint and hair plastered to
his scalp. Will, on the other hand, just looked stunned, although dripping wet.

"You're damn lucky I happened along," Lester said, a little unnecessarily.

"No kidding." Aaron gave a shuddering look over his shoulder at the cross
he was to ride and the pile of metal spikes that still lay next to it.

Lester's gaze traveled up to the four crosses already erected, carrying the
pathetic remains of the Priestess's last victims, and his brows drew together.

"Well, hell," he said, in a voice that was quiet but filled with anger. "I know
them. Reverend Wiltz and his wife, and his daughter and son. Minister of the
Astoria First Bible Church, where I attend. Or did, before everything went to
hell. Shoulda done what I could to protect 'em. That woman and her crazy
followers threatened to kill 'em six months ago. Didn't like the competition, I
s'pose. She didn't wait long for her opportunity."

"I'm sorry." Kerri shuddered.

"Me, too. They were good people, and his son couldn't'a been eighteen years
old. Nice boy. They're in Jesus's hands now." He gave a harsh sigh and with one
toe prodded the body of the man who had been about to drive a nail through
Aaron's wrist. "At least them two won't be able to hurt anyone else, ever again."

"Amen to that," Will said.

"Any case, let's not stand here jawin' about it in the rain. Power's out up at my place, so all I got's cold hand-pumped well water to wash with, but it's better than nothing. At least you can get dried out a little and recover. I live up in Vermont, it's not far."

"Vermont?" Will echoed, frowning.

"Vermont, Illinois, not state of Vermont. Otherwise it'd be a hell of a drive."

"Before we go, we need to find our car keys, and if we can, our guns," Kerri said. "They took both when we got captured."

Lester nodded. "Any idea what they did with 'em?"

"I'd guess the Priestess kept them," Aaron said, glancing over at her corpse, face-down on the muddy ground.

"Priestess?" Lester spat on the ground. "Yeah, I heard that's what her people were callin' her. When I knew her, she was Alice Kuhlau. Got a little full of herself, I guess. But we can talk about that later. Where did she keep her belongings?"

Kerri shrugged. "We never saw where she slept. The whole time we were here, we were kept tied up outside."

"Whenever she appeared, she came from that direction." Will pointed to a gap between two scrubby oak trees.

"Worth a look-see," Lester said.

The rain was coming down in sheets, and the ground squelched underneath their feet. There was no sign of the other cult members. Their leader gone, they must have scattered, directionless, like the ants in an anthill when the queen is killed. At least Allison and Aidan had gotten away. With any luck, far away from people who would torture a mother to death in front of her own child for daring to rebel.

Beyond the gap between the trees was another, smaller clearing, at the back of which was a tent, palatial by comparison to the small, leaky shelters the rank-and-file had apparently occupied. Kerri hung back, out of a habit of caution—there was no certainty that all of the leaders had been killed—but Lester strode right up and unzipped the flap.

It helped, Kerri reflected, to have a high-powered rifle under your arm.

But the tent was empty of people. Inside were piles of seemingly random objects—clothes, books, kitchen implements, packets of dried fruit and beef jerky, two canned hams, several Bibles, a variety of hunting knives and pocket knives, and a stack of notebooks, each of which had Journal written on the front. There was no order to it, just a chaotic mess of the fragments of people's lives. Whether they were the Priestess's own belongings, or those taken from her followers and victims, was impossible to tell.

Kerri looked with curiosity at the journals. Were they the Priestess's personal diaries? What sort of thing would a profoundly diseased mind like hers write? Kerri decided she didn't want to know and let them lie.

They found their guns in short order, tossed aside in one corner of the tent. The car keys proved more difficult, but eventually those were found, too, lying underneath a soggy fleece vest with a long tear in the side.

Thunder rolled in the distance.

"We'd best get out of here," Lester said. "Weather's getting worse, and I wouldn't count on those loonies not comin' back and tryin' to visit revenge on us for takin' down old Alice." He snorted. "Huh. Priestess, my rosy red ass. Can't believe she ever got anybody to listen to her, much less that many. Lot of dumb people out there."

There didn't seem to be any arguing over that. They followed Lester back up the hill, then across the corner of a cornfield. Near where a long, narrow dirt road dead-ended was an aged pickup truck that probably used to be silver but now was a dingy gunmetal gray.

"Hop in," he said. "My house is only a coupla miles up the road."

Despite their experiences and their vow to be more cautious about trusting people, fatigue and relief effectively cancelled any hesitation they had about going with Lester Poole. All three of them climbed into the truck without question.

"Known Alice for a long time, and she's been weird the whole time," Lester said, as the truck bumped and splashed itself down the dirt road between the cornfield and the woods. "We went to the same church for a while, but she kept gettin' in arguments with the Reverend, like she knew better about such matters than he did. She took to preachin' the Bible in her living room—she lived with her mom, who was as nutty as squirrel shit too—and somehow got people to come listen to her. Bunch o' folks from the Astoria First Bible Church split off and useta go listen to her. She was always preachin' 'bout the End Times, how we had to watch out 'cause Satan was plannin' to round us all up and have a big ol' barbecue."

"She wasn't wrong," Will said. "Look around you."

Lester gave a grim chuckle. "I'll grant ya that. But she didn't help none. She went further and further off the deep end. Said Reverend Wiltz was Satan's minion, she knew God's will and what Reverend Wiltz said was devil's talk. She didn't like most of us, but she hated the Reverend, because he challenged her. Guess she got her revenge." He paused, his face registering deep grief. "Still can't believe anyone'd do that. I guess you get power, you start to use it, you know? I heard 'bout a year ago, her followers were callin' her 'Priestess' and bringin' her gifts and all, and then a bunch of 'em went and were livin' at her house and in her mom's barn and in tents and such like. Finally her mom got fed up and ran 'em all off—the police had to get involved, wasn't pretty. But they took off and went to live in the woods, guess that was about three months ago. We heard tell that she was doin' some pretty crazy shit, like when one of her followers disobeyed or sinned or whatnot, she'd have 'em stripped naked, tied to a tree, and whipped. But you know, I wasn't gettin' involved, not at that point. I figured, hell, they joined up, they can walk away any time. If they stand there and let her or her cronies flog 'em bloody, well, that was their business."

"She had them brainwashed to the point they'd let her do anything," Aaron said. "She told one of them he had to sacrifice his hand, and he did it. Walked up, let them tie his arm to a stump, and cut off his hand with an axe. Guy ended up bleeding to death."

Lester shook his head. "I don't get it. I mean, I'm a religious man myself, read the Bible daily, and attend church, or at least did until all this stuff come down in the last week or so. But I also got enough sense that if Reverend Wiltz had told me I had to let him cut my hand off, I'd get up and walk out."

"She convinced them if they disobeyed, they were going to burn in hell. After that, you obey because you're terrified."

"Guess you're right. But still seems to me God gave us a brain so we can use it." He turned off onto a narrow country road. The windshield wipers slapped out a rhythm as rain thrummed against the windshield, but it seemed to be slackening, and the western sky looked lighter than before. "Anyhow, I just fought off another bunch o' them black-eyed bastards this morning, added the bodies to the bonfire, and thought for some reason, 'I better go check and see what them crazies in the woods are up to.' Don't know what made me think of that, but I did it, and lucky I did, I guess. The Lord musta spoke a word in my ear."

"What do you know about the Black-eyed Children?" Aaron gave a curious look at the man.

"Know about 'em? Only that they're tryin' to catch me nappin'. I been holdin' 'em off for a week, now. They attacked a coupla neighboring farms. Took whole families away to God knows where. I saw 'em fightin' with Doug Claiborne, next farm north of mine. Guess they'd already got the rest of his family, his wife and his three kids, or leastways that's what I figure, because when I went up there, the house was empty. I heard the commotion and run up there to see what was goin' on, and there was big ol' Doug—tough as nails, built of muscle—wrestlin' with this kid who looked like he couldn't'a been more than twelve, and what's more, losin'. And before I could get there, the kid got Doug in a chokehold, dragged him toward the barn, and went inside. But when I got there, the barn was empty, and so was the house. Everybody gone."

"And they attacked you next?"

Lester nodded. "Yeah. But I was ready. I'm not gonna look for a fight, but someone comes for me, I'm gonna defend myself. And also defend someone else, if they're in trouble, like you was this morning. So I drove around a little and saw the same thing everywhere—all up and down the road, empty farmhouses. The whole area, not one person left, but lots of these kids lurkin' around. But they ain't kids, not really, you know that, right? Demons from hell is what I think they are."

"Oh, yeah," Kerri said. "We know. And your guess is not far wrong."

"When they came for me, I just started pickin' 'em off. I was a sharpshooter in the Army, won trophies for marksmanship, so it wasn't hard. That's when I found out they wasn't what I thought, you know—gangs, like they have in big cities, teenagers takin' advantage to go out lootin' and killin' people. But I saw them eyes, and I knew they was somethin' different. Also, they don't bleed when you shoot 'em, did you know that? You can blow a big ol' hole in their gut, and nothing."

Aaron nodded. "We found that out."

Lester gave him a canny look. "Sounds like you know a good bit more about 'em than you're lettin' on."

"Once we get dried off and cleaned up, we'll tell you what we know. Let me just say this—you're damn lucky to have survived this long. The Black-eyed Children don't like losing, and they don't give up."

"Bring it on. I noticed when I shoot 'em, the bodies always disappear after, so I figure they take 'em away for some reason. I started burnin' 'em. They didn't like that. Hiss like snakes when they're angry. Scariest damn thing I ever seen. Doesn't even look human."

"They're not," Will said.

Lester turned off the road into a long driveway up to a neat white farmhouse with a gabled roof and dormers, and coasted to a stop. "Welcome to the homestead. Be careful getting out, till we check to see if those black-eyed bastards came for a visit while I was gone."

Kerri looked out of the side window, where, despite the rain, a bonfire was burning. A column of smoke rose from the center, and the flames shot sparks up spiraling into the air.

On to where the purifying fires burn. Kyle Tauriac's words rose again in her mind. *Find help where you seek it. You will know him by a pillar of smoke, a heat and light that cleanses.*

Did that mean that they had already passed the iron and blood, the snakes with their fangs dripping poison? Looking back, she could only assume that referred to the Priestess and her followers.

Kerri had never believed in the supernatural. Claims of psychic abilities always seemed to her to be hocus pocus, foolishness that would only dupe the gullible. But now… the Children themselves could apparently communicate using something like telepathy. And Kyle's prophecy was, so far, eerily accurate. Or was she simply taking his words and twisting them to fit what had happened?

She got out of the pickup, looking at the fire sizzling and spitting as the rain fell, but still hot enough to glow nearly white at its center.

Did that mean that the rest of Kyle's prophecy was going to come true, too?

Find the one who was captured, then save the one who was lost. There you will find a door, which all of you must step through without question. If the door closes, you will be trapped. That is all. Do all of these things, and you will complete the circle.

A door. What *kind* of door? And who were "the one who was captured," and "the one who was lost?"

It was all too vague to be helpful. Kyle's pronouncements were no more useful than the things Saul had said if all you could do was make sense of them in retrospect.

The four of them did a slow circuit of the house, guns drawn, looking for any sign of the Children. Nothing. They climbed the front stairs, and Lester unlocked the door and swung it open with a creak.

The foyer was empty, and a quick, furtive tour of the house, splitting up into pairs and searching every room, turned up nothing unusual.

"But they can show up fast, and out of nowhere," Aaron said, as they re-entered the living room. "We can't let our guard down."

Lester nodded gravely. "Yup. You don't need to tell me that. But buddy, before you sit down on any of the furniture, you need to wash off some of the mud. Rainwater's one thing, dirt is another. You're a mess."

"Nearly being crucified will do that to you."

"I guess it would. Bathroom's down the hall, just before you come to the kitchen. I've got a coupla five-gallon buckets of water in there, and clean towels for when you're done."

"What about clothes?"

Lester frowned. "You don't have a change of clothes?"

"Nope. We've been traveling for days with only what we've got on our backs."

"Huh. Okay, I guess there's a story behind that, but it can wait. I've got an old bathrobe in there you can wear. Rinse your clothes, we can hang 'em out, at least once the sun comes out."

"Probably not a good idea for any of us to be alone," Kerri said.

Aaron grinned. "You volunteering?"

It was such a relief seeing a smile on his handsome face that it took Kerri's breath away. She pictured him spread-eagled on that horrible wooden cross, about to have a nail driven through his arm, his face full of anger and fear and desperate anguish, considered how close she'd come to losing him.

Maybe their luck hadn't run out after all. She pushed the mental image away.

"Sure. I can cover you while you're cleaning up."

"Bet you can."

Will shook his head and rolled his eyes. "Guys, get a room, okay?"

"We're gonna." Aaron took Kerri's hand and led her off down the hall to the bathroom.

She closed the door behind them, and Aaron began to strip off his filthy, wet clothes.

"Do you think it was God's intervention that brought Lester Poole to the clearing at exactly the right time?" Kerri asked.

Aaron dipped a washcloth into one of the buckets of water and began to clean the mud off his skin. "I dunno. Do you?"

"I'm not sure. My parents are Sunday Christians, you know? They attend the First Methodist Church, but I don't think they take it very seriously. My brother is the religious one in the family. He married a Baptist minister's daughter."

"And you?"

She shrugged. "I haven't thought that much about it. Noah was agnostic and honestly didn't seem all that interested in the question. But it's things like this that make me wonder."

He wrung the cloth out, dipped it in the bucket again, then put one leg on the rim of the tub and wiped away globs of mud that clung to his leg hair.

"You got cut," Kerri said, pointing.

Running up Aaron's calf was a long but shallow scratch. "I don't even remember when I got that."

"Other things to worry about at the time, probably—like how not to end up dying horribly."

"Exactly." He rinsed the rag again. "But in answer to your question—I don't know. Sometimes it certainly seems like fate is leading us by the hand. Other times—like with Greg and Jason Lantz—not so much."

"God works in mysterious ways."

"Too mysterious for me." He stood, stretched, arching his back. "Am I clean enough to get a hug?"

"You're naked. You think it's gonna lead to something else?"

"Not right now. I mean, Will probably thinks we're in here fucking like bunnies. But right now I just need to hold you, convince myself that we're still alive and unharmed and that you still love me."

"Of course." She went to him and slipped her arms around his middle, and for a time they just held each other, relaxing into the contact between their bodies. There, in a stranger's bathroom in the middle of nowhere, Illinois, at least for a few minutes there was nothing that mattered but each other.

Finally the embrace broke, and Aaron took an old terrycloth bathrobe from a hook on the wall, slipped it on, and knotted the belt around his waist.

"You want a turn washing?"

"Nah, not right now. I will towel off a little, though. Mostly, I'm just wet. There's only one robe."

Aaron took a moment to pour some of the water from the bucket over his soiled clothes. Mud and grime and grit swirled down the drain, but his t-shirt would probably never be the same again.

Oh, well. There were more pressing issues than clean clothes. They couldn't be more than two or three more days' drive from New York. Unless they ran into another obstacle, in only a few days this would all either be done—or they would be dead or captured by the Black-eyed Children.

Whatever that implied for the survival of humanity.

Kerri gave herself a cursory toweling, then decided it was warm enough it didn't really matter, and she and Aaron returned to the living room.

Will and Lester looked up as they entered.

"You look a little more human," Lester observed.

"I feel a lot more human. I left my clothes in the bathtub, maybe we can hang them out like you said once the sun's out."

"Sure. Say, Doctor Will here has been telling me about everything that's going on, and all that you've been through. You're really Homeland Security, are you?"

"I suppose," Kerri said. "As of a few days ago, I don't think DHS exists any more, but that's how we got involved in this, yes."

"And these bastards, they're aliens? Like from another planet?"

"That much we don't know. It's our best guess, yes."

"Aliens." Lester raised an eyebrow. "I always figured aliens'd look like one of them creatures from *Star Trek*, sorta like a regular ol' human with a rubber nose, funny hair, and a fake Russian accent."

"They use the innocent look to get victims," Aaron said. "Or at least they did. Now, it's all-out war. But my impression is that they could look differently if they chose. If I'm right, we have no idea what their actual form is."

"If they can change what they look like, why don't they do anything about the eyes?" Lester frowned. "You see them eyes, you'd never mistake a real kid for one of them."

Aaron shook his head. "I don't know. There's a lot we don't know about the Children. In fact, when you think about it, there's damn little in the way of concrete information we do know. They can jump from one place to another through portals they create. They're fantastically strong. They don't eat or drink, they feed on neural energy they siphon away from sentient life forms, leaving the victim emptied of memories. They seem to communicate with each other by something like telepathy and may be able to read our minds using the same power, although that's not certain. And… that's about it. We're fighting an enemy we basically know next to nothing about."

"Well, you got enough to start on. And Will here, he was telling me they regenerate, or something?"

Kerri nodded. "We were on a mission in Issaquah, Washington, before the invasion started. We were able to kill a Child with a gunshot to the chest and get the body back to a lab, where it was autopsied. Their internal organs are nothing like a human's. They looked… I dunno, like they were one big muscle. No heart, lungs, stomach, kidneys, nothing. And their brains had these green fibers that were similar to what we saw in an autopsy of a human collaborator."

Lester shook his head and scowled. "I can't believe there are people who are siding with these sonsabitches."

"It doesn't seem voluntary," Aaron said. "The closest we can come is that their brains have been invaded by a parasite that controls their actions."

"But in answer to your question, Lester, yes—they can regenerate, and recover from amazing amounts of damage," Kerri said. "The Child I watched being autopsied—a day later it kicked its way out of a storage locker in the morgue, created a portal on the wall, jumped through it, and got away."

"Lord save us."

"So it's a good thing you've been burning the bodies. That seems to be one of the only things they can't recover from."

"I don't know why I started doing that." Lester frowned and rubbed one work-hardened hand across his brow. "When they started showing up, it was maybe three days ago, o' course I killed the first couple. I knew they weren't human, leastways not a human like you and me, although they got a human shape. And I thought, 'Better get rid of the bodies.' It wasn't because I was afraid of the police or whatnot. I knew I could make a case I was defending myself, which I was. So I dragged the bodies to the barn, figured I'd decide what to do with them later, and when I came back that afternoon, they were both gone. So when the next attack happened, I thought, 'I'm gonna burn the bastards. See what they think about that.' I got a lot of firewood stacked up, more than I'll need in five winters, so I started a big ol' fire and threw the bodies on it. That's another thing—they burn up to cinders. No bones left. Nothing."

"It's a good thing you did that," Will said.

Lester nodded. "Like I said, I don't know why I thought of it. But the next day, they attacked the farm with maybe a half-dozen of 'em, chargin' me, but like I said, I'm handy with a rifle. I shot four of 'em, and the other two ran for it. I was draggin' one of the bodies to the bonfire when one of the ones that got away turned and looked at me, and when he saw what I was doin', he bared his teeth and hissed. It was a sound I never heard a human make. I grabbed my rifle, and he and his friend ran around the back of the barn and disappeared. They've tried twice more, and each time gave up after I killed one or more of 'em. I figure at some point they'll decide one old hick farmer's not worth the trouble and give up."

"Hope so," Will said. "But I wouldn't count on it. Don't let your guard down."

"Never have," Lester said. "Never will. I've been told not to."

Aaron gave him a puzzled frown. "Told? By who?"

"The messengers. The Pleiadians. That's what they call themselves."

"You know about the Pleiadians?" Kerri couldn't keep the astonishment out of her voice.

"Well, yeah. How do you think I was ready for them black-eyed devils and knew they wasn't real human children? I been talkin' to the Pleiadians for, oh, maybe six months now. They said I needed to be on the lookout for 'em when they got here."

The three all stared at Lester Poole, mouths hanging open in shock.

Lester looked from one to the other. "The Pleiadians…. you do know they're angels, right?"

CHAPTER
14

WILL GAVE LESTER POOL AN incredulous look. "Angels?"

If Lester was put off by the clear skepticism in the doctor's voice, he didn't show it.

"Well, sure. What else are you gonna call 'em? They warned me to be ready to defend myself, told me about the black-eyed demons that was comin', and also how I was to be on the lookout for people who needed help. They didn't tell me specifics, like when you'd arrive and where, and I honestly just had a hunch this mornin' that I should go down to the clearing and check up on Alice and her band o' crazies. I get hunches that way. Always have."

"So you knew we were coming?"

"Not you three for sure. Like I said, they tell me stuff but are short on details sometimes. But they told me to keep watch—'keep vigilant,' is the way they said it—that if I didn't, it would be the end of everything. I told 'em, 'How can that be? I'm nobody special.' And they said, 'If you fail, it will have repercussions that will echo across the whole Earth.' Sounds crazy, I know, but that's how they said it. I told 'em I didn't like puttin' on airs and makin' myself important. After all, that's what Alice Kuhlau and her crazy followers did, decided she was anointed by God or whatnot, and that they had to do what she said or God would smite 'em. Me, I know I'm a simple man and a sinful one, so I didn't know why them Pleiadians were comin' to me particular. But I guess if you three are on a mission to stop them black-eyed bastards, maybe I turned out to be important after all, because if I hadn't been there, you'd be in a world of hurt right now."

Kerri stared at the old farmer in amazement. He seemed to take what he called a "visitation by angels" as something that could happen to anyone. But the Pleiadians, with their ability to manipulate time, had picked him out, and without him, all three of them would be dying on crosses right now, along with Allison, tortured and executed in front of her own son. Had the Pleiadians, Lester Poole's angels, foreseen all that, and sent him to intervene?

On one hand, it was heartening. They were fated to succeed, at least this far. But it was also a little terrifying. A powerful group of timeline-manipulating aliens had engineered a brink-of-time escape, but that didn't mean they did it out of any kind of personal kindness toward Kerri and the others. Will had said, it seemed like ages ago, they might be playing their own game—that the Pleiadians wanted the Black-eyed Children to be defeated for their own reasons and not out of any particular compassion for humanity and were moving Kerri and Aaron and Will around like pieces on a chessboard to make certain that happened.

If that was the case, Lester Poole's characterization of them as angels was not particularly apt.

———————————

BY NOON, THE SUN WAS out, but the morning rains had left the air heavy with humidity. Lester hung Aaron's clothes out to dry, but Kerri couldn't escape the feeling that they needed to get moving again.

"We already lost a day to the Priestess and her cronies. We need to put some miles behind us."

"I understand," Lester said. "I can drive you back to your car, 'cause otherwise you'll have to cut through the woods, and who knows if any of Alice's friends are still hangin' around. But if you want to find a detour around the Sugar Creek Bridge, you'll have to go a few miles out of your way. Pisses me off that them nutcases blew it up. I have no idea where they got the dynamite from, not sure I want to know."

"They used the rubble to block the roads, so cars would have to come all the way to the end," Aaron said. "We'll have to backtrack for miles."

Lester gave a dismissive gesture of one hand. "Naw. Not necessary, if you can help me clear enough of the rubble away from where the Vermont Road hits Route 24 so's your car can get through. Maybe give your clothes a while to dry, and then we'll go see if it's possible for us to get through the blockage without a scoop truck."

An hour later, Aaron was able to change back into his clothes, which were still clammy, but at least not saturated with mud. They exited back into the yard, where a quick search showed no apparent activity by the Children, nor any sign of the Priestess's scattered followers.

"You think they'll gather back together, try to rebuild their cult?" Will asked as he climbed into the back seat of Lester's battered pickup truck.

"Could be." Lester shook his head. "You can't change people's minds that quick, not when they been swallowing the same line o' nonsense for months or years. They invested that much time into it, they're not gonna let it go, even if it's poison." He put the truck in drive and made a big loop around the oak tree in the front yard, then headed back out onto the road, this time turning south.

"I know one person who isn't going back, if she can help it," Kerri said.

"Who's that?"

"All I know is her first name's Allison. She's the fourth one they were planning to execute this morning, along with the three of us. She tried to help me last night, tried to untie my wrists and ankles but got caught. The Priestess had also threatened to kill her son. I think she, at least, isn't going to fall for it again."

"Could be," Lester said again. "But you know, you'd be surprised. It's like women who keep going back to the husband that beats 'em. Each time, they think it'll be different, it won't happen again, things'll be better this go round. People are funny animals."

"That they are," Aaron said. "If there's one thing we've found out on this mission, it's that people don't respond like you think they will."

After only four miles, they came upon the mound of rubble the Priestess's followers had piled at the intersection with Route 24. It was mostly chunks of asphalt strewn with tree branches and other debris.

"I think we can handle this, if we all give it some elbow grease," Lester said. "All you need is a big enough gap for your car to fit through."

A concerted effort for a half-hour cleared a narrow gap on the left side of the rubble pile. A couple of the pieces of blacktop were big enough to require all four of them to lift. Kerri wondered briefly what earth-moving machinery the cult members had used to move all of this—and where it was now.

But Lester's truck was able to bump and rattle its way through, and they turned left onto Route 24, back toward the remains of the Sugar Creek Bridge and the gravel pull-off where Aaron's car was parked.

Will was the first one to spot what had happened. All he said was, "Oh, fuck, now what are we going to do?"

Aaron's car was mangled. All the windows and windshields shattered, the sides dented, and worst of all, the tires slashed. When they pulled over, Aaron got out first, a devastated look on his face, and walked to the car, gave it a solemn pat on the hood.

"Damn it all. You were a great car."

"It's them crazies did this," Lester said firmly. "Count on it."

Will shook his head. "Revenge for the Priestess's death. Striking back at us the only way they could, once we were out of their clutches. Or maybe they did it before the Priestess died, to prevent our escaping."

Aaron turned toward them, his face showing a combination of frustration and hopelessness. "But what do we do now? Where the hell are we gonna get a car? We damn sure can't go to New York on foot. It'd take weeks."

Lester gave them a thoughtful look. "Well, now. I think I know the answer to that."

"Yes?"

"Take my truck. I'm not gonna need it. Gettin' you back on the road is the only way we've got a chance against the black-eyed devils, far as I can see. And like I said, when I talked to the Pleiadians, they told me when people come along who were fightin' the Children, I was supposed to help 'em in any way they needed. Seems to me like this is the only thing I can do to help you now."

"But…." Kerri regarded the old farmer, with his stained baseball cap, his face lined and weather-worn from years of working in the sun, and words failed her.

Who would have thought, looking at him, that he'd spoken with angels?

Kerri didn't consider herself religious and in fact hadn't given the question much thought. The Sunday school lessons and vacation Bible school had, on the whole, little effect on her. But standing there, in the presence of this simple man who had saved their lives and now looked as if he was going to save their mission, maybe his characterization of the Pleiadians as divine servants wasn't that far off after all.

It was Will who said what she was thinking. "But how will you get around? You'll be stuck on your farm. You'll run out of food."

He regarded the doctor for a long moment, and it was obvious he was considering his words before he spoke. "Well, I haven't told you everything the Pleiadians told me. Best I tell you the rest. But let's not stand here. I got the sense that there are some o' them crazies still lurkin' around. Feelin' of bein' watched, you know? No reason to stick around, now that your man has said goodbye to his car."

Aaron unlocked the trunk and moved the tranq rifle and cartridges, then the gasoline cans and the hand pump, into the bed of Lester's truck. They got back in, Aaron giving one more wistful look at the remnants of the spotless blue Renault he'd cared for so assiduously.

"What did the Pleiadians tell you?" Will asked as Lester turned the truck around and they headed back down the highway.

Lester seemed reluctant to speak, even though he was the one who had brought it up. "I was talkin' to one o' them, the one I saw the most often, calls himself Cassiel. And he says I have to keep fightin' as long as I can. I asked him,

'Am I gonna survive all this?' So he tells me he can't tell me my fate, it's not good for people to know the future, all that kind o' stuff. But I keep at him. I tell him, 'Ain't gonna change what I do, I just want to know, so I can make my peace with God and ready myself,' you know? If I knew I was gonna die at sundown tonight, wouldn't change a thing I was gonna do, 'cept I might not worry about takin' my arthritis medication." He laughed at his own joke. "Long and short of it is, I finally convinced him. And he says, 'When the others show up, the ones you are to help, your days will be short, so do not hold back. Give them what they need. Then make your peace, or whatever it is you need to do, for you will have accomplished what you were created to do.' Those were his exact words. So when I saw you there in that clearing, and that asshole was about to hammer a spike through your arm, I thought, 'This is it. I'm gonna die soon.' But like I said, didn't change a thing. I knew I had to save you three, and see you safely on your way."

"Dammit," Will said under his breath. "That's just not right."

"You could come with us—" Kerri started, but Lester frowned, shook his head, and gave a dismissive wave of his hand.

"Won't make no difference, you know? The angels, they know past, present, and future. Fact is, I don't think they even see it like we do. It's all one thing, you know? It's like we're watchin' the movie, but the angels know the entire plot ahead of time. So wouldn't matter much if I did come along. The angels tell me I'm gonna die soon, I'm gonna die soon. I'm all right with that. I ain't led a perfect life, and done my share of sinnin', but I'm guessin' God'll be willin' to let bygones be bygones over the small stuff. And truth be told, I'd rather die in my old farmhouse, where I grew up and lived all my life, than takin' off with you and headin' out to New York or wherever you're goin', and dyin' anyhow."

"Now wait a minute," Will said. "If the Pleiadians are angels, like you said, can see the whole plot, why can't they save you? You know, step in and stop whatever it is that's going to… going to…." He trailed off, gave a frustrated shake of the head.

"Not how it works, Doc." Lester smiled. Kerri had never seen someone look so completely serene. "We gotta trust that it's working out how it should. They can't stop every bad thing from happening. Probably'd be a lousy idea if they did. Some people gotta die so others can live. That's the way of it."

Will hitched a sigh. "God. I keep hoping this whole situation will start sucking less, and it never does. So you're telling us we just take your truck, wave goodbye, and drive away, leaving you here to die?"

Lester gave a belly laugh. "Well, son, I wouldn't'a put it that way, but basically, yeah, that's what I'm tellin' you. I've done what I was supposed to do. I'm not gonna lie down and give up, so don't you worry—those black-eyed bastards come back, I'm gonna keep fightin' till I run out of bullets. They want me, I'm not gonna make it easy on 'em."

"Even knowing you're going to die in the end."

"Hell, we're all gonna die, right? And Cassiel, he didn't say if the Children were gonna get me, or if I was gonna fall down the cellar stairs and break my neck, or drop dead of a heart attack, or whatnot. Don't you worry about it. It's the fate of man to suffer death. But I got no special fear of where I'm goin' afterward, so I'm not scared." He turned into his driveway, put the truck in park, pulled the hand brake. "And no use draggin' it out. You got to get back on the road."

He left the motor running.

They said their goodbyes there under the bright sun on his front lawn. Kerri knew they would never see him again, whether or not Cassiel's prediction of his death was correct. She gave the old farmer a hug, which he returned a little awkwardly, patting her back and saying, "Glad to help you. Now, don't delay. Get to New York and do whatever it is you're supposed to do." He pointed up the road. "Keep goin' north, maybe another five miles or so. You'll pass the little village of Vermont, basically nothin' more than a couple o' shops and a post office. Keep goin', the road ends at Route 136. Head east on 136 for maybe another ten miles, and there's a little dogleg just past Duncan's Mills. After that, 136 strikes off east, and it's a straight shot across damn near the whole state."

He shook hands with Aaron and Will. Will looked like he couldn't quite fathom a man who was so calm about his own impending death and gave him a wide-eyed glance as he climbed into the back seat of the truck. Aaron took the first shift behind the wheel.

Kerri turned and looked over her shoulder as they drove away. Lester Poole raised one hand in a solemn farewell, then turned back toward his house, every movement radiating a peaceful acceptance that she had never seen in anyone before.

That kind of trust in a higher purpose—whether you called it God, or the angels, or the Pleiadians, or fate, or something else entirely—must be comforting. Kerri couldn't imagine accepting her lot with such tranquility.

But if you knew, honestly knew, that you had done what you needed to do, maybe it was the only response you could have. She remembered a hymn from her childhood in the Methodist Church, the lyrics and melody buried in her brain untouched for years.

All my troubles will be over, since I lay my burden down
Lord, I'm feeling so much better since I lay my burden down
I am climbing Jacob's ladder, I feel like shouting hallelujah,
Every round goes higher and higher, since I lay my burden down

And the truck crested a low rise, and Lester Poole and his house were lost to sight.

———————

"DO YOU THINK THERE'S ANYTHING to Lester's claim that the Pleiadians are angels?" Will's question made Kerri jump. Her reaction, however, was not only because Will had suddenly broken the silence, but because she'd been about to ask the same thing.

"I mean," he continued, when no one answered, "I was raised Catholic. My mom's like the Cajun Mother Theresa. Hasn't missed a Holy Day of Obligation in maybe thirty years, says her rosary daily, doesn't eat meat on Fridays even now that the Pope says it's okay. So we grew up praying not only to God and Jesus and the Virgin Mary but to a bunch of saints and angels. My mom's favorite was the Archangel Michael."

"Why?" Kerri asked.

"Dunno. My sister claimed it was because the stained glass window in the church we attended had a picture of Michael, with a raised sword and ripped biceps, and really badass wings, and my mom thought he was sexy. Mom never would have admitted it, of course."

Aaron gave Will an incredulous smile. "So you think Michael and all the rest are real?"

"Well, no, not as such. But maybe the Pleiadians have been interfering with human affairs for centuries, just like the Black-eyed Children have. It'd be no surprise if the people back in the day thought the Pleiadians were angels."

"You're not about to go all Ancient Aliens on us, are you, Will?"

"A month ago, I'd have laughed in your face. In fact, I used to watch *Ancient Aliens* and *Monster Quest* and all of those shows just because they were hilarious. But maybe there was something to it, after all. Lester Poole was convinced."

"I guess."

Will grinned. "Okay, Aaron, I get it. But I've had my capacity for belief stretched so far out of shape in the last few weeks that I can't even recognize it any more. I stopped going to church as soon as I moved out and went to college, and all through college and med school I considered myself an agnostic. Didn't give it much thought, honestly, except when I went home for a visit and attended church out of filial duty, but even then it was just, 'Wow, I'm glad I don't have to believe all this anymore, and get to sleep in and eat meat whenever I want and not feel guilty every time I masturbate.' Imagine being a teenage boy and having that hanging over your head all the time. Every time, I felt like all the saints were staring at me in disapproval."

Aaron guffawed. "That'd be a buzzkill."

"You have no idea."

"I still have a hard time imagining why people are so convinced that if God exists, he's mostly concerned with what people do with their genitals in the privacy of their own bedrooms."

"I know, right?" Will gave a gesture with one hand, his face earnest. "And being gay added a whole other layer onto all of it. Most of the people in church, at least the ones my age, knew I was gay. I mean, I didn't exactly make a secret of it. My friends knew since we were in high school. But with my parents—especially my mom—it was That Which Must Not Be Spoken Of. Certainly didn't make me fond of organized religion. So there was no hesitation about jettisoning all that shit. But what if at its basis, there's something to it? Not all the trappings and regalia and rules and regulations, but the basic idea of beings out there who are so advanced as to seem divine to us?"

"I don't even know how to answer that," Kerri said.

Aaron frowned thoughtfully. "Well, Arthur C. Clarke said that any sufficiently advanced technology would be indistinguishable from magic."

"That's it exactly. I mean, think of what we've seen just in the last few days. The Earth invaded by an alien race that can create portals through space and communicate telepathically. A prophet who can predict the future. A cult that thinks the End Times are here and crucifies people who don't agree."

Aaron frowned thoughtfully. "You're putting the Priestess and the Prophet in the same category. I don't think that's right, you know? They're more like opposites."

"How's that?"

"Kyle Tauriac downplayed it, but he really was channeling something real, wherever it came from. He claimed he wasn't divine, but he was, at least in some sense. The Priestess, though? She was just Alice what's-her-name, who had a psychotic break and decided she was the Chosen One of God. She claimed she was divine but wasn't. The Priestess's cult was pure human fuckery. Like nine hundred people in Jonestown drinking the Kool-Aid because he told them they should. Nothing supernatural about it."

"Okay," Will said. "I'll grant you that. But what about Lester Poole, knowing exactly when to show up to stop you from having a spike driven through your arm, and saying he knew to watch for us because the angels told him?"

Kerri smiled. "Maybe it's just a matter of admitting to ourselves that we don't have all the answers."

"I think that's it exactly. And if I ever go back to religion, it won't be my mom's brand of it. It's got me thinking, that's all." Will paused. "We've been given a lot to think about, is all I'm saying."

"That much I can't argue with."

THE DRIVE ACROSS ILLINOIS WAS uneventful. More depopulated towns, wrecked cars, dead bodies of humans who apparently thought that an alien invasion wasn't a sufficient threat and decided to turn against each other. They passed through the town of Havana, Illinois, then headed northeast. Ten miles out of Peoria a dark smudge hung on the horizon, at first looking as if the bad weather was returning, but as they approached, they could smell it.

Not rain clouds. Smoke.

They navigated a careful loop around the majority of the city, but even at that distance they could see that it was burning. The air tasted hot and acrid, and Lester's truck didn't have an air conditioner, so they had no recourse except to drive with the windows down and put up with a bitter, ashy smell that persisted for nearly an hour after they'd left Peoria behind and once again struck off due east.

They switched drivers just after crossing the border of Indiana near the town of Kentland, with Kerri taking the wheel and Aaron napping in the back seat. The afternoon wore away as mile after mile of flat farmland fell behind them, and there was quiet in the old truck except for Aaron's occasional snore.

It was only as evening was drawing down, and the oranges and crimsons of a fiery sunset gleamed through the smudged back window, that Will spoke again.

"Why do you think the Pleiadians told Lester he was going to die?"

Kerri shrugged. "I don't know. I've been wondering that, too. Saul was adamant that he wouldn't tell us the future, even those parts of it he knew, because by telling us we might try to do something to change it."

"Maybe they knew Lester wouldn't do that, that he'd accept it and keep on doing what he was doing."

"Maybe." She looked east into the darkening sky. "I don't have Lester's faith, but I think we need to trust that Saul and the other Pleiadians know what they're all doing. If we don't accept that, this whole trip has been one long pointless exercise in futility."

Will nodded. "Would you want to know your future, even if meant knowing all the bad things that were going to happen? If it meant knowing when and how you'd die?"

She thought for a moment, then shook her head. "No. I'd rather not know. I'd like to think I could take that knowledge and do what Lester's doing—make sure I was prepared, that I'd done what my grandparents called 'putting your affairs in order.' That's how my grandpa talked about it when the doctors told him he had terminal cancer. He was cool with it, or as cool as you can be with such news. He said, 'I've had a good run. Now I need to make sure I tie up any loose ends.' But in this case, when I know my death is likely to be at the hands of another, whether it a Black-eyed Child or one of my fellow humans, I don't think I could handle it. It's better we don't know."

"You're probably right." He looked out of the window at the wheat fields and silos and barns slipping past in the failing light. "How much farther you want to go tonight? We talked about not driving after dark because the Children, or anyone else, could see our headlights. Also, think about the bridge that was out. In the dark, we might not have seen it till we went over the edge."

Kerri didn't answer for a moment. "I was hoping to make it into Ohio."

"That's where your brother lives, right?"

She nodded.

"How much farther, do you think?"

"Not absolutely sure. I looked at the road atlas when we stopped for lunch.

He lives in the town of Findlay. I think it's maybe another hour or so after we cross the border of Ohio."

"I wouldn't tell you no. We lost a day's travel to the End Time nuts, so it's probably a good idea to keep going. But Kerri, you…." He trailed off, closed his mouth tightly.

"What?"

He turned toward her, his eyes full of concern. "I don't know how to say this right. But you probably… you shouldn't get your hopes up."

Kerri had been telling herself the same thing, as the nondescript plains of Indiana rolled past and Ohio approached. But hearing Will say it was like a knife blow.

"I'm sorry," he said. "I'm not very tactful."

She shook her head. "No. I know. But I looked at our route, and it will barely take us out of our way at all. He lives in a suburb on the west side of Findlay. I couldn't just pass by without… without…."

"I get it. I think about my parents and sibs maybe a hundred times a day. Not being able to find out how they are is agonizing, but knowing you can't know doesn't stop you from wanting to know. Let's keep on. We'll get as far as we can."

It was almost eleven o'clock by the time they passed the city limits of Findlay. Aaron had taken over the driving not long after they crossed into Ohio, and although he voiced many of the same reservations Will had, he acquiesced to the detour.

"If they're there, at least we'll have a comfortable place to sleep," Kerri said.

"And if they're not?"

But Kerri had no ready answer for that.

They exited I-75 onto West Main Cross Street, and a slow, meandering loop took them onto a cul-de-sac with a long row of nicely-maintained ranch-style houses with tasteful plantings and neatly mown lawns and basketball hoops over the garage doors. There were none of the signs of chaos Kerri had been fearing—the broken windows, bullet holes, and dead bodies they'd passed too many times in the last few days to recall. She pointed off to the left.

"There. That's it."

Aaron pulled into the driveway, and shut off the engine.

"I know everything looks quiet." Aaron spoke in a whisper, as if he was afraid to break the unearthly silence that had descended without the grating rattle of Lester Poole's aged truck. "But we can't let our guard down."

"I'm not walking up to my brother's front door with a gun drawn." Kerri knew it was stupid the moment the words came out of her mouth, but she didn't say so. Drawing her gun seemed to be an acknowledgement that Jake and his wife Susan, and their three kids, Devin, Anthony, and Katie, were gone, that the maelstrom drowning the world had taken her brother's family down, too.

When Aaron spoke, his voice was gentle and patient. "Okay. But Will and I will be behind you, covering you. Do not go inside unless you know for certain it's safe."

Kerri nodded, and they got out of the truck. The moonlight was silver on the dew-laden grass, and they cast sharp-edged, pitch-black shadows on the driveway as they approached the front steps.

She stepped up, pulled open the storm door, and knocked.

The impact of her knuckles pushed the door open with a creak. It not only hadn't been locked, it wasn't latched. Kerri gave a frightened glance over her shoulder at Aaron, then turned back and shoved it open wide.

"Jake?" she called into the dark interior.

No one answered. And she knew, without going inside, that her brother and his wife and children were gone, and the modest house on Utah Avenue, Findlay, Ohio, was abandoned.

CHAPTER
15

THEY RETRIEVED FLASHLIGHTS FROM THE truck and made a thorough search of the house. No signs of the Children. Also, no signs of Jake Elias and his family, nor why they weren't here. Jake was a tough, no-nonsense type, fiercely loyal to his friends, implacable to anyone who threatened the people he loved. The fact that he was gone and there was no sign of a fight made it look like wherever they were, they'd gone voluntarily. No way would Jake stand by while the Children took his wife and children, leaving not so much as a piece of furniture out of place.

Kerri and Aaron took the main bedroom for the night, Will one of the boys' bedrooms. Kerri shuddered as the flashlight beam swept across what had been obviously occupied by a teenage boy. A t-shirt draped on a chair, football gear piled next to the closet door, a small desk with a notebook, pencils, and a bright green textbook labeled *Prentice-Hall Algebra I.* An OSU Buckeyes banner on the wall. A cork board displaying an Earth Science test with a bright red *100, Well Done!* on the top, a ticket for a Keith Urban concert, and a photograph of a smiling, well-built blond boy in swim trunks with his arm around a laughing, bikini-clad girl with black hair, standing in front of a water slide.

"Devin," Kerri said, in a near whisper. "Didn't know he had a girlfriend. He was fifteen."

"Don't use the past tense unless you're sure," Will said.

She shook her head. "They're gone, can't you feel it? All of them. Looks like the whole neighborhood. Gone. Vanished."

Will didn't respond.

"Make sure your gun's within reach," Aaron said. "I'm hoping our little detour with the Priestess's merry band may have thrown the Children off our trail, but I'm not counting on it. If they come through, shoot. Don't hesitate. We'll be right next door."

Kerri and Aaron returned to the master bedroom, and Kerri gave a solemn look around the place where her brother and his wife slept. It was a reflection of Jake's and Susan's life—orderly, clean, a little unimaginative. The walls had a framed painting of a generic-looking landscape, photographs of their wedding and their kids as babies, photographs of Kerri's and Jake's parents at their fortieth wedding anniversary, three years earlier. It had been right before Kerri joined the Boundary, she recalled, and she looked wistfully at she and Noah sitting at a picnic table, mugging for the camera, no clue of how their lives would be overturned in only a few short weeks.

"Come to bed, babe," Aaron said.

She turned toward him, nodded, and walked over to sit next to him on the spotless duvet cover, perfectly aligned with the bed frame, smooth as if it had been ironed in place.

"I'm just in shock, you know? You realize they could be gone, but then when it turns out to be true, it slams you over the head."

"Do you wish we hadn't come?"

"No. Of course not. I wanted to know. I had to know."

He nodded, and slipped an arm around her waist. "I'm sorry."

Another nod. "We've lost so much. All of us. Even if we somehow defeat the Children, things will never be the same."

He pulled his shirt off and stretched, arms behind his head. "I feel like I could sleep for weeks."

"Hasn't exactly been a relaxing trip. Especially the last couple of days." She took his hand, brought his arm toward her, and kissed the inside of his wrist.

"I think watching that evil man ready to torture you, drive a nail through your arm… it's one of the most horrible moments of my entire life. I couldn't handle it if someone hurt you."

He drew her to him. "We escaped, though. And I don't know if you'll agree, but I think what Lester Poole told us is the most encouraging thing I've heard on this whole trip. If he was sent by Saul's people to save us somehow, if that was his purpose for staying alive, like he seems to think—then it makes me optimistic about our making it the rest of the way."

"And then what?"

"I can't think any farther ahead than that at the moment. I'm trying to adopt Lester's attitude. Do what you have to do, accept that what should happen will happen."

"Faith of any kind doesn't come easily to me."

He stroked her back. "Me, either. But one thing I do know for sure—things always seem more hopeful after a good night's sleep. C'mon. For tonight, let it go. We'll handle tomorrow's problems when it's tomorrow."

They undressed silently in the dark, and she climbed into bed next to him, curling up against his warm body, skin on skin. At first, she doubted she could relax, but the terrible come-down from the constant fear of the past twenty-four hours won, and minutes later she was asleep, her cheek against Aaron's chest, her arm encircling his middle, drowned so deeply that even dreams could not reach her.

———————

SHE AWOKE TO SUNLIGHT SLANTING in through a gap in the curtains and Aaron still sleeping with one arm protectively around her. All was quiet, despite her conviction they would face an attack from the Children or their fellow humans before the night was over.

Maybe Aaron was right. Maybe the delay had thrown the Children off their trail. Until proven wrong, Kerri decided to keep that happy thought in her mind.

After making love, they got up and dressed, joining Will in the kitchen where he was munching on a granola bar while looking out into the sunlit back yard.

"Hi, guys," he said as they entered the room. "All quiet on the western front?"

"Far as we can tell," Aaron said. "See any signs of movement out there?"

"A couple of goldfinches, some sparrows, and a squirrel. Other than that, nothing. Sleep well?"

"Like a rock. I don't think I've slept that soundly since the night we spent in Rose Dawson's motel."

"Me, either," Kerri said.

"So, Kerri." Will spoke slowly, as if he were hesitant to say what was on his mind. "Do you want to… you know, search for your brother and his family?"

She gazed out into the neat back yard, with its square of patio, barbecue grill, lawn furniture, bird feeder hanging from a well-pruned crabapple tree. Everything around her shouted out her brother's influence, his determination to lead an orderly middle-class life. But that life was over, if not literally, then figuratively. Whatever had happened, wherever Jake and his family were, that existence would never be again.

"No. No, we need to keep moving on. I needed to come and see if he was still here, but now that I know he's not… well, either he and his family are alive and in hiding, or they've been captured or killed. In either case, there's nothing I can do about it. If we were to look for them, where would we start? They didn't leave any notes saying where they'd gone, not even a hint of what might have happened. It would be pointless to try to find them with nothing to go on."

Will nodded, his face registering sorrow. "I'm sorry, Kerri. I think it's about the thousandth time I've said it, but this fucking sucks."

"Yes. Yes, it does." She sighed, and straightened her shirt. "You found food?"

"Yeah, there's a good bit of food and stuff in the cabinets. Looks like nobody's come here since your brother and his family left, or the pantry would have been emptied, especially considering they left the front door open. Oh, and I also thought to look in the medicine cabinet in the bathroom."

"Good thinking," Aaron said. "What'd you find?"

"Some leftover antibiotics, looks like for one of the kids. Erythromycin. Not a full course, but better than nothing. Some ordinary painkillers and antiseptics and stuff. I also swiped your brother's deodorant, which God knows I've needed for days."

"I'm sure you don't smell any worse than we do," Aaron said. "And hell, back in medieval days, everyone smelled bad. I guess you get used to it."

"Well, I'm gonna forestall the body funk as long as I can. Anyhow, I found some shopping bags and loaded up the useful stuff I could find so we could bring it along. There's some yogurt and cheese and eggs in the fridge, but we don't know how long the power's been out here, so I left it. But I cleared out the pantry and also found a hand can opener for the canned stuff."

"Good thinking."

"When do you want to set out?" Kerri asked.

"Want?" Will chuckled. "What I want is a hot shower, a big pot of strong coffee to myself, and the morning newspaper filled with what we used to think of as 'bad news,' but what is now seeming to me like some kind of paradise on Earth compared to what we've dealt with in the last week and a half."

"I know what you mean," Kerri said. "I feel the same way."

"But since I'm not gonna get any of that, I'd say let's hit the road as soon as possible. No particular reason to delay. The longer we stay in one place, the more likelihood we'll be seen by any of the various bad guys we've had to contend with. So let's give a quick check for other stuff that might be useful, then beat feet."

They were pulling out of the driveway twenty minutes later. In the clear sunlight of morning, the emptiness of the neighborhood was even eerier than it had been at night.

"You ever read the book *A Wrinkle in Time?*" Kerri asked as Will wound the truck back through the maze of roads that led out of the subdivision.

Will smiled. "Yeah. Madeleine L'Engle. I loved that book as a kid."

"This place reminds me of Camazotz."

The smile vanished. "Jesus, Kerri. Scariest scene in the whole book. You think so?"

"I mean, not really. There aren't any little boys bouncing balls in every driveway in perfect unison, mothers all stepping out of the house at the same time, and so on. But it's unearthly, the silence and the… I dunno, the neatness. It's only been a little over a week, so the lawns aren't even overgrown yet. It's frozen, like a time capsule. Like a fly trapped in amber."

Will was thoughtful for a moment. "Maybe the analogy is pretty accurate. Remember, we were wondering if the Children were like the cells of an organism, and if so, maybe there was a central brain controlling what they did? Remember at the end, the disembodied brain that was running the show on Camazotz?"

Kerri nodded. "It."

"Yeah. And for my money, It was scarier than that motherfucking clown of the same name. Pennywise just wanted to eat you for lunch. It in *A Wrinkle in Time* wanted your eternal soul."

"If I can interrupt this cheerful reminiscence," Aaron said from the back seat, "let's see if we can loop around the main part of the town. From the map, it looks like we want Highway 224 East. Eventually we'll have to get on the interstates again—from the look of it, there's no easy way northeast across Pennsylvania without jittering around on back roads. But I'd like to delay that as long as possible. I'm still leery of major highways. More likely to be watched by the Children."

"Oh, because that's a cheery thought," Will said.

"Better than talking about freakin' Camazotz."

MORE EMPTY TOWNS AS THEY crossed Ohio. More blockaded exits with threatening signs, guarded by no one. They picked up I-71 toward the Ohio Turnpike to avoid the city of Akron, but just outside of a little village called Remsen Corners they came upon the worst battlefield yet. What had once been a cornfield was now a torn-up mess, ground into a muddy wasteland by vehicles and feet and, apparently, explosives. The place was pocked with craters and littered with the bodies of the dead, all of whom looked human.

"No Children anywhere," Will said.

"They'd have regenerated, anyhow," Aaron replied. "Or at least had their bodies removed by their comrades. So no way to know whether this was a fight against the Children, or yet another example of our species's determination to wipe itself out."

"Looks like photographs I've seen of the battlefields of World War I," Kerri said.

Aaron nodded. "I was reminded of the photographs taken by Mathew Brady during the Civil War. The one that stands out in my memory is the two guys looking down into a trench filled with corpses after the Battle of Antietam. It was in my American history text in high school, and I remember staring at it, trying to imagine what it was like to be there, standing on the edge, gazing down at the remains of my comrades and enemies, thrown together into the same pit. I've heard that the Brady photographs changed people's attitudes about war, because it was the first time non-combatants saw the aftermath up close and personal."

"Didn't stop us from waging it," Kerri said.

"No." Aaron looked out of the window, and shook his head. "Jesus, how far does the devastation stretch? This is horrifying."

They crested a low rise, and hanging from a crooked pole was an American flag, shredded by bullets. At its feet were about a dozen dead bodies. Nearby was a truck riddled with bullet holes, not a window intact, lying on its side.

"Whatever happens," Kerri said, "the United States will never again exist as it did."

"The same could be said about any other country," Will replied. "This is the last stand for the human species. We either triumph and defeat the Black-eyed Children, or we get wiped out completely. No middle ground."

Kerri tried to shove back the hopelessness that had been bubbling close to the surface ever since this trip began, and when she spoke, it was with a forced lightness that she knew the two men recognized as false. "Then we have to make certain we succeed. We don't have another option."

The remainder of Ohio passed with little sign of the invasion except for the overwhelming emptiness. The Ohio Turnpike was wide open, four lanes of blacktop with not a single car except for the few that had run off the road. They passed hundreds of empty farmhouses, and more than one town that was crowned by the dark, acrid reek of smoke.

They crossed the Pennsylvania state line at a little before three in the afternoon, near the town of Sharon. The route looked clear, cutting straight east across the center of the state on I-80 until Lock Haven, then north toward New York and whatever awaited them.

A jackknifed semi just past Clarion required a careful drive through the sloped median, but Lester Poole's old truck bumped through without hesitation.

The absence of other humans, as horrifying as it was, did present one advantage. They became less nervous about stopping to pilfer gasoline from filling stations along the way. They still posted sentries—one of them filling the tank and the gas cans, the other two with drawn guns, ready to meet any resistance—but they didn't see a single other human being for the remainder of the day.

Night was falling by the time they reached Lock Haven, a small college town in the middle of nowhere in central Pennsylvania. Kerri wondered briefly what had possessed someone to site a college there, in the middle of wooded hills and scraggly-looking farms and rundown houses. Little hope of ever finding that out, not that it mattered. Aaron exited I-80 onto Highway 220, and before they reached the town center, turned into a parking lot with a sign that said, Grayhaven Motel.

"Weren't the Grey Havens the place in *Lord of the Rings* where the Elves went to catch a ship out of Middle-earth?" Will said as he got out of the truck, holding a heavy-duty flashlight in one hand. The slam of the door closing echoed in the pervasive, all-encompassing silence.

Aaron looked at the key ring in his hand. "No auto-lock. Gotta do it the old-fashioned way." He pushed down the lock button on the door and lifted the handle as he closed it. "But I don't remember for sure, Will. And I'm not sure if that's encouraging or discouraging if you're right."

Kerri looked up at the darkened front of the motel building. "Maybe the Elves had the right idea. Things get nasty, clear right the hell out."

"Yeah, well, they were pretty badass even so." Will went up to the door marked Office and jiggled the handle. "Locked," he said, and with no hesitation, used the back end of his flashlight to smash the window.

"We're becoming savages," Kerri said. "We want something, we take it."

"The owners of the Grayhaven Motel can come argue with me about it if they want to." Will turned on the flashlight and aimed it into the window, then pushed aside the curtain and peered around. "Looks all clear to me."

"Let's not get complacent," Aaron said as Will climbed through the broken frame, then trotted around to unlock the office door and let them in. "Remember that just because it seems quiet isn't a sign that it's safe. Or because it's safe now doesn't mean it'll be safe an hour from now."

"You're just a regular ray of sunshine." Will stepped aside to let them in.

"A realistic ray of sunshine," Aaron corrected. "One room or two?"

"I'm fine with two," Will said. "We haven't seen hide nor hair of the Children since what, Missouri? You two need your privacy, and I wouldn't mind some, myself."

"Gonna make the saints and angels look at you in disapproval?" Aaron gave him a salacious grin.

Will shrugged. "Hey, a man's gotta do what a man's gotta do. You find me a hot-looking guy to hook up with, maybe I'll come up with a different solution."

"WE'RE OUT OF PROTECTION," AARON said in a breathless voice, as they twined together on the bed, clothes strewn in a random tangle on the floor.

"I know."

"We can… there are other ways to make love."

"No." Kerri kissed him. "I need you. All of you. If I get pregnant…."

"Yes? If?"

"Then it gives us both one more reason to survive this."

He looked down into her eyes, and she pulled his body to her, and all conversation ceased.

As they lay together after the first time, their bodies still coupled together and trying to return breathing and pulse to normal, Kerri chuckled.

Aaron smiled down at her. "What?"

She ran her hand down his back, eliciting a little shudder of pleasure. "I hope Will's not too jealous. I think we rattled the windows."

He shrugged. "He's up to dealing with it, I think. I bet he's already given the saints something to frown at."

"When all this is over, we need to find him a nice boyfriend."

"Yes. I can't imagine how much harder this would be if I didn't have you in my arms each night." He gave her a gentle kiss. "You're right. Will deserves someone. He's been an amazingly good sport about all this."

"That's putting it mildly. Every situation we've been thrown into, he's met head on. We couldn't have found a better person."

Aaron's face became serious. "We should reach Colville tomorrow. We're right on top of it now. Are you ready?"

"Ready? Hell no. I'll never be ready. But like everything else we've had to deal with, we'll take it as it comes. How about you?"

He kissed her neck. "No. Right now, what I want is to stay here, in your arms, forever." He began to move slowly inside her again, and she tightened her embrace around his middle, letting the strength of his body flow into her.

"Tell me we'll make it through this, that this won't be our last night together."

"I can't—"

"No. Promise me. I need to hear it."

He stopped, and for a moment they were still, linked as deeply as a man and woman can be. His heart thrummed against her, and he whispered in her ear, "I promise. We will see through tomorrow. I swear this won't be our last time."

"Hearing that makes me feel like it's real." She buried her face in his neck. "I have to believe it's true, or I couldn't face what we're facing. But I needed to hear you say it." Then she pressed her mouth against his, and once more there was no more talking in the darkened motel room.

THE NEXT MORNING DAWNED GRAY and threatening. The wind blew leaves across the parking lot as Kerri peered out through the curtains.

Aaron slipped on pants, zipped and snapped them. "How's it look out there?"

Kerri turned and gave him an appreciative grin. "Not nearly as good as it looks in here. Jeans and no shirt is a good look for you."

"Woman, you are insatiable."

She shrugged. "Only when you're around. I don't hear you complaining."

"Hardly." He pulled his t-shirt over his head. "Man, this shirt smells bad. We still haven't found a change of clothes."

"Hasn't been a priority."

"It'll have to be at some point, or the Children will smell us coming a mile away. And speaking of the Children, it's time to hit the road."

"Are you scared?"

"Shitless."

"Me, too. I keep thinking I'll get used to the fear, but it's not happening."

He stretched and yawned. "I don't think that's the way it works. My dad used to say that courage wasn't about not feeling afraid, it was about feeling afraid and doing what you had to do anyhow."

She opened the door, letting in a gust of cool air and the autumnal scent of falling leaves. "Is it September?"

"Beats the hell out of me."

They peered outside then stepped out onto the sidewalk in front of the row of motel rooms, but there was no sign of anything out of the ordinary. No Children, no other humans, no sign that Lock Haven, Pennsylvania was anything but a ghost town.

Kerri knocked on the door of Room 2. "Hey, Will? Wakey-wakey. Time to get going."

No answer.

She knocked louder. "Do I need to come in there and roll you out of bed? Because I will."

Still nothing. Kerri's smile faded, and her eyes met Aaron's.

She turned the doorknob. The door wasn't locked, and swung open without a sound.

The sheets and blankets were turned down, and there was a pile of clothes on the floor. But otherwise the room was empty.

Will Daigle was gone.

CHAPTER
16

KERRI AND AARON CHECKED IN the bathroom, closet, even under the bed.

"You think he went outside?" Kerri said, trying to quell the panic rising in her belly.

"Naked?"

"Maybe he needed to pee, like last time."

Aaron shook his head. "He'd be back by now. It doesn't take that long."

"Look." Kerri lifted an empty holster from the nightstand. "At least he's got his gun."

"And he was wearing his boxers." Aaron toed the pile of clothes aside. Will's t-shirt and jeans lay tangled together, on top of socks and a pair of disreputable-looking sneakers.

"Fuck. This is bad. What do we do?"

"What *can* we do?"

"Well, we sure as hell can't abandon Will."

Aaron ran his fingers along the wall, looking up and down the painted and peeling plasterboard.

"What are you doing?"

"Trying to see if there was a portal into here. At least then we'd know if it was the Children."

"Who else could it be? Will's smart enough to lock the door, so whoever it was got in here quickly enough to subdue him without making a sound. We'd have heard if he'd shouted for help."

"I hope so." He looked over at her, the guilt heavy on his brow. "We were kind of… occupied."

"God, I hope we didn't leave Will to his fate because we were too busy fooling around to hear him."

About three feet to the left of the television stand, Aaron's probing fingertips went right through the drywall with a crunch. "Well, I think we've got our answer."

He punched at the wall over and over—probably as much to relieve his own anguish as to prove to himself that it had been the site of a portal. In minutes, he had a vaguely rectangular hole driven into the wall, and the remains of the rotten plasterboard lay piled on the worn carpet and around his feet.

He stared at the wall, the exposed studs like the bones of some animal, a nervous system of wiring running up and along the ceiling, and then slammed both hands against what was left of the wall. "Fuck!"

His shout was so explosive that Kerri jumped.

"Aaron…." She put one hand on his upper arm, but he shrugged it off.

"No. We knew better. We let him take a separate room because we were thinking with our gonads and not our brains. Him, too, but we should have nixed it. He's new to this, despite all he's been through. Us? This isn't our first rodeo. It was all very well when we thought the Children had lost our trail, but we knew that wasn't true."

"Why didn't they attack us both, then?"

He shrugged, a frustrated, angry gesture. "One is easier than two. Divide and conquer. I dunno. Maybe because they knew I had the tranq rifle."

"They have a high opinion of our reflexes."

He gave a derisive snort. "No kidding. Hell, they could have gotten us in *flagrante delicto* more than once. But if they knew Will was alone, it was a safer bet."

"So like I said. What do we do?"

Aaron met Kerri's eyes, and they were filled with grief. "We keep moving."

"And leave Will?"

"What choice do we have? It's like with your brother and his family. Okay, maybe they're all being held captive somewhere. Where? We stick around Lock Haven and search every building? These are creatures that can build a portal to wherever the fuck they want. They may not even be on the planet anymore. We can't afford to waste time scrambling around looking."

"Jesus, but just to get in the truck and leave…."

"I know. You think I don't know? I like Will a lot. If I knew what to do, I'd sure as hell do it. But right now, getting to Colville is more important."

"Dammit."

"You know I'm right. And you know that Will would agree."

A single tear coursed down her cheek, and she dashed it away angrily with the back of her hand. "You're right. But I still feel like shit doing it."

He nodded. "I won't argue with that. But the longer we stay here, the longer we're inviting the Children to come back and try to get us, too. Let's go before we join Will wherever he is."

He walked out of the open door into the gray light of the parking lot. The clouds in the west were dark and heavy with rain, and the wind had picked up, lifting Kerri's hair and blowing it across her face. She brushed it back.

"Who drives first?"

"I will." Aaron went around to the driver's side. "The interchange through Lock Haven and Flemington looked kind of weird. We should check the road atlas before—"

His voice stopped. Kerri stood by the passenger side door waiting for Aaron to unlock it, peered around the windshield. "What? What's wrong?"

"Come here."

She jogged around the front of the truck.

Aaron was holding a piece of paper, and it fluttered in the gusts of wind. He held it out to her.

Written on it, in a handwriting so neat it could have been typeset, was a message with no salutation or closing. None was needed.

Your friend is being held in a Walmart store near here. We trust that you will be able to find it. If you fail to show up by noon today to negotiate terms for your surrender, we will kill him in as painful a way as we can manage and will make certain that his bleeding corpse is returned to you so that you can see what your actions have done. Come unarmed. If you are seen approaching with a weapon, we will take this as a sign of your faithlessness and will kill your friend immediately.

"It was under the windshield wiper."

"You realize how much the Children sound like the Priestess and her cult?" Fear flushed over her, tightening around her chest like a belt.

"They both want the same thing. To win at any cost. Evil, at its base, is always about dominance."

"What do we do? You said if we knew where he was…."

"I know."

"Terms of surrender, my ass." Kerri snorted. "They don't want surrender. They want us dead."

"So we march in there and give them a shot at us?"

A few big raindrops splatted against the pavement. "It's that or leave Will to his fate."

"Fuck. This is suicide."

"I'm willing to take the risk." Kerri looked at the empty highway, spooling off toward the center of town, where Will was being held. That the Children would follow through on their threat, she had no doubt. "I know it's stupid. I know it's dangerous. And I know it could result in our mission failing. That's what the Children want. But knowing where Will is, knowing what they're planning to do to him, we can't leave him behind. Once one human life becomes expendable, we're no better than they are."

Aaron nodded slowly. "I can't believe we got this close, only to—"

She reached out and touched his face. "Don't give up yet. You promised me last night, remember? You promised it wouldn't be our last night together."

"Yeah. I remember." He gave a deep sigh. "Okay. Let's do this."

They consulted the telephone book in their motel room to find the address—Aaron's phone had died, so the GPS was finally, and probably permanently, unavailable.

"Nice while it lasted," he muttered, frowning at the Yellow Pages advertisement. "At least they provide directions."

"How far?"

"Not very. Next town south of here. Mill Hall. Looks like it's right on the main drag."

"Let's do it."

"Yup. But one thing."

"What?"

"I'll be goddamned if I'm walking in there unarmed."

"They said they'd kill Will if they see us coming with weapons."

Aaron grinned. Once the decision was made, the hesitation and the anguish were gone, and the fierce laser-like intensity had returned to his green eyes. "That's assuming they'll see us coming."

———————

THEY PARKED AT A FARM supply store from which the Walmart sign was visible in the distance. The building itself was shielded from view by a belt of trees and a strip mall with a sign saying Millbrook Plaza. Aaron filled the six remaining hypodermic cartridges with colchicine, loaded one into the tranq rifle, and slipped the other five into his pocket.

"Don't forget you have those in there, sit down, and impale your leg."

Aaron gave a grim chuckle. "No kidding. I'm guessing I wouldn't melt, but I'd rather not know what a shot of colchicine would do to human tissue."

By now it was raining steadily, and within minutes they were both soaked. Kerri found herself wishing for the dry heat of the southwestern desert, or even the dust and continuous wind of her childhood home in Nebraska. These damp climates, it was a wonder people didn't mildew.

On the other hand, maybe it masked the sound of their approach. May as well think positively.

They made their way through the belt of trees then behind the strip mall, keeping as much as they could to the shadows, and peering out before running across a clear space. They met no resistance—in fact, there was no movement of any kind.

"Do they really think we'll walk in there and calmly surrender?" Kerri whispered, as they ducked behind a dumpster against the back wall of a Little Caesar's Pizza.

Aaron shrugged. "I don't think they understand human nature very well. From the contact we've had with them, they always seem to sneer at our compassion for our fellow humans as weakness. Who knows? From the note, it was obvious they thought we'd come. Otherwise, why not just kill Will and be done with it?"

There was a scrubby field of grass, each blade bent and dripping, between Millbrook Plaza and the Walmart. Kerri peered out from their hiding place. Fortunately, there were no windows on that side of the building. After a quick check to make sure there were no Children posted at the store's corner, they sprinted across the gap, only stopping when they flattened themselves against the back wall.

Kerri gave a quick jerk of her head. "There's probably a service entrance along the back."

"Okay, and then what?"

"Like we're planning to do in Colville. Improvise."

At intervals along the wall were heavy doors. All closed, including a huge corrugated metal rolling door large enough to get a forklift through.

The first two were locked.

Kerri was becoming increasingly jittery. The Children had to know they were here. They'd shown over and over their superior senses, brains, and strength. The only advantage they had was surprise, but did they even have that?

Aaron jiggled the handle of the third door, and surprisingly, it turned. He pulled it open. It swung outward on silent, well-oiled hinges, and the pallid gray light that was able to seep its way through the cloud banks illuminated a long row of shelves, each stacked to the ceiling with boxes. But the light faded quickly, and the end of the row was in complete darkness.

"How the hell are we going to find Will in the dark?" Kerri said, as they stepped inside. At least they were out of the rain, although no closer to a plan of how to accomplish what they'd come here to do.

"I have an idea," Aaron said. "But if it really is pitch dark in the store itself, it's not gonna work."

They walked forward as silently as they could, into a twilight, then evening, then the absolute dark of night. The door showed as a distant rectangle of gray. They began to feel their way forward, stopping only when they got to the end of the row of shelves and an open space.

Off to the left was another faint glow, and the shelves nearby showed as indistinct, soft-edged shadows. They inched along, expecting at any moment to be attacked, but everything was quiet. In short order they were next to an open doorway with hanging strips of plastic, separating the warehouse from the store itself.

Kerri peeked around the edge of the opening. The interior of the store was poorly lit, but at least not pitch black as the aisles of the warehouse were. There appeared to be skylights—which made sense. Without them, people would be in complete blackness every time the power went out.

"Okay, so what's your idea?" Kerri whispered.

"Electronics department."

"Um… there's no electricity."

Aaron just rolled his eyes.

They stepped through the plastic strips as silently as they could and slipped along the back of the store, cautiously peering around the shelves each time they reached an aisle. There was still no sign of the Children—nor of Will.

It was obvious that once Aaron was committed to the idea of rescuing Will, he had no further misgivings about it. Kerri, however, was filled with doubt. It was certain that this was intended to be a trap, to catch all of them and be done with the trio that had eluded the Children so long. But had Aaron's initial inclination been right—that they should keep going, leave Will behind, that one man's rescue was not worth risking their lives, and more importantly, the failure of their mission? Was what she had told him mere soft-heartedness?

Too late now. One way or the other, they had to see this through.

Although what Aaron could possibly want in the electronics department, Kerri had no idea.

They threaded their way through the rear of the store, and ahead, hard to read in the gloom, a sign appeared that said Electronics along with the locked glass-fronted cabinets designed to stop shoplifters from taking small but valuable items like iPods, Fitbits, and phones. Aaron scanned the shelves and after a moment pulled a box down with a satisfied smile.

"Batteries," he said in a hissing whisper. "Find batteries. C and double-A."

She gave him a perplexed look, but didn't want to get into a conversation long enough to figure out what the hell he was trying to do.

In short order she found a rack of batteries, and took a package of Cs and double-As as Aaron had instructed. She was getting increasingly jittery. Could the Children read their thoughts as easily they apparently read each other's? If so, surely they would know she and Aaron were here and would have attacked.

Or were the Children right now stealthily approaching, stalking their prey like a hunter targeting a deer?

When she returned, Aaron was sitting in the middle of the aisle, the tranq rifle next to him, and had opened the container, pulling out… a boombox?

Another questioning look, but Aaron only responded by sticking out his hand for the packages of batteries, which he sliced open with a pocket knife.

He put two C batteries into the boombox itself, and two double-As into a remote. Then he looked around for a moment, and with a grin crawled forward toward a rack with CDs, returning in a moment with one in his hand.

Justin Bieber?

He grinned at her and shrugged, popped the CD in and closed the cover, turned the volume knob up to 10, then stood, picked up the tranq rifle, and motioned for Kerri to follow him.

They edged their way farther along the back wall, then turned toward the clothing department. Here there were no shelves, only racks of shirts and pants. Poor cover unless they were on hands and knees, and that was hardly conducive to speed. But before they got out of sight of the boombox, Aaron held out his arm, aimed the remote, and pressed play.

A guitar riff, sounding absurdly loud in the silence, rang through the store, followed by Justin Bieber's voice singing something about your mama getting the job she wanted. Aaron ducked down and sprinted through the clothing department.

And finally, Kerri heard the sound of running feet, bare feet slapping on the tile floor.

The Children were here after all.

They wouldn't have much time. Once the Children recognized it was a ruse, which they would in short order, they'd know what Aaron and Kerri were trying to do.

Here, luck took their hand. At the front of the women's clothing department they peered out around a rack of blouses on sale and saw in the wide space between the cash registers and the door, Will Daigle.

He was clad in nothing but his boxers and tied hand and foot, a gag across his mouth. From his expression, he had no idea what was going on, why Justin Bieber had suddenly started singing in the back of the store.

He was being guarded by only two Black-eyed Children, who looked around warily. They had to know what was happening.

Aaron ran to a line of about a dozen shopping carts, neatly nested and waiting for shoppers who would never come, got behind them, and pushed.

It started slowly, and Aaron groaned, the muscles on his arms standing out like bands of iron. But once they began to move, it only remained to run behind them and continue increasing their speed. The two Children guarding Will turned toward them, a startled look in their obsidian eyes.

One moved quickly enough to get out of the way. The other was struck head on, the momentum of the carts knocking it sprawling.

Will made a muffled grunt of surprise.

In one swift motion, Aaron reached down, the pocket knife still in his hand, and cut the cords around his ankles, then all three of them sprinted for the front of the store.

The Child who had avoided the carts gave chase. It did not shout out, but Kerri was certain it was calling its comrades telepathically. She pulled down whatever she could grab to toss in its way—racks of candy, a pile of plastic hand baskets, a stack of lawn chairs, a cork board on the wall with bright green letters on top saying *Employee of the Week*. The obstacles slowed it down long enough for them to get through the front door and out into the rain-slicked parking lot.

But they were a good quarter mile from the truck, and within seconds, a dozen Children poured out after them, their faces twisted in unmistakable expressions of rage.

Aaron whirled, aimed the tranq rifle, and fired. The lead Child, the one who had been standing guard over Will, dropped. Aaron didn't pause to watch the slow dissolution that followed. He fired and reloaded again and again, striking one after another, and finally they halted the charge.

As one, the Children turned. A glowing portal appeared on the brick wall of the store, and there was an answering white blaze from the beacon in Kerri's pocket. Moments later, Kerri, Aaron, and Will were alone in the parking lot.

Will held out his arms, still tightly bound with a length of yellow nylon rope.

Aaron cut it, and Will yanked the gag from his mouth and said, "Fuckin'-A." He rubbed his wrists. "I have got to stop getting myself tied up. Uncomfortable as shit."

Aaron gestured toward the road. "Let's go."

"Clothes," Will said. "I've got to get some clothes. I know I've got a great physique, but no sense showing it off and making everyone else feel inferior. And we're here at Walmart, right?"

Kerri laughed. Could anything dampen the man's sense of humor?

"Okay. But quick. They'll be back. They've got to know we're running low on tranq cartridges."

Will nodded, stood, and they ran back toward the store entrance.

A mad grab for clothes and whatever else they could lay hands on, then they sprinted back out into the rain. And they had only reached the edge of the parking lot and the grassy field between Walmart and Millbrook Plaza before the glow of another portal shone on the store wall, and what looked like hundreds of Children poured through.

Kerri had run track in high school and college but had never sprinted so fast in her life. They reached the parking lot of the farm supply company, saw the truck at the far end, as the first of the Children were no more than a hundred yards behind them. Aaron turned the key in the ignition. She had a momentary panic that the truck wouldn't start—and wouldn't that be the ultimate irony, to rescue Will and get caught because of an unreliable vehicle? But it coughed itself into life, and Aaron slammed the shift into reverse and peeled out on the wet pavement. Lester Poole's ancient truck did what was probably the first donut it had turned in its entire existence, then he shifted into drive and stomped on the accelerator.

Kerri had noticed before that the Children didn't waste time continuing a pursuit that they knew they'd lost. The onrushing crowd stopped, almost in unison. She twisted over her shoulder and the last thing she saw, before they shot out onto the road, was a Child in the lead that she recognized, staring at them with cold hatred in its polished black eyes.

C H A P T E R
17

I F THERE WAS ANY DOUBT about where we were going before this,"
Kerri said, as they cleared Lock Haven and were heading north on Highway
220, "there can't be any now."

Aaron nodded but didn't respond.

"Hey, guys?" Will sat in the back seat, clad in brand new cargo shorts, a Penn
State sweatshirt, and running shoes with no socks. "Thanks for rescuing me."

"No worries," Kerri said. "You'd have done the same for either of us."

"Of course. I mean, I'd have tried to. Most likely I'd have been so terrified I'd
have pissed my pants then had a stroke. That's the first time I've seen the Children
up close and personal. And you know what? Those motherfuckers are scary."

"Can't argue with that."

"How'd you know where to find me?"

Aaron picked up a piece of paper and handed it over his shoulder to Will.
"They left a note for us."

Will read it in silence. "You do know what they were trying to do."

"Catch all of us."

"And you thought I was worth risking the whole mission for?"

"Like Kerri said. You'd have done the same for us."

"That doesn't make it smart." Will paused. "Look, y'all. I consider you
friends, and I hope you feel the same for me. But if Saul is right—and if he's

not, this has been one huge damn waste of time—it's way more important than any one of us. If one of us is captured, the other two need to give serious thought to cutting losses and moving on."

"The subject came up." Aaron gave a quick glance in the rearview mirror before returning his eyes to the road.

Will's eyes widened a little. "Oh."

"But we decided we had to risk it. I'm committed to seeing this through, and as long as it's in my power, I'll keep trying to get to Colville and accomplish whatever it is we're supposed to be doing. But we're in this together. If there's a chance of rescue, we have to take it. The way Kerri put it was that otherwise we're no better than the Children, and she was right. We're also no better than the Priestess, offering her devoted followers up to die like they were worthless garbage, rather than even considering if she could be wrong. That way lies the worst the human race has ever created—fanaticism, fascism, terrorism. Once you've decided that a single person's life isn't worth saving, there's no turning back."

Will was silent.

"Anyhow," Kerri said, "it's done. We rescued you, with a little help from Justin Bieber."

"I have to admit I was completely baffled when I heard the music start." Will laughed. "Good choice, by the way. If ever there was a voice that would sow disarray into the enemy that has to be it."

"First CD I happened to grab," Aaron said.

"I figured." He paused. "The Child that was in charge—he was creepier than the rest of 'em, and that's saying something. Some of the others wanted to use me for… you know, for food. Suck my brains out, or whatever it is they do. He wouldn't let them. He said, 'This one needs to be kept intact.' Then he looked at me with a terrifying smile, and said, 'All three of them. They're wanted for other purposes.'"

Kerri shuddered. "Other purposes."

"And I'm thinking it wasn't extra players for a pickup basketball game. My guess is they want information, specific information, that they think one of us might have. Especially you, Kerri. He said to me, 'I gave her a choice to stop fighting once, and she rejected it. Very shortly she will find herself regretting that decision.'"

She thought back to the Child they'd captured in Issaquah, Washington, who had hinted that she in particular was going to be their target if she didn't abandon the Boundary, give up working against the Children. The thought that she might have some central role in thwarting them had seemed then, and still mostly seemed, pure arrogance.

But here it was again. The Children themselves knew who she was, were gunning for her specifically.

"At least we defeated them this time," she said, trying to keep the tremor out of her voice.

"And I'm damn glad of that. That note sounded like they had something special in store for me. I've got to stop getting myself into situations where people want to torture me to death."

"So what's our plan?" Kerri looked out the window at the rain-swept, tree-covered hillsides slipping past them. The transition had been gradual, but they'd left behind the flat and featureless plains and were headed into craggy uplands, where the rocky bones of the Earth protruded through the soil, and the rolling terrain was thick with mountain laurel, rhododendron, and dogwood. "We'll be in New York by late afternoon, if I'm counting the miles correctly. Early evening at the latest. So this is it, guys. Whatever we're going to do, we're going to do it soon."

"As a battle cry, do you realize how lame that sounds?" Will said. "Forward, men! Let's go and do something or another, I'm not sure what!"

Kerri gave a grim chuckle. "Well, once again, we're back to trusting the Pleiadians. Saul implied we'd know what to do when we saw it."

"At the moment, I'm thinking he's vastly overestimating our intelligence. No offense."

"No, I know what you mean. So Aaron, do you know how to find the place we're looking for, once we get to Colville?"

Aaron nodded. "I don't know why I thought to do this, but glad I did. Before the battery on my laptop crapped out—that's back in New Mexico, before we picked up Greg Lantz and his son—I got into the database and wrote down the address, then checked the GPS and jotted down some directions."

"Good thinking," Will said earnestly. "I have to admit I never thought of doing that. I've been more focused on trying not to get killed."

"It looks like it won't be hard to find. I'm not sure what kind of place it is—a business, a house, whatever—but it's only a couple of blocks off the main drag, which is Route 12. There's a grocery store nearby. That was big enough to show up on the GPS. Lauxman's, or something like that. I wrote it all down."

"If we could find a way to charge your phone, is the GPS even still working anymore?"

Aaron shrugged. "Not sure. Like Kerri said a while back, GPS runs off satellites, and isn't directly connected to what the Internet is doing. So probably. And it sucks, but we'd have been able to recharge my phone if only I'd been thinking. I had a car charger in the Renault, but that's one thing I didn't think to grab and toss in Lester Poole's truck."

Will leaned back in his seat. "You know, this has thrown us back—I don't know, not just pre-Industrial Revolution, but like, medieval times. Back then, hardly anyone traveled anywhere. Your average peasant probably spent his whole life and never went more than twenty miles away from where he was born. He not only didn't communicate with people in the next town over, he didn't even know they existed. This has cut us off from each other completely. No Internet, no cellphones, no telephones at all. Hell, no snail mail, for God's sake. Even if the Children go away tomorrow, we'll still be little pockets of survivors, cut adrift from each other. It'll be years before we're able to connect again."

"It makes you realize how much we all relied on that network," Kerri said. "Not just for connecting to other people but for knowledge. You needed to know something? Twenty second Google search. Without that, we're back to trying to find a book with the information. If there is one."

"Maybe if we do defeat the Children, the Pleiadians can give us a hand up," Aaron said.

"Maybe." Kerri frowned. "I wonder if that's against their rules, like their insistence on not telling us the future. Kind of like the Prime Directive in *Star Trek.*"

"They broke that rule with Lester. They told him his future. Bad news, but they told him."

"Yeah." Kerri sighed. "I'm still banking on their seeing the big picture, that this is all progressing like it's supposed to. But minute to minute, that conviction seems pretty thin."

NEAR WILLIAMSPORT, PENNSYLVANIA, THEY SAW one of the few groups of living humans they'd seen since the Priestess and her insane followers in Illinois. The rain had slowed to a drizzle, the showers sweeping off to the east, but the sky was still overcast and threatening. Between the road and the flat, gunmetal-gray surface of the Susquehanna River shimmering in the distance was what looked like a school building, and in front of it were a few furtive-looking people—a woman of about forty-five, a teenage boy, an elderly man, and a toddler who couldn't have been more than three. The woman and the boy were filling buckets from a gutter spout off the roof.

All of them turned in unison at the sound of the truck. The woman dropped her bucket, where it dumped, spilling its contents over the ground. She ran to the toddler and scooped him up, and the four of them dashed around the side of the building, the old man hurrying despite a pronounced limp, the boy still lugging the heavy water bucket.

"Wish we could stop and reassure them we're not dangerous," Kerri said.

"Thing is," Aaron replied, "we are dangerous. The Children have been after us from the get-go, but you know after this morning they're gonna be gunning hard for us. I get the impression they're not used to losing, not even for a little while. It's why they were cocky enough to leave a note to lure us in and not kill Will or attack us directly."

"That tranq rifle stopped 'em," Will said.

"True. But I don't think they're really scared, not in any sense that they might be about to lose the entire game."

"Are they?"

Aaron shrugged. "Don't know. I hope so. But even so, we shouldn't stop to help anyone, not unless it's a dire emergency. Right now, we'd be putting them in more danger rather than the reverse."

———————

THE MILES SLIPPED PAST. THEY took Highway 15 North, which was nearly a straight shot toward the town of Colville. The terrain climbed into the forested foothills of the Alleghenies, with trees, stone-sided bluffs, wide-ly-spaced small towns, and not much else. Twice more Kerri saw people—once in the little village of Blossburg, where a white and frightened face peered at them out of an attic window as they passed, and then in the even smaller village of Tioga Junction, just shy of the border of New York, where an old woman sat in a porch swing, cane in hand and a defiant scowl on her face, as if daring the Children—or anyone else—to come for her.

Not far past was a big sign that was supposed to be encouraging. *Welcome to New York. The Empire State.* The cheerful words sent a shiver twanging its way up Kerri's backbone. By this time the sun, hardly visible for the clouds, was low in the western sky. A quick dogleg just past the border would take them onto Route 12, which passed right through the town of Colville.

And then what?

It had come up over and over again. They were relying on Saul's assurance that they needed to go to Colville, and when they got there, they'd know what to do. Kerri had been the one all along who had been the most insistent about Saul's good intentions, and more, his knowledge of what had to happen to defeat the Black-eyed Children. But now, only an hour from their goal, that confidence was leaking out of her like water from a cracked bucket. Right now, what she wanted was to hide, to find a place to secret herself, Aaron, and Will away, leave the heroics to someone else.

But what if there was no one else? In the end, who a task falls to has more to do with random chance than choice. She'd always insisted, right from the moment she and Mike Rivers had found the box buried in the sand on the top of a hillside near Deming, New Mexico, that despite the evidence, there was nothing special about her. She was a rank-and-filer, and given her penchant for disobeying the orders of her superiors, not even a very good one.

But here she was, with another agent and a doctor who had for some crazy reason thrown his lot in with theirs, heading toward what was likely to be a strongly-defended center of the Children's activities.

Insane. That's what it was.

But she didn't tell Aaron to stop driving.

They made one last stop for gasoline just outside of Corning. By then it was full dark, and getting the cover off the fill spout and slipping the hose of the suction pump into the gas tank took a lot of fumbling about. They only risked the flashlights for long enough to find the set screws, and did most of the rest by feel.

Aaron and Will stood guard as Kerri pumped the gas into the truck. All too quickly, there was a gurgling noise—they'd hit the limit of what the intake hose would reach.

The gasoline was running out. Everywhere. No more would be forthcoming. Which brought a new and anxious question to Kerri's mind—if they were still alive after this evening, where would they go then? And how?

Cars and trucks were soon to be less than useless. Travel would be on foot, or at best, on bicycle, if they could find one. So for all intents and purposes, once tonight was over, they'd either be dead, or trapped, more or less permanently, in the northeast.

With winter coming.

Kerri forced that thought away, and pulled the intake hose out of the tank. "That's all she wrote."

"It'll be enough to get us there," Aaron said. "We'll worry about getting away afterward."

Minutes later, they were underway again. They didn't bother putting the cap back on the tank. There was barely anything there to steal, anyway.

A steep drive, winding out of the valley of the Chemung River and back into the uplands. The wind rose and tore the clouds to shreds, pushing them east across a velvet black sky. Every once in a while there was a glimpse of a moon just past full, and the countryside would be illuminated by a ghostly silver light that made the fields and trees and houses look surreal, like something out of a fever dream. Then the clouds would cover it up again, and the darkness descended like a curtain.

A twisted, slow climb, past a turnoff to the village of Lamont, then what Kerri had dreaded—the headlights reflected from a bright green sign that said, *Colville 15 Miles*. Seeing the words made her heart rise into her throat.

No. Too late to back out. In fact, it had been too late the moment they left Las Cruces on the day the invasion began. Her pathway was already laid out before her feet, even though she'd been unable to see it.

Ten minutes later they crested a hill and ahead, glimmering in the intermittent moonlight, was the end of a long, narrow lake. From her study of the road atlas, this must be Carlisle Lake, with Colville huddling around the arc of its southern shore. She turned and looked into the back seat. Will was evidently able to sleep regardless of any worry he might have. He leaned back in the seat, eyes closed and mouth open. Of course, he'd had hardly any sleep the night before, snatched from his room as he was getting undressed for bed, so it was understandable.

But Kerri was so ramped up she couldn't imagine relaxing, much less falling asleep.

A yellow caution sign saying, *STEEP GRADE. Trucks MUST use low gear,* and Route 12 curved its way down the face of the hill. More houses, and closer together. A motel, a Home Depot, a Pizza Hut. Petrillo Ford, the windshields of its now-useless inventory reflecting moonlight at them as they passed. Robin's Nest Florist and Greenhouse, wedged into a narrow spit of land between the highway and an access road leading to a Staples and a Lowe's.

Then, on the left side of the road, a low, blocky building, its sprawling parking lot dotted with shopping cart returns.

Aaron turned off the highway, coasted across the lot, and braked to a stop but didn't say anything, simply continued to stare out of the windshield of Lester Poole's truck as if he couldn't quite believe what he was seeing.

"Okay," he finally said, in a voice that sounded as if he were keeping it steady and light only with a supreme effort. "We're here. This is it." He paused, swallowed. "God help us."

CHAPTER
18

THE GROCERY STORE SPORTED A dead neon sign, glinting faintly in the moonlight, that proclaimed it had once been *Lauxman's*. Like so many buildings they'd seen in the past week, its front windows were smashed, and Kerri knew what they'd see if they went inside. Emptied shelves, anything edible or useful gone, everything else in chaos.

There was only one other vehicle in the lot—a truck with *Lauxman's* written on the side, stopped at an angle by a shopping cart return. Its back doors were open, as well as the driver's door. In the light of a nearly full moon Kerri thought she could make out the silhouette of what had probably been the driver, hanging limp, halfway out of his seat and supported only by the shoulder harness, arms dangling toward the parking lot.

It was crazy how little this affected her. In only a few weeks, she had become inured to death. What would have shocked her, jolted her with adrenaline, only registered now as a curiosity and a source of diffuse pity.

Or maybe she already had enough adrenaline in her bloodstream that there was none left to jolt her with.

"How far?" Will whispered.

Aaron gave a jerk of his head. "GPS said the road curves around the back of this store. Another maybe eighth of a mile or less, it tees out. Left at the T, then the target's on the left."

"You okay going in unarmed, Will?" Kerri said. "You lost your gun in Lock Haven."

Will shrugged. "Not much choice, is there? What am I gonna do, stay in the truck by myself and listen for screams? And wait for how long? Fifteen minutes, forty-five, an hour? No, I'll figure something out." He gave her a cryptic smile. "Plus, I have a trick or two up my sleeve that even the Children won't have anticipated."

Kerri gave him a curious grin. "I'm looking forward to it."

"Okay, then." Aaron reached behind the back seat of the truck and hefted the tranq rifle, still loaded with a cartridge full of colchicine, and picked up the one remaining filled cartridge left. He shook his head. "We should have realized we'd run out of hypodermics before we ran out of our magic flower juice. Stupid."

"I don't see how we could have foreseen any of this." Kerri closed the door. "We just have to improvise and then do the best we can."

"Lock and load," Aaron said.

They walked off toward the sidewalk that curved along with the road around the back of the grocery store. All was still. As far as she could tell, they were entirely alone.

A cool breeze stirred, chilling Kerri's skin, making her realize she was soaked with sweat. Maybe she wasn't as calm as she'd thought. And, after all, this was it. This was what they'd been aiming at the entire time, somehow getting to Colville, then somehow doing something. It had never been more concrete than that. They had trusted Saul's pronouncement that when they got there, they'd know what to do.

And now they were here. In the next half-hour, they'd either knock out the Children's command center or else be captured or killed. It was as simple as that. The waiting was over.

The road rose slightly as it arched across a small bridge underneath which a shallow stream chattered against its rocky bed. The breeze carried the scent of earth, dampness, the crisp smell of dead leaves. She concentrated on walking as silently as possible, hoping that the occasional footfall as one of them stepped on a patch of gravel or a fallen twig wouldn't give them away.

The t-intersection Aaron mentioned was barely visible in the deep darkness under the spreading branches of a row of trees. Left onto an even more cracked and uneven sidewalk, for perhaps another five hundred yards.

Ahead and to their left was a low, sprawling building with a sign in front saying *Colville Collectables*. It took Kerri a moment to notice the oddest thing about it.

The lights over the door were on.

She had not seen anywhere that had power since the night they spent in Rose Dawson's hotel in Vaughn, New Mexico, over a week ago. It was strange how quickly she'd gotten used to its absence. The explanation for the lights here was quickly apparent, however. There was a low humming noise, apparently from a generator, emanating from somewhere behind the building. This was good and bad. They wouldn't be stumbling around in the dark and could see any Children who were about.

But the Children could also see them. And from what she'd observed, their night vision was far better than a human's to start with.

Kerri frowned, looking at the building that had been the target of their long, difficult voyage across the United States. It was very far from her mental image of a fiercely-defended stronghold, surrounded by Children waiting for them to arrive.

Was this really the place they were supposed to attack? And if so, why?

They moved forward stealthily for another few feet, but then Aaron put out one hand as they were about to step out from the shadow of a tree into the better-lit space in front of the building, and stopped them.

Then he pointed.

Standing in front of the building was a single slim, waif-like figure. There was something alert in its posture, as if it were a predator ready to spring.

Had it seen them? No way to be sure, but it didn't move and did not appear to be looking toward the spot where they stood.

"I got this one," Aaron whispered, lifting the tranq rifle to his shoulder.

"Don't miss," Kerri said. "We've only got one cartridge left after this."

The Child in front of the building suddenly tensed and swiveled its head toward them. They must have preternatural hearing to have picked up the whispers from a hundred feet away, but apparently it had. It began to walk, then run toward them.

Aaron fired the rifle.

The cartridge caught the Child high in the upper chest. It made a low grunting noise and stumbled to a halt. And just as they'd seen before, a wet spot, looking black in the pallid moonlight, spread across its ragged shirt. It gagged, raised its upper lips in an animalistic snarl, and fell to its knees.

Then its whole body collapsed in on itself. In less than a minute, there was nothing left of it but a puddle of whitish slime and the remnants of its clothing.

"I don't care how many times I see it," Will said under his breath, "but that is by far the grossest fucking thing I've ever seen. And I used to do autopsies for a living."

Any reply was cut off when the door to the building flew open with a bang, and a half-dozen other Children ran into the parking lot, looking around wildly. It took no time at all for them to locate the three Boundary agents, frozen in the shadow of the trees.

Aaron slammed the last of the hypodermic cartridges into the tranq rifle, raised it, and fired. Another Child went down, and he tossed the rifle aside and drew his gun. Kerri took down three with her own weapon. Although she knew this would only be temporary—the Children had fantastic powers of regeneration—at least for now, it stopped their headlong charge.

One of the Children, however, was able to dodge and weave past both Kerri's and Aaron's bullets, and ran straight for Will, arms straight out in front of it, long fingers reaching for the doctor's face. Kerri turned toward him, bringing her gun up.

Before she could fire, Will calmly pulled a water pistol out of his pocket, and said, "Yippie-kai-yay, motherfucker," and squirted the Child right in the face.

It was carried forward by its momentum and knocked Will spinning, but he was able to keep his feet. Kerri watched as the Child pitched to the ground, clawing at its face as its features dissolved. Its head liquefied first, but as with the others, the effect spread until its entire body was gone.

"Holy shit," Kerri said under her breath.

Will shrugged. "I shoplifted it from a sale bin in the Walmart in Lock Haven while we were grabbing clothes, then filled it with colchicine. I figured if we weren't going to be able to use the tranq rifle, it was a pity to let it go to waste."

They stared at the building. No more Children were in evidence, but long experience told her not to trust the seeming calm. Plus, she had seen behavior that indicated the Children had some sort of telepathic link. If this were true, there was no way that the death of seven of the aliens would go unnoticed.

So far, the little warning beacon in her pants pocket was dark. This didn't guarantee there were no more Children in the area, only simply that there was no portal.

Good news, as far as it went. But it didn't make Kerri's pulse slow down any.

They crossed the parking lot, still moving as quietly as possible, but met no further attacks. A low set of wooden stairs led up to the open front door, through which a dim, yellowish light shone.

As they stepped through, Kerri realized that whatever purpose the building had served prior to the invasion—most likely an antique store, judging from the sign—there was no trace of it left. The interior looked like a mad scientist's laboratory. Nearby were tables with equipment of uncertain purpose. Metal prongs, wires, loops, clamps. Glass flasks with multiple spouts, from which protruded hoses leading to shining silver canisters. Clear-sided tanks, hundreds of them, filled with a greenish, viscous liquid, in which floated clumps of tissue that looked like overcooked meat.

They fanned out, Kerri and Aaron with guns drawn, Will still holding his ridiculous-looking plastic water pistol that was probably deadlier to the Children than any other weapon they had.

As she walked down the aisle between the tables, the contents of the tanks changed. The lumps of tissue were larger, more defined. They looked less like undifferentiated blobs, and more like…

… embryos.

With a clench of nausea, Kerri recognized what the aquariums were.

Incubation tanks.

There was a sudden shuddering on the far wall, something Kerri recognized all too well. The portal shimmered, and simultaneously the beacon in her pocket lit up like a miniature sun.

She shouted, "Will! Aaron! Behind you!"

From the portal streamed Children, dozens of them, pouring into the room like a ragged army, their faces lit with triumph as they surrounded the prey that had eluded them for so long.

Will raised his gun to fire, but Kerri shouted, "Wait!"

Instead of aiming her own weapon at the Children, she pointed it at the nearest row of tanks. Her voice rose over the chaos of movement.

"Stop. Don't move. I'll take them all out. You may bring me down eventually, but by then hundreds of your young will be nothing but slime and broken glass."

There was a hissing intake of breath from the Children, but they stopped. One looked at Kerri, a smirk on his narrow face, and she instantly knew him. The Child they'd captured, only to have him freed, the one who had engineered the ambush that led to the death both of Danielle Tauriac and of Kerri's abducted boyfriend, Noah. The Child she'd seen staring at them with icy hatred just that morning, in the parking lot of a Walmart store.

"So much for humans' professed reverence for life," the Child said, contempt in its voice.

"I'm not going to argue philosophy with you."

The Child laughed. "Then why did you come here? To make a brave stand before you died? I thought that suicide was discouraged among your people. Or was it to kill a few of us, a few out of millions?" He nodded toward Will. "The chemical weapon is clever. Like every species, we are not invulnerable. But do not try to convince me that you plan on trying to overwhelm all of us with a single water gun full of poison."

"I'll be satisfied if I can take a few of you with me," Will said. "So bring it on."

"I've been issued an ultimatum." The Child sounded completely unconcerned. "Kerri Elias is correct that we value our young, and that threatening them is an effective deterrent. But you cannot keep up that defense forever. Whatever damage you inflict, either to ourselves or to the incubators, you must see that the end result will be precisely the same."

Will snorted laughter. "Oh, kiss my ass, you pompous bastard. Go ahead. Come at me, bro."

"As you wish," the Child said with a sneer—but did not move.

That was when Kerri realized their mistake. There was only one thing that could mean.

There was another entrance to the room.

She whirled. Coming up from a narrow passageway between the aquariums was at least a half dozen other Children. The three of them were surrounded. The thought, *This is it, then,* flitted across her mind like a leaf blown on a high wind, and a strange calm settled over her. She raised her gun, fired, and the nearest Child fell. She heard other gunshots, and more than once the gurgling dissolution brought by the contents of Will's water pistol. One thing worked in their favor—the bodies of the fallen lying on the floor slowed down the attackers, but as they watched, another Child came through the portal, and another, and another.

Aaron grabbed Kerri's upper arm and spun her around. There was a gap in the ring—one of the fallen Children had collapsed into the passage between the incubators and blocked it, for a moment halting them. They ran down the aisle, leaping over the bodies of Children struck by bullets, Children who would regenerate, repair the damage, and come back at them an indefinite number of times.

Words chased each other through Kerri's mind. *Implacable. Unstoppable. Undefeatable.*

But now there was at least a moment's respite, and they seized it. She didn't dare turn but could hear Will panting behind them, and the slapping of the Children's bare feet on the plank floor as they gave chase. She turned, ran down another narrow passage between banks of incubators, and through a door. Once Will was through, Aaron slammed it shut, shot home a bolt, just as the first of the Children collided with it hard enough to shake the entire building.

"That won't stop them for long," Will gasped out.

"They can just create another portal." Aaron had never sounded that despairing, that hopeless. "And now we're trapped. There's no exit other than the door we just came through."

But Kerri was facing the back wall, which glowed green, not from incubators but from long transparent tubes. All of them were empty but one.

There was a moment that hung suspended as she stared at the occupied tube.

No. It couldn't be. Was this what they'd been sent to do? Her mind rebelled, tried to disbelieve what she was seeing. She felt disembodied, unreal, and it was almost a surprise to hear her own voice.

"Guys, I think you'd better come over here."

The hammering on the door continued, but Kerri barely heard it.

In a clear cylinder, perhaps three meters long, a naked man was suspended in the same viscous greenish liquid that was in the incubators. His hair was overlong and almost white, he had two months of scraggly beard on his face, and what had been a powerful physique had dwindled to a pathetic scarecrow figure, with stick-like arms and legs. His eyes were open, focused on nothing, but as she approached the tube, his head swiveled toward her, and they opened a little wider in recognition.

Aaron was behind her now. "You know this man?"

She nodded, and forced herself to say the words. Her voice sounded thin and strained in her own ears.

"Yes. It's Mike Rivers." She stopped, swallowed. "My former partner in the Boundary, who was abducted right under my nose in Deming in July."

"Dear God," Will said in a breathless whisper. "What can we do?"

"Break the tube," Kerri said quietly.

"What?" Aaron looked at her, aghast. "Kerri we don't know what that will do to him!"

Her voice rose to a shout. "It doesn't matter! Break the fucking tube!"

And as she watched, Rivers's mouth formed two words—*Help me.*

Aaron and Will were both still glued to the spot. Kerri looked around her for something heavy enough and finally found a sturdy metal lab stool in one corner of the room. She ran to it, grabbed it, and sprinted back toward the tube that held Mike Rivers, holding it by one leg and swinging it as hard as she could.

The first blow, astonishingly, only caused a single long crack. She reared back for another strike, then a third, by now crying out in desperation at each impact. At the fourth strike, the side of the tube shattered, and the mass of the liquid inside did the rest. The green goo rushed out in a sticky flood, filling the room with an acrid, biting odor. Rivers slithered downward, carried by the flow of fluid, sliding headfirst out of the tube, and slumped to the floor.

At first, he seemed to be dead. Which was all right. She knew he would prefer being dead to being trapped in one of the Children's evil scientific experiments. But he gave a rattling cough, vomited up about a quart of the green liquid, and then lay there in the puddle, hacking and gasping for breath.

And that was when another portal formed in the wall behind them.

"Fuck," she said under her breath. Aaron had been right. All they'd done was delay their demise by a few minutes. At least they'd freed Rivers—that by itself counted for something.

But no one came through the portal. In fact, the portal itself was flickering, as if it were incomplete or intermittent. Maybe the Children's technology wasn't flawless after all? They'd stopped hammering on the door, but Kerri couldn't recall when it had happened. It didn't matter anyway. When the Children finally made their way through, all four of them would die, and that would be it.

Then she remembered Kyle Tauriac—or whatever had spoken using Kyle's mouth—saying, *Find the one who was captured, then save the one who was lost. There you will find a door, which all of you must step through without question. If the door closes, you will be trapped. That is all. Do all of these things, and you will complete the circle. I will say nothing more.*

And in a blinding flash, she understood. The one who was captured—Will Daigle, rescued from a Walmart in Lock Haven, Pennsylvania. The one who was lost—Mike Rivers, stolen away from a desert path a thousand miles from here.

And now, a door. Which, if it closed, would trap them.

Without any conscious volition, she ran to Rivers, and picked him up into a fireman's carry. She shouted, "Come on! Now! Don't stop, don't ask, just follow me!"

There was a momentary thought, a certainty that she didn't have time to argue with them, that the two men would make it through the portal by their own will or not at all. At the same time, she half-registered a second portal forming on the opposite wall.

So where had this one come from? And where did it lead?

When she saw the first Child step through the other portal, she realized she didn't care. In a moment, anywhere would be better than here.

She went through at a dead sprint, not daring to look behind her to see if the two men had followed. She landed in a dark space with a smooth, hard floor. What light there was—from the shimmering of the portal—winked out only seconds later, leaving her in absolute blackness.

She set Rivers down. He hadn't moved since she'd picked him up, throwing his weight over her shoulders as easily as if he'd been a child. She felt around the space, and bumped into someone else doing the same thing. For a moment their arms entangled, and there were two simultaneous gasps in the dark.

"Is that you, Kerri?" came a hushed voice.

"Will? Thank heaven you made it through." Kerri tried to bring her pulse back to normal, and gave a convulsive shiver. Her clothes were wet with the acrid green slime, but at the moment she hardly gave it a thought. "Where's Aaron?"

His voice, sounding exhausted. "Over here."

She gave another shudder and ran toward him, and was enveloped in Aaron's strong, loving arms. For a moment, they simply clung together, like two people lost at sea, hanging on to each other in a desperate attempt to cheat death.

"Where are we?" Will said.

"No idea."

Then a female voice—a blessedly familiar one—said, "You are in the Boundary Headquarters Building, in Las Cruces." An unseen hand struck a match, and the flame was applied to the wick of a candle.

The feeble, fluttering light illuminated the astonished face of the woman who had trained Kerri when she'd joined the Boundary, over three years ago.

Asha Choudhary.

CHAPTER
19

AN HOUR LATER, KERRI, AARON, Will, and Asha huddled together in a dimly-lit examination room on the fourth floor of the headquarters building. Rivers lay on his back on a bed near one wall, a blanket pulled up to mid-chest, eyes closed, breathing softly. They had cleaned him up as well as they could—Asha insisting they scrape a sample of the green liquid from his skin and keep it for testing—and settled him in bed, where he was asleep in minutes.

"I don't want to think about what that poor guy's been through," Will said. "Can you imagine? I'm kind of glad I don't know the details."

"How was he breathing in that stuff?" Aaron asked. "Why didn't he drown?"

Will shrugged. "Speculating, here, but there are some liquids that can be hypercharged with oxygen. The Navy was experimenting with one a while back, called Fluosol. It's still used as a blood substitute in cases of carbon monoxide poisoning and sickle-cell anemia but ended up being pretty expensive to manufacture. The thing is, there's nothing inherently bad about having a liquid in your lungs. The air you breathe is a fluid, too. The problem is, we're used to breathing a fluid that's twenty percent oxygen, but even highly oxygenated water—like in fast moving, cold streams—has a concentration of way less than one percent. But if you could raise the concentration of oxygen in a liquid to near twenty percent, you could breathe it."

"It'd probably hurt like hell," Kerri said. "Getting even a little water up your nose is pretty painful."

Will gave her a somber look. "I doubt the Children were worrying about his comfort levels."

"What I'm wondering," Aaron said, "is how you escaped, Asha. What happened when headquarters was attacked?"

Asha looked at him for a moment, her lips tight. It was apparent she didn't want to revisit that horrible morning that the invasion began, but when she spoke, her voice was steady.

"It seemed like there were hundreds of portals. They appeared everywhere at once. We've never seen that many Children in one place—it was easy enough to picture them as we'd seen them before, one or two, and tending to flee rather than engage. Here, they went all out. It must have been planned for weeks. It was coordinated, quick, and ruthless. What they call a surgical strike. There were a few people who were killed outright. Shayna Vallejo—she was thrown into a wall when she tried to fight them. You probably know how strong they are. Her neck was broken. She died instantly."

"My God," Kerri said quietly, suddenly realizing she was fighting back tears.

"I'm sorry. I know she was a friend of yours. But a lot of the others were pulled through portals. Taken away. We don't know where—whether they're even…." She hesitated, her dark eyes looking from one of them to the other.

"Whether they're even still on the Earth," Aaron finished.

Asha nodded. "It's hard to look upon this as anything but a complete defeat. A few of us managed to hide and simply waited them out. When they'd cleared the entire building, or thought they had, they left. My fear was that they were planning on staying here, using this as a command center, which would have made it impossible for any of us to survive. Fortunately they had other ideas."

"Who else survived?" Kerri asked.

"Evan Reed. He's on guard duty down on the first floor. I know that must seem ridiculous—since the Children can simply create portals when they want to get in, it's hard to imagine their using the front door. Cameron Sterling from

Research also survived. He hid in a chemical storage locker that luckily the Children didn't think to open."

"Kevin Salerno?"

Asha shook her head. "Vanished. Early in the raid. He and a few other guards tried a frontal assault, hoping to drive the Children back. They underestimated the scale of the attack. We all did."

She bit back tears. The thought of friendly, easy-going Salerno as a captive was heartbreaking. He always had a smile on his face, whether he was fighting next to you or sharing a pint of beer. He and Will would have liked each other.

No chance of that now.

"Who else?"

"There are a few others. We're not sure if anyone got out of the building when the raid started, so there may be survivors we don't know about. Of the ones who got trapped inside, only ten people total. Since then, we've been hiding out here. There's back-up electricity from solar panels, enough to run most of what we need, but we follow a strict policy of lights out at sundown. The quickest way for the Children to find out they didn't get us all would be for them to see lights in the windows at night."

Kerri nodded but couldn't stop a shiver running up her backbone. In only a few days, the world had changed irrevocably, and their actions would have to change as well. They'd moved down a notch on the food chain and would have to start thinking like prey.

Then she frowned. "Where's Rendell?"

"Unknown. He's not here, that's for certain. Whether he was killed or captured, we have no way of knowing, but the latter is far more likely."

"Shit. I never liked the guy, but I wouldn't have wished that on him."

Asha gave Kerri a long look. "I cannot think of anyone I have known in my entire life that deserves what the Children do to human beings."

Aaron held out his hands, palms upward. "What do we do now?"

"I wonder if this is what Saul wanted us to do?" Will gestured toward Rivers, lying peacefully asleep on the bed. "Rescue Rivers?"

"I can't imagine anything else it could have been," Aaron said. "Otherwise, it would just have been a clumsy and poorly-prepared raid on a place where the enemy outnumbered us ten-to-one. That wouldn't be a mission. It would be suicide by Child."

"But why Rivers?" Kerri glanced over at the man she had worked with for three years. Their relationship had been fractious at best. Rivers was a domineering, arrogant man who had more than a touch of the male chauvinist in him. He had never considered Kerri as an equal. Hell, he hadn't even considered her useful. He had always treated his partnership with her as an annoying inconvenience.

"Was it because he's a leader?" Will ventured.

"So were a lot of the people who were captured," Asha said. "Rendell ranked higher than Rivers. Saul must have had a reason to believe bringing Rivers back was important." Again her gaze moved across their faces, and it was clear when she spoke that she chose her words carefully. "That is, if we still believe Saul is on our side."

"Don't you?" Kerri said.

"I am unconvinced," Asha responded. "I do not put my full trust in people easily, and I will say that I have wondered for some time what Saul and his people get out of helping us. Why put themselves at risk? Why not just step back and let the invasion happen? The fate of our planet surely cannot mean so much to them."

"Do you have any guesses?" Aaron said. "I have to admit we've been wondering the same thing ourselves."

Asha nodded. "My fear is that they're using us to achieve their own ends, whatever those are. If they truly had our best interests at heart, why didn't they warn us of the attack on headquarters in time for us to halt it, or at least defend ourselves more effectively? Saul and his people can seemingly jump back and forth from present to past to future, so surely they must have anticipated it. We've lost hundreds of agents here—and at the same time, they induced you to cross the country to rescue one man."

"You're right," Aaron said. "It doesn't make much sense."

"I'm not ready to abandon Saul just yet," Kerri said. "I don't understand why he's doing what he's doing. If Rivers is the reason for the raid in Colville, I'm not seeing what possible use he can be. But there has to be some reason. I don't believe that Saul sent us out there, risked our lives, to accomplish nothing."

She looked over at the man in the bed, a thin, wretched husk of what he had been only a few months earlier. His once powerful muscles had wasted away, his hair was white, his skin lined in a way that made him appear twenty years older. The hands folded on top of the clean sheet were nearly skeletal.

What possible use could he be to them in this state? Did he know something about the Children, learned during his captivity?

Finding that out would have to wait until he awakened. For now, it was more critical that he be allowed to sleep as long as he needed to.

———————

THE POWERS-THAT-BE HAD evidently foreseen the possibility of the headquarters building being a stronghold, or at least for being under a state of siege. There was a storehouse of food in a room on the fifth floor, and it included hundreds of different sorts of canned food, including refried beans, soups, beef stew, spaghetti and meatballs, vegetables, fruit, and more. Shelves with shorter-lived items—dried fruit, crackers, tortillas, and the like—were already half empty, but it made sense to use those first and turn to the less perishable foods later as needed. There was one whole wall lined with what looked like thousands of bottles of water.

Yes, someone had been thinking ahead. Fortunately.

As a result, they dined better the following day than they had in almost two weeks. They were joined by Evan Reed, the tough, taciturn agent who had been dating Shayna Vallejo. Kerri had a pang when she thought of passionate, vital Shayna, imagining her being thrown into a wall, killing her instantly. This was chased by an even more somber thought—if given the choice of having her neck broken or being drained of neural energy by one of the Children, used for food and then tossed aside like refuse, she would have chosen death in a heartbeat.

They all would.

Cameron Sterling, the young scientist who had first thought of colchicine as a possible weapon against the Children, was there, too. He was a tall man with chestnut-brown hair and hazel eyes behind rimless glasses and a slim runner's build. When Cameron heard about Will's use of colchicine in a two-dollar kid's water pistol, he laughed and shook his head, then clapped Will on the shoulder.

"You, sir, are a serious badass. I bow to your magnificence."

At the moment, he was in earnest conversation with an agent she hardly knew, a serious-looking young woman named Jana Liang, discussing if it were possible to broadcast colchicine more widely. Kerri heard him say, "… like with a crop duster!" before she turned her attention elsewhere.

Aaron sat across from her, shoveling food in with his usual gusto. Of course, he had reason—they had been on short commons the previous week.

She took a sip of boxed orange juice and said to him in a low voice, "Last night you asked, 'what now?' Any ideas?"

He shrugged and gave a sigh. "It's hard to see what we could do without going outside the headquarters building, and if there are any Children around, that'd give away the fact that there were some survivors. Pure suicide."

She nodded. "So do we just hunker down here and wait to see what happens? What Rose Dawson said she was doing?"

"I dunno. At least one high-ranking agent survived. You speak highly of Asha. Maybe she'll know what to do."

"Maybe." She glanced around the sprawling common room where she and the other agents had come while off duty, to relax, have a cup of coffee, shoot the breeze, even have a friendly game of table tennis. It seemed like that was in another life. Now, the survivors were huddled close together, talking in low tones, as if afraid their voices would carry into the outdoors, give them away. "Where is Asha, anyway?"

"She was here earlier. Not sure where she went."

"What I'm wondering is what's going on outside these walls. I mean, think of it. Remember Topeka? A whole city of what, a hundred thousand people? Gone. Cleared away. A ghost town. How could all this happen this fast?"

Aaron leaned back, stretching out his long legs in front of him. "Saul was right. The Children are an implacable enemy. Think of how long they've been feeling us out. What did Dwayne Constantin tell us? There were records of historical contacts with the Children going back maybe a thousand years? And those are just the ones we know about. They've been planning this for a long, long time. Maybe waiting, letting our population grow, the way you would farm animals, before… harvesting us."

A surge of hopelessness rose in Kerri's chest, one she'd been forcing down over and over. During the past week, a combination of the necessity of keeping focused on the task and the omnipresent danger had allowed her to distract herself, but now, finally at rest, she couldn't ignore it. She, Aaron, and Will had come through the ordeal substantially unscathed and accomplished what they were apparently meant to accomplish. But what kind of future did they have? And if all they had to look forward to was defeat, capture, and death, what good had all of the struggle been?

Aaron looked up and over her shoulder, and Kerri turned to see Asha approaching them, her face expressionless.

"Kerri," she said quietly. "Rivers is awake. He wants to speak with you."

"Probably wants to thank you for rescuing him," Aaron said.

"No," Asha said. "No, I don't think that's it."

Kerri rose and followed Asha from the room. She wondered if Aaron was going to come with her, but he remained seated at the table, watching her leave with a concerned frown.

They walked up the stairs to the fourth floor in silence. Asha was a quiet woman at the best of times—a calm that belied a sharp and incisive mind, not to mention physical power and fighting ability that no one would guess from her small stature and economy of movement. In the midst of this crisis she was even more guarded, her face betraying nothing of what she thought.

Kerri wondered briefly if Asha had the same feelings of futility and hope-lessness she did. If so, she almost certainly would never let it show, much less admit it openly.

The door to Rivers's room was a little ajar, and Kerri knocked lightly on it. Receiving no answer, she pushed it open and walked in. Asha remained in the corridor.

Evidently Aaron was not the only one who felt that this conversation, what-ever it was to be about, was for Kerri's ears alone.

Rivers was still lying on his back in bed, but the upper half was tilted to allow him to sit up. He was wearing an old t-shirt, but the blanket still covered him from the waist down. He turned slowly toward Kerri as she entered, a look of recognition entering his eyes.

Whatever the Children had done to him, at least he still had that much of his memory left. Better than the poor unfortunate they'd found by the side of the road in a park near El Paso, who had been drained of every last memory, and left as a mindless husk, an empty shell.

"Elias," he said in a hoarse voice, then cleared his throat, wincing a little.

"How are you feeling, Rivers?"

He shook his head. "Like roadkill. But better than yesterday this time."

Kerri pulled a chair up near his bed and sat down. "I'm glad we were able to get you out. It was a near-run thing."

"I know. I can't believe the three of you took those kinds of risks. I'm grateful, but to be truthful, I'm not worth it."

"Has Asha told you what's happened since you were abducted?"

"Yes." He looked away toward the small window, curtains pulled back to reveal a patch of flawless blue sky. "Hard to escape the feeling that we're screwed, isn't it?"

"A little, yeah."

There was silence for a moment, then Rivers said, "So why did you do it? Asha told me some kind of nonsense about being contacted by an alien who supposedly knows what's going on?"

"Saul."

"Right. Him. So he told you to come find me?"

"Yes. He's the one who directed us to go to Colville."

"Why did he want me rescued? At this point, we have to think of numbers. Sending three agents across the country to rescue one doesn't make any sense. I'm not that important."

"I believe there's a reason."

He gave her a thoughtful look. "The Children were experimenting on me. I'm not sure why. I know they didn't do it to everyone they abducted. Some of them they simply…." He paused, face twisting for a moment, then regained his composure. "Some they fed on. They get their sustenance from our thoughts."

"I know. I've seen it happen." She didn't add that it had happened to her, a memory pulled from her brain at the touch of the Child's hand, gone as if it had never been.

"Others they killed. I got the impression that some of us have brains that are more compatible with them than others. It's like when you're raising chickens, you know? If some of them are sickly, or aren't laying, you cull them without a second thought."

She shuddered. The analogy was all too apt.

"But me, and I think a few others—they weren't drained, and they didn't simply discard us. They did… tests."

"Like what?" She paused. "I mean, if you don't want to say…."

He shook his head. "No, I need to tell you. There's a reason you should know. After I was abducted—well, I was unconscious for a while. I don't know how long. But I woke up in the lab where you rescued me. Where did you say it was?"

"Colville, New York."

"New York." He licked his lips, frowned. "They'd stripped me, and I was on my back strapped to a table. They examined me, every square inch of me…." His cheeks colored a little. "It was obvious they wanted to know how the human body works. Funny how all the movies about alien abduction got that part right."

"Makes sense. They may superficially look like humans, but internally there's no similarity at all."

"Asha said something like that. Anyway, once they were done with that, they put something in my eye. I couldn't see it. It was too close, you know? It felt like a piece of thread."

The hairs on the back of Kerri's neck stood up. "A thread? What color was it?"

"Green."

She stared at him in silence for a moment, recalling the green fibers that had covered Dr. Paul Chauvin's brain, fibers that had tried to impale Will Daigle in the finger, presumably as a way of parasitizing him as well.

"What did it do?" She tried to make the question sound offhand but couldn't hide a tremor in her voice.

"It slid to the corner of my eye and slipped down my tear duct. It hurt. But only for a moment." A trace of the old shrewd look, so familiar from their days as partners in the Boundary, came into his expression. "But it sounds like you maybe know more about this thing than I do."

"A little."

"It's still inside me, you know." His gaze focused on her face with a trace of the intensity she remembered from before his abduction. "I can feel it. It's trying to access my thoughts. It keeps trying, but I'm able to resist it."

"We met people who had been completely taken over by it." Should she be telling him this? If he'd been parasitized, wasn't he one of the collaborators, like Jennifer Martinez and Paul Chauvin and Ramon Gil, who had led a perfectly normal life until he had blown himself up on the side of a New Mexico highway in a failed attempt to kill her, Aaron, and Danielle?

But Rivers didn't seem to recognize her shock of understanding—and her fear. "It was obvious the Children were upset by the fact that the thing hadn't worked. I could hear them, you know? Faintly. Like they were talking in my brain. It wasn't English, but I could understand, at least a little. Something went wrong, and they wanted to know why." He looked away again, then took a deep breath. "They put us inside those tubes. Me and two others, one man and one woman. I'm guessing the same thing had happened with them, and they wanted to find out why we were different."

"Did they?"

He shrugged his narrow shoulders, shoulders that had once been clothed with muscle. Hard to see how he'd ever be able to return to the man he once was. That man was gone, as surely as if the Children had killed him outright. "I don't think so. The woman, and the other guy—eventually they just died. Me, I thought I was going to die of fear when they started filling the tube with that green goo. I watched it rising, engulfing more and more of my body. I tried screaming at them that they were going to drown us, but they didn't pay any attention. I held my breath as long as I could, certain I was minutes from dying. Most terrifying experience of my life. When I finally exhaled and took a big breath of that liquid, I thought, 'This is it. This is death. Oh, well, better than whatever else they had planned for me.' But I found I could breathe the stuff. It hurt, and it was harder to push in and out of my lungs, but I could somehow breathe it."

"Will thought that must have been the case."

"He's a doctor, right?"

"Yes. We were lucky to find him."

Rivers nodded. "So they just kept us there, suspended. Like they'd put us in cold storage and forgotten about us. I don't know what that glop was, but I guess somehow it kept us fed, too. I could feel it flowing upwards over my skin, so they had some kind of way of pumping it through the tube. I was hungry, because my stomach was empty, but I didn't starve even though I wasn't eating." A momentary frown creased his forehead. "Didn't stop the other two from dying. I remember when the guy died. Somehow, I was able to hear something of what they were thinking, too—not specifics, just feelings and traces of thoughts. His kind of faded out, like moving out of range of a radio station. Then it just winked off. I looked over at his tube, and his eyes were closed, his face peaceful. I knew he was dead. The woman died not long afterward."

"How did you survive?"

"Not sure. I got the impression that the other two just gave up. Me, I was determined. I remember thinking that if I died, I was gonna make the bastards kill me outright, not leave me in a glass tube waiting to die of despair."

"Can you…." Kerri stopped, swallowed. "Can you still hear them? The Children, I mean?"

"Yes. A little. It's in the background, like hearing a television in a nearby room. I've gotten to where I can ignore it. It doesn't control me like it did the others, the ones you mentioned who had been taken over completely."

"Do you think it goes the other way? Can the Children hear your thoughts?"

"I'm not sure, but I don't think so. I sent some pretty violent thoughts in the direction of my captors, you know? Daring them to kill me. Picturing myself ripping them to shreds with my bare hands. They never reacted one way or the other." He gave her a canny look. "I know why you're asking. You don't need to be subtle. I've been through too much for you to have to pussyfoot around."

She nodded. "If they can hear what you're thinking, we have to be exceptionally careful what we say around you."

"Not only that." Rivers opened his eyes wide. "If they can, you should kill me. Quickly. Because if they can hear what I'm thinking, they'll know there were survivors from the raid on headquarters. They'll find you."

Kerri looked at him in silence for a moment. "We can't do that."

"Why the hell not? I mean, I'm glad you rescued me, kept me from shriveling away in an observation tank, surrounded by the Children. I'd rather die among friends. I'd rather have friends… put me to death, than that." There was just the faintest hint of a hesitation, then his voice became stronger. "You can't let sentiment stand in the way of any chance you have of surviving."

"No, it's not just sentiment," Kerri said. "We went on that whole cross-country trip because Saul said it was necessary. And that means we were supposed to rescue you. I'm certain that's why we went to New York. That reason and no other. So I flatly don't believe that after risking everything we did to bring you back, the right thing to do now is to put you to death."

He regarded her steadily for a moment. "But what good can I possibly be in this condition? I can barely stand unassisted. It's anyone's guess how much of my strength I can ever hope to regain."

"I don't know. I think we have to figure that out. I think we have a lot to figure out." She gazed out of the window again, into a bright world that, for the moment, was completely inaccessible to them. "Like how a portal appeared in the lab in New York, exactly at the right time to rescue you—and brought us back to headquarters, the place we needed to go."

"I think…." He shifted slightly in the bed, ran one thin hand across the scraggly hair on his chin. "I wonder if I might have done that."

Kerri goggled at him. "How?"

"I don't know. But when I saw you, I recognized you. I couldn't remember your name, not at first, but when I saw your face, I thought, 'She can help me.' And once you broke the tube, all I could think of was, 'We need to get out of here. Back to headquarters.' That's when the portal appeared."

"Can you…." She paused, frowning. "Have you tried to do it again? Just to see if you can?"

He nodded. "Several times. I tried to create a portal on the wall. Nothing. I have no idea why."

"Maybe it wasn't you the first time."

"Why else would a portal have appeared right there, and going to the right place, like you asked?" A hint of his old asperity returned to his voice. "C'mon, Elias, the Children aren't that stupid. It's not like they just leave portals around for their enemies to use. If it wasn't me, where did it come from?"

Kerri had no answer for that. Had their partial parasitism of Rivers's brain—infiltration that he was somehow able to hold at bay—give him some of the Children's abilities? If so, that could certainly explain why his rescue was important.

It hadn't been a humanitarian mission at all, saving one lone agent. The critical thing was to bring him back, where he could be used…

… for *what*?

Listening in to the Children was one thing, but it wasn't like they didn't already know their enemies' intent. And it was hard to see how an intermittent and unfocused ability to create portals was going to give them any kind of significant advantage.

But all she said was, "I guess that's one more thing we have to figure out."

He nodded. "Hey, Elias?"

"Yes?"

"Thanks."

She took his hand, gave it a squeeze. "Look, Rivers, I know we never got along that well. But there's one thing I never doubted. If the situation was reversed, you'd have done the same for me in a heartbeat."

He nodded slowly. "I hear you have a new boyfriend."

"Aaron Vincent. He's one of the ones who helped rescue you."

"That's what Asha said. She also told me what happened to Noah. I'm sorry."

She met his eyes for a moment, then looked away. "He didn't deserve that."

"None of us do. Like Danielle. That one hit me hard."

"Me, too. I still can't believe she's gone."

"It happens in war. Doesn't make it any easier, but we're not all going to survive this." He paused. "But I'm glad you've found someone. Asha said he's a good man." He gave her hand a return squeeze. "Take care of each other."

"That's all we can do. Look after the ones we care about." She felt tears rising and forced them back. "Maybe that's the only important thing we *can* do. Ever. And I guess for now, it'll have to be enough."